...ries

"Meg's ... er own without any experience makes her an admirable character, as she faces each new challenge with good humor and a smidgeon of exasperation. A reliable cast of characters support Meg and make this a strong series that continues its streak of compelling plots." —*Kings River Life Magazine*

"Sheila Connolly continues to include fascinating facts about apples and orchards within her stories . . . Not only will you get hooked on the mystery, but you will be racing to the kitchen to bake an apple treat!"
—*Cozy Mystery Book Reviews*

"Fans will enjoy the heroine taking a bite out of crime in this fun regional cozy." —*Genre Go Round Reviews*

"Really well written . . . I was constantly kept guessing. This series is in its stride, and I'm eagerly awaiting the next book in this series." —*Fresh Fiction*

"Meg is a smart, savvy woman who's working hard to fit into her new community—just the kind of protagonist I look for in today's traditional mystery. I look forward to more trips to Granford, Massachusetts!" —*Meritorious Mysteries*

"An enjoyable and well-written book with some excellent apple recipes at the end." —*Cozy Library*

"A wonderful slice of life in a small town . . . The mystery is intelligent and has an interesting twist . . . *Rotten to the Core* is a fun, quick read with an enjoyable heroine, an interesting hook, and some yummy recipes at the end."
—*The Mystery Reader* (4 stars)

continued

"Full of rich description, historical context, and mystery."
—*The Romance Readers Connection*

"Meg Corey is a very likable protagonist . . . [A] delightful new series." —*Gumshoe Review*

"An example of everything that is right with the cozy mystery . . . A likable heroine, an attractive small-town setting, a slimy victim, and fascinating side elements . . . There's depth to the characters in this book that isn't always found in crime fiction . . . Sheila Connolly has written a winner for cozy mystery fans." —*Lesa's Book Critiques*

"A warm, very satisfying read." —*RT Book Reviews* (4 stars)

"The premise and plot are solid, and Meg seems a perfect fit for her role." —*Publishers Weekly*

"Meg Corey is a fresh and appealing sleuth with a bushelful of entertaining problems . . . One crisp, delicious read."
—Claudia Bishop, bestselling author of the Inn at Hemlock Falls Mysteries

"A delightful look at small-town New England, with an intriguing puzzle thrown in."
—JoAnna Carl, national bestselling author of the Chocoholic Mysteries

"Thoroughly enjoyable . . . I can't wait for the next book and a chance to spend more time with Meg and the good people of Granford."
—Sammi Carter, author of the Candy Shop Mysteries

Picked to Die

Sheila Connolly

BERKLEY PRIME CRIME, NEW YORK

THE BERKLEY PUBLISHING GROUP
Published by the Penguin Group
Penguin Group (USA) LLC
375 Hudson Street, New York, New York 10014

USA • Canada • UK • Ireland • Australia • New Zealand • India • South Africa • China

penguin.com

A Penguin Random House Company

PICKED TO DIE

A Berkley Prime Crime Book / published by arrangement with the author

Berkley Prime Crime Books are published by The Berkley Publishing Group.
BERKLEY® PRIME CRIME and the PRIME CRIME logo are trademarks of
Penguin Group (USA) LLC.

For information, address: The Berkley Publishing Group,
a division of Penguin Group (USA) LLC,
375 Hudson Street, New York, New York 10014.

ISBN: 978-0-425-25711-1

PUBLISHING HISTORY
Berkley Prime Crime mass-market edition / October 2014

PRINTED IN THE UNITED STATES OF AMERICA

10 9 8 7 6 5 4 3 2 1

Cover illustration by Mary Ann Lasher.
Cover design by Annette Fiore Defex.
Interior text design by Laura K. Corless.

Acknowledgments

Even in small towns, everyone doesn't know everyone else. That's particularly true for one nearly invisible community in Granford, Massachusetts, the town I've created in the Orchard Mysteries: the Jamaican pickers who arrive each year to harvest the crops from the fields and orchards of Massachusetts. Their visas allow them to stay no longer than 364 days each year, so they never become part of the town, even though the same workers return year after year, sometimes for generations.

This book is, in a way, about that community, without whose members farmers would struggle to earn their living. It's also about people's assumptions about others—and how often they may be wrong.

I need to thank Janice McArdle, librarian at the Granby Free Public Library (which recently moved to a wonderful new building), and Terry Johnson, former president of the Granby Historical Association, for providing so much useful information about the real town that Granford is based on, and for being so supportive of my efforts. Thanks also to all the townspeople who have stopped by to talk to me at the annual Granby Town Wide Fall Craft & Tag Sale and tell me about their own memories of the town. You can be sure you'll recognize a few of your stories in future books!

The town of Granford would not exist without the ongoing help and guidance of my agent, Jessica Faust of Book-Ends, and my editor, Shannon Jamieson Vazquez of Berkley Prime Crime, and I owe them many thanks. And the series would never have happened or gone forward without the guidance of Sisters in Crime and the warm enthusiasm of the Guppies.

Thus let me live, unseen, unknown,
Thus unlamented let me die

—Alexander Pope, *Ode on Solitude*

1

"This whole town has gone crazy," Seth Chapin said as he dropped heavily into a chair across the kitchen table from Meg Corey.

Meg looked at her fiancé in confusion. "Fiancé": such an odd, somehow old-fashioned word. She kept forgetting that they were now officially "engaged" in the eyes of the world. Well, the small world of Granford, Massachusetts, at least— it wasn't like she was announcing it in the *Boston Globe*. She didn't feel like a fiancée, which she'd always thought was an equally silly word. They hadn't gotten any closer to setting a date. They hadn't discussed where or when or how. They hadn't even worked out where they'd live, though currently Seth was spending most of his time at her house, which made sense, since his office and storage space were in her barn. On the other hand, Meg also had her housemate to consider—Briona Stewart, who was also Meg's orchard manager, and indispensable to keeping the apple orchard running. Given how little Meg could afford to pay, the position came with a free room, and she couldn't just toss Bree out into the local student-driven housing scene. There were many things Meg and Seth needed to talk about, maybe when they were less busy and exhausted—she with the apple harvest, Seth with his fast-growing renovation business. Not the best time to make happy plans.

"What are you talking about?" Meg asked now. "Did I miss something? What's going crazy?"

"Everyone in town wants to tear things down and put things up, all at once." Seth sighed. "You have anything cold to drink?"

"Of course. Water, iced tea, even some sports drink, if you want electrolytes." After a recent brush with heat exhaustion, Meg had been scrupulous about keeping plenty of liquids on hand. Since it was harvest season, she was also always reminding her pickers up in the orchard to stay hydrated, too.

Seth hauled himself up and got a bottle of water from the refrigerator. He sat and downed half the bottle. "That's better. So, basically, I think everybody in town looked up, noticed it was September, and said, 'Hey, we'd better get something done before winter.' Of course, we could argue about whether there'll even be a winter this year, what with the weird weather we've had. Or maybe there'll be a six-month winter."

Meg sipped her own drink. "Back up—who's 'everybody'?"

"Well, first there's the library. Did you hear about the new one?"

Meg racked her brain and came up blank. She hadn't had

time to read the local paper since . . . June? And it was only a weekly. She'd been so busy for months, first with fighting the drought, which had meant a lot of hand-watering of her eighteen acres of apple trees; now with managing the harvest, which had begun in August and would run through November, depending on when the apples decided to ripen, which was kind of unpredictable. But a new library was a major step for Granford, Massachusetts, and she felt like she should have known. Besides, Seth, a town selectman, usually kept her up-to-date. "Uh, no?"

"And you a concerned citizen!" Seth joked. "Okay, last year one of the old families in town donated a part of their property to the town to use to build a new library. It's out near the high school, on Route 202. Plenty of space for parking, and it's big enough to build what they want, assuming they can figure out how to pay for it. They've already got some state grants, and the fund-raising is going well." He stopped to drink some more water. "The building site is set back pretty far from the road, so you might not have noticed it if you drove past it. But there was a formal ground-breaking a few months ago."

"Sorry I missed it. Should I make a contribution? But building a new library doesn't sound at all crazy to me."

"I'm not finished," Seth said. "Then there's the Historical Society."

"What are they doing?" Meg asked. Now, the Historical Society *was* someplace she was involved with. They owned a nice but too-small one-story building that faced the village green, just down the hill from the church. When she'd first visited almost two years ago now, as a newcomer to Granford, it had been an unheated space filled with a hodgepodge of unrelated collections. She wasn't surprised that the director, Gail Selden, had bigger plans. Gail had also become a friend, and had helped Meg more than once to find information about her own eighteenth-century home. "Don't tell me they're moving!"

"No, not that," Seth replied. "They own that building outright, but as you've probably noticed, it needs work. And it's not really big enough to serve the public the way they'd like."

That was true. Gail had worked wonders cleaning it up and creating exhibits that made sense, but it was still small and unheated.

Seth went on, "The Society has collections stashed all over town, wherever they could find storage space, and Gail really wants to get them all under one roof. But still the same old roof."

"So what are they planning?"

"Basically, they had two choices: build up or build down. The Historical Society board didn't want to change the profile of the building by adding another story, even a partial one, so they've decided to dig out under the building."

"Wow—that sounds ambitious. Is it even possible?" Meg got up to help herself to another bottle of water, laying an affectionate hand on Seth's shoulder as she passed. She was still getting used to having him around more or less full-time, but with their busy schedules, it was nice when they saw each other at all. "Want another?"

"Sure." He laid his hand over hers, briefly. "They have an architect who says it's possible, if it's done carefully, of course. At least it's not too big a building. They'd have to put supports under the existing building, then excavate, then pour a foundation and finish the space so it can be used for document and collections storage, which means special considerations for moisture and ventilation. Oh, and

Gail really wants a bathroom in the building for staff and volunteers."

Meg laughed. "I can certainly understand that!" While her own colonial house had four bedrooms, it had only one bath, which really wasn't enough with three people living in the house—especially when they all needed showers at the same time after a working day. She had to keep reminding herself that when the house had been built by one of her Warren family ancestors, there had been *no* indoor plumbing beyond the well in the basement, which had provided water for the kitchen above by way of an old hand pump. But standards for personal hygiene had been different then. "So what's the time frame there?"

"Yesterday," Seth said. "Seriously, they want to get it roughed out before the ground freezes, so it's a pretty ambitious schedule. But they more or less have the money in hand, so they don't want to wait."

"They do?" Having money in hand was an unusual situation for most historical societies.

"Yeah. The Society also owns the house across the street, which they rent out for income, and Gail told me that when they talked to a financial advisor he told them that they could take out a mortgage on the rental house, and voilà! They'd have the cash for the renovations. The rent gives them enough income to cover the mortgage payments. Once they figured out how much money they had to work with, then they started thinking about building plans."

"I'm impressed. So, that's the library and the Historical Society—are you finished yet?"

"Not quite. There's also a school building that needs some serious work, and nobody can decide whether to try to fix it—with state money—or to tear it down and start over. So we put together a committee to study it, but there's a deadline coming up shortly."

I really am out of the loop, Meg thought. Of course, not having any children, she hadn't paid much attention to school-related issues, but still. "Is that all?"

"Almost. This is off the record, but the town is also thinking about selling the town hall building."

"What? I like that building!" Meg protested.

"It's a lovely structure, but a lousy municipal building. It was built as a private summer home at the height of the Victorian era. The wiring isn't up to code, so it's hard to use computers and printers and the like."

"Where would the town administration go? Is there some other building that would work? Or do they want to build, too?"

Seth shook his head. "Not clear. They might be able to move into the old library when the new one opens."

"This really is a game of musical chairs, isn't it?" Meg said. "Where do you stand on all of these? I mean, you're a selectman, so in a sense, you are the town, or part of it." Meg knew there were only three members on the select board, plus a town manager. Who voted to approve projects like these?

Seth leaned back in his chair and stretched. "Caught right in the middle. The library and the Historical Society have their own funding, so they don't need our approval, apart from permitting and inspections and such. The school project does, and obviously selling town hall would. Theoretically, I'm in favor of all and any of these, as long as the financial numbers make sense and they meet all construction requirements—which could be challenging, at least for the Historical Society."

"Are you going to be personally involved?" Meg asked. When she'd first met Seth, he'd been managing his family's plumbing business, but his real love was building restoration and renovation. Although plumbing was a good fallback when no one could afford historically accurate renovations to their older homes.

"If I had my choice, I'd help out with the Historical Society project. It's an interesting challenge, and I'd like to be sure they retain the historic character of the building. As you know as well as I do, when you start jerking around an old building, you always end up finding other things you need to fix, like rotting sills or termite damage. And if they're putting in an HVAC system—which, by the way, would be a first in that building—there are issues of windows and insulation and making the building more airtight while still keeping it authentic, at least in appearance."

"And you don't have to vote on that project, so there's no conflict," Meg mused, almost to herself.

"Exactly. The library doesn't need me, and the school project probably wouldn't either. The town hall question is anybody's guess. So that leaves the Historical Society. By the way, I pointed Gail toward an architect who specializes in this kind of project, so they've already got plans in hand."

"Can it be done before winter?"

"It's a tight schedule, but it could work, if everything goes well."

"And if it doesn't?"

"We seal it up as best we can and hope for a mild winter. At least the collections will be stored off-site."

"Speaking of the collections, I know she's got more documents about this house that I'd love to see, but I haven't had the time. Maybe when the harvest is over." Winter,

Meg knew from last year—her first as an apple grower—
was the slowest time for the orchard. She'd have some long
days to fill.

"How's the harvest going?"

Meg shrugged. "I don't have a lot to compare it to other
than last year, but Bree says we're doing okay. We were
lucky that the drought broke when it did. Another couple of
weeks and we'd have lost a lot of apples." *Along with most
of my very thin profit margin.*

"Everything working out with the pickers?"

"So far. Most of the regulars are back, bless them,
although we lost one to a competitor over in Belchertown
who could offer a little more money, and there are fewer and
fewer people who want to do this kind of manual labor."

Meg was lucky that although *she* was new to running an
orchard, the orchard itself was well established, and in
recent years had been overseen by the local state university.
Which was also how she'd come to employee Bree, a recent
graduate of the university who'd studied orchard management. The fact that Bree was Jamaican-born also helped
her in managing the mainly Jamaican pickers who had
been working the orchards in the Connecticut River Valley
for generations—at least it helped once they got used to the
idea of working for a woman, and a young one at that, and
one who'd spent most of her life actually living in Massachusetts rather than Jamaica. But Bree had earned their
respect and things were going smoothly; the loss of that one
picker was in no way her fault. "That's why Bree and I are
both up there most days, just to fill in. It's hard to know in
advance from week to week what's going to be ripe, and
sometimes we get swamped. Plus, it's demanding work.
Thank goodness the new trees we planted in the spring

won't be bearing for a couple more years. Maybe by then I'll have figured out how this all works."

"Can you take a short break tomorrow? I'm going to talk to Gail about the excavation process in the morning, if you want to tag along."

"I'd love to see Gail, and this project sounds really interesting. I don't think we've got a lot on the schedule for tomorrow, so I can probably sneak away. But I'll have to check with Bree."

"You talking about me?" Bree came in through the back door.

"May I take an hour or two off tomorrow morning, please, ma'am?" Meg said, smiling. "The Historical Society is planning to add a basement under their building, and I'm curious to see how they're going to do it."

Bree rummaged in the refrigerator and pulled out a bottle of water. "I guess. We're just about caught up with the Cortlands and the Empires, but the Galas aren't ready yet and we're waiting on the Baldwins. Did you order the new crates?"

"Oh, shoot, I forgot." The old wooden crates that Meg had inherited when she moved into the house were wearing out fast, and they'd been replacing them as needed with more modern plastic ones. Not nearly as pretty, but much more practical. "I'll do that in the morning."

"Then you have my blessing for the morning—*after* you place that order," Bree said in a mock-serious tone. "What's happening with dinner?"

"Not a clue," Meg replied. "Seth, you have any ideas?"

"There's a new pizza place in the shopping center on 202. Want to try that?"

"How did I ever miss seeing that? Let's go!"

2

The pizza last night had been good, and Meg sent up a silent cheer that Granford had one more place that served food. The only "real" restaurant in town, Gran's, was more upscale, though far from fancy. Meg loved eating there, especially since she'd had a hand in creating the place, and even more so because she now counted the owners, Nicky and Brian Czarnecki, as friends, but she wasn't always in the mood for a sit-down meal. A pizza place, and one only a mile or two from her house, was a great quick-and-dirty alternative.

When she awoke the next morning, Meg checked the clock, then rolled over and nudged Seth. "Hey, what time are you meeting Gail?"

He answered without opening his eyes. "As soon as she gets the kids off to school. What time is it?"

"Seven."

Seth opened his eyes, then sat up quickly. "I've got to get some paperwork together before we head over there. You are still coming with me, right?"

"Sure. Nobody's started anything at the Historical Society, right?"

"Not yet, but they're hoping to begin this week. Right now we're still at the talking stage, and looking at plans."

"You going to do the plumbing?" Meg asked.

"Maybe. First step is to find someone to do the digging. I can recommend builders to pour the foundation, but shoring up the building and removing the soil is trickier and it takes more skill." He was pulling on jeans and a T-shirt as he spoke. "I'll go start coffee, and then walk Max. See you downstairs?"

"I won't be long."

Meg could hear stirring noises from Bree's end of the hall, so she darted into the bathroom quickly, emerging ten minutes later after a quick shower. She threw on her clothes and joined Seth in the kitchen, where he handed her a cup of coffee. Max, his Golden Retriever, greeted Meg enthusiastically.

"Drink it before it gets cold," he said. They toasted and buttered a couple of bagels, and Meg scanned the first page of the daily paper. Why did she keep subscribing, when she rarely had time to read it? Oh, right, to put under her cat Lolly's litter pan. As if on cue, Lolly appeared from somewhere, butting her head against Meg's leg, looking for her own breakfast.

After she'd fed Lolly, Meg ventured, "Okay, so remind me—how old is the Historical Society building?"

"The building dates back to the mid-1700s," Seth said. "Actually, it was the first meetinghouse in Granford. There was some infighting going on within the church in South

Hadley about where to put the new church they needed, and in the end they decided to split the parish. It took them thirteen years and fifty local meetings to arrive at that decision—makes our current process look lightning fast, doesn't it? Anyway, the short answer is that the new parish was created in 1762, before Granford was even an official town, and before they had an official place to meet. So the building is about the same age as your house. By the way, South Hadley had another fight about churches starting in 1820, and that time it took them *sixteen* years to work things out. And then in the 1820s Granby had its own tiff and actually built two churches, but only the one survives, the big one that's there now. The other one was closer to the cemetery where all those Warrens are buried, but the cemetery is older than the church."

"But the meetinghouse had no heating and no plumbing."

"Nope. Those old New Englanders were tough birds," Seth replied cheerfully. "And sermons were long in those days. Of course, if most people in town showed up, they would have generated some considerable body heat. And, I've read, they used to have 'singing.'"

"Which means what?" Meg asked.

"Got me, but the town paid the princely sum of thirteen dollars for it in 1792, and by 1798 they even had a bass viol."

"You're making this up. Aren't you?"

"Nope. Read Judd sometime."

Meg recognized the name as the author of a monumental history about the town of Hadley, published in the nineteenth century. "Seth, when do you find time to learn all this stuff?" Meg said plaintively. She could never catch up. She couldn't remember reading to the end of a book in months—either she had no time or she fell into bed exhausted, so there was no way to study the history of Granford. Maybe come winter she'd try again.

"I like old buildings, and I've been passing by most of these all my life. You'll learn."

"Yeah, as soon as I have a spare year or two. Are you ready to head out?"

"Sure. I think I'll leave Max here—there's too much interesting stuff to smell at the Historical Society."

It took only a few minutes to drive from Meg's house to the center of Granford, which still boasted its original town green ringed with maple trees. The church—which Meg now knew was the "new" one, not the original one—anchored one end of the green, with a parish house and then the Historical Society on the slope below. A pharmacy-slash–general store occupied space across the street, and up toward one end, on the highway, loomed the ornate Victorian town hall. The relatively new restaurant, Gran's, had moved into what had been a nineteenth-century home at the top of the hill, with a nice view of the green, as Meg knew well. There was little traffic.

Gail Selden was sitting on the Historical Society building's steps waiting, and stood up when they pulled into the church parking lot. Knowing that there might be changes coming, Meg studied the building quickly: single story, low-pitched roof, two massive granite steps leading up to the entrance. And the majority of the town's population had squeezed inside? Not a very large town back then.

When she saw them, Gail called out, "Hey, Seth. Hi, Meg—did you get dragged along?"

Meg smiled at her. "No, he described what you wanted to do and I had to see for myself. He said you plan to dig *under* the building? There's no basement?"

"Looks like it," Gail replied cheerfully, "and no, they never included a basement. As for the project, our board is on board, so to speak, so all we need is the go-ahead on the structural issues, which is where Seth comes in."

"You talk to those excavation contractors I told you about?" Seth asked.

"We've talked to a couple, and they offered two options for the excavation process. I wanted to ask you which one makes more sense."

"Let's go inside," Seth said. Gail opened the door with an old key, and they followed her through it.

"Wow," Meg said when they'd entered the main room. "You've cleared out a lot of stuff since the last time I was here. The first time I saw the place, there were stuffed birds and animals all over the place. What happened to them?"

Gail grinned. "Uh, let us say they retired. The local taxidermist left something to be desired, and they were molting or shedding all over the place."

"I can imagine." Meg smiled back. "You're really serious about going through with this plan?"

"We sure are! Let's sit at the table in the kitchen exhibit—it's open now that we've stowed away some of the tools and antique appliances." Gail led the way to the table, where she had already laid out what looked like architectural drawings. She waited until they were seated before beginning.

"Seth, you can probably follow this stuff a lot better than I can, but as I understand it, the idea is to shore up the building from beneath with leveling jacks and steel beams—"

"Assuming your substrate can support them," Seth interrupted.

"Of course," Gail said quickly, "and we'll check that out

first—or our contractor will, I guess. And then we dig out the soil to a depth of ten feet, which gives us space to pour a slab down there and still have adequate headroom."

"Go on," Seth prompted. "You know where your HVAC system will go? And what provisions have you made for moisture control?"

Gail held up both hands. "Seth, I know only the big picture. You'll have to talk to the architect and the contractor about that stuff. But they've both done jobs like this before. I've talked to several of their clients, and I haven't heard any complaints."

"What's the plan for removing the soil?" Seth asked.

"We're still debating about that. There's good old-fashioned manual labor—a bunch of folk with shovels, which would be historically correct but a lot of work. Or we see if we can fit a baby Bobcat excavator in there, once we get it started. Or somebody mentioned using what they called a vacuum extractor—like you stick a big hose down into it, and the dirt is sucked right out and then deposited in a dump truck or even left on-site. I don't know what you think about that, but it sounds like fun to watch."

"Let me ask around. I have heard that it's effective in a small, contained area, and getting rid of the dirt immediately would be a big plus. Both make sense in your case. When do you want to start?"

"This week."

"Wow," Seth said. "But you're lucky it's a small building. Most excavators could be in and out in a day, once the shoring is in place, and could fit it in between their other projects."

"Yeah, I know it's fast, but please, *please* don't tell me

to ask the board to slow down. Do you know how long it's taken to advance the project this far? And we'd really love to be able to be open this winter. We've never been open in winter before."

"Do you expect a lot of visitors?" Meg asked.

"Not swarms, but I'm hopeful we could attract a few. There are often parents visiting their kids at the colleges around here, and we're seeing more of them in Granford since Gran's opened. And genealogists will trek through anything to get their research done. We've calculated that the entry fees or memberships paid by the new researchers should offset the additional cost of heating the place in winter—which should be done anyway, to preserve the collections. Working quickly now won't impact the cost of the project, will it, Seth? The excavators didn't seem to think so, and as you said, for them it's not a big job."

"Probably not, as long as you don't run into anything unexpected, like a rock ridge running under the building, or a spring." Seth looked at his watch. "I've got a job in Easthampton, so I'd better go. Meg, you want a ride back?"

"I can take you home, Meg, if you want to hang around a little longer," Gail volunteered eagerly.

"That sounds good," Meg said. "You go ahead, Seth."

"I'll take the plans and proposals with me to look over, Gail, and I'll try to get back to you by tomorrow. Fast enough for you?"

"That's terrific, Seth. My board is really excited about this, and I'd hate to lose the momentum. I appreciate your help. Which reminds me: if we ask nicely, will you do the heating and plumbing stuff?"

"Sure, although I might have to bring in a couple of extra people. I'll try to keep the costs down, though."

"I know you're fair, Seth. Thank you so much for making this work!"

Seth gathered up the papers from the table and as he headed for the door, Meg could hear him whistling. He was a man who truly loved his work.

Gail turned to Meg. "Hey, I haven't had a chance to say congratulations to you guys."

"Oh, about our engagement? Thank you. Apparently everyone in town knew we were getting married before we did."

"You make a great couple. Seth's a terrific guy."

"I know—everyone keeps telling me that." Meg smiled. "Before you ask, no, we haven't set a date. I've got to get through this harvest, and he's crazy busy with all the projects going on in town."

"I know! It's like a contagious disease—everybody suddenly wants something new, or at least renovated. But I think it's time for all of us. The plans for the library look wonderful. Since they're going to have a dedicated genealogy room, I'm going to get together with their staff and sort through the documents we each have and see what's the best distribution of materials."

"Great idea! What're you planning to do with the records during construction?"

"More of the same thing we've always done—parcel them out around town. I thought maybe you'd like to take some of them, the ones about the Warren family and the settlement of the south end of town."

"I'd love to, at least for a while, although I don't know when I'll have time to look at them. Not until December, I'd guess."

"Don't worry, I know where to find you. So, you want to see what else we're planning?"

"That's why I'm here. Seth tells me your building is about the same age as my house. Maybe I'll learn something useful about colonial construction. I'll keep my fingers crossed that you don't run into anything unexpected!"

"Amen to that!" Gail replied fervently.

3

"How did your board decide to do this now?" Meg asked Gail, as Gail led her around the room, pointing out changes. "By the way, how many people are on it?"

"There's the president, the vice president, the secretary, the treasurer, and four additional trustees. You've probably met them all at one time or another."

"You're not on the board?"

"Nope, I just run the place. But back to your first question, about the timing?" Gail giggled. "I kind of drove the point home when I suggested they hold a board meeting here one evening. You'd be surprised how rarely board members actually set foot in here."

"They got cold?"

"No, that wasn't too bad. But then the board chair really,

really needed to go, if you know what I mean, and I pointed out that we didn't have any facilities in the building."

Meg stared at her blankly for a moment until she figured out what Gail meant, then she laughed. "Oh, you mean 'go,' not leave."

"Exactly. Let me tell you, the meeting broke up pretty fast after that, but I think I'd made the problem clear. So we started talking about how we could add a bathroom, and I told them retrofitting plumbing like that could get expensive, and if we were going to spend that kind of money, we really ought to do as much as we could all at once."

"Makes sense. But adding a bathroom and digging a whole new basement aren't exactly the same thing," Meg commented.

"No, but by that time I'd jump-started the discussion. Like I've said, right now our collections are scattered all over town, and frankly, we aren't even entirely sure what we have and where to find it. That's just not right. If we're supposed to be a public institution, serving the people of this town by preserving our history—not to mention attracting a few outsiders—then we're falling far short. But the icing on the cake was discovering that we could actually afford it."

"Seth mentioned something about that. What's the story with the other house?"

"We were 'gifted' that house across the street almost twenty years ago now. I'm glad that people want to see their heritage preserved, usually a home or building that's been in the family for generations, but any property brings its own problems with it. Taxes, maintenance, and so on. Still, this one was close by and right on the green, so we couldn't say no. Anyway, it came with no strings attached, and we hold the title."

"And you didn't want to use it for display or storage space?" Meg asked.

"Hey, it's a nice house and in good shape, so we rent it out and make some money that way, although we do reserve the right to use the barn behind it for storage. But it wasn't until we added a new board member who works for a bank that we realized we could take out a mortgage on it to finance our other plans. Not a big one, just enough to cover expenses. And the rent covers the mortgage payments. Everybody wins. He's already drawn up the papers, and he's just waiting until we have a firm plan and a final figure."

"Sounds like this project is meant to be," Meg said. "You know, even if you do have the money, it might not hurt to do a small fund-raising campaign. You don't have to ask for much, but buying a board or a brick or getting their name on a plaque gives people a sense of ownership in the project. Maybe it will attract more attention."

Gail looked off into a dusty corner, thinking. "We'd be competing with the library fund-raising, but I think we could make it work, especially if we pitch our appeal to local historians and genealogists. I'll talk to the head librarian. Thanks for the suggestion." She looked over at Meg. "How're you doing with the orchard?" she asked.

Meg knew Gail was truly curious, not just asking a polite question. "Busy, as always. My trees came through the drought well enough, although it took a lot of work from Bree and me just keeping them watered. The apple crop may be down a bit from last year, but I don't know if this is normal or last year was. The house hasn't fallen down around my ears—yet. And the wildfires this summer missed us, thank goodness." Gail didn't know the half of that story, and Meg didn't plan to share it with anyone.

Gail laughed. "Well, you'll have Seth to help keep an eye on things, won't you? I'm assuming he'll move into your place, but where's Bree going to go?"

"That's one of those questions we've been putting off. We kind of mentioned the idea of her moving into Seth's house, but that's a lot of space for one person. On the other hand, it would be free housing and she could still walk to work. It might be better all round to find a family to buy his place, but since it was built by his ancestors and has been continuously occupied by Chapins for the last two hundred–plus years, Seth isn't exactly eager to sell. So we're still thinking about it. You've seen his place, haven't you? It's a lot like mine. And like his mother's house, too. Those early Chapins and Warrens probably all shared the work on all those houses, since they were near neighbors. Most of the other old houses in Granford are pretty much the same."

"Ah, but that's part of the charm, isn't it?" Gail said. "I shudder to think what would happen if some mogul decided that Granford was the perfect place to build his latest McMansion and all his friends followed him out here."

"Don't worry—Seth would lean on the Zoning Commission to stop them."

"Nothing like having friends in high places!" Gail agreed, laughing. "So, you ready to go home?"

"I'd better be, or Bree will skin me alive. She gave me the morning off, but we're smack in the middle of picking, and shorthanded. One of our pickers found a better job this year."

"I sure don't want to trade places with you," Gail said fervently. "Manual labor is not my thing."

The drive home took only minutes. They passed Meg's

orchard, where she saw the pickers working steadily. Each one would reach up to deftly remove an apple from a branch with a quick twist, then place it carefully in the bag strapped to his chest. When a picker's bag was full, he would then transfer the load to a nearby bin, taking care not to bruise the apples.

"You still haven't decided to try your hand at cider-making?" Gail asked as they pulled into Meg's driveway.

"Not yet. Maybe someday. I figured I'd better get the basics down before I add anything else. At the moment I'm selling the less-than-perfect apples to a local cider-maker for next to nothing. At least, I *think* he's making cider. He mentioned something about trying to make apple vodka . . ."

"Nothing new under the sun," Gail said. "In case you've wondered—and I'm sure you haven't—there used to be not one but *five* whiskey distilleries in Granford in the early 1800s. Didn't last long, though."

"Don't tell me this was a dry town?" Meg asked in mock horror.

"No, nothing like that. After all, hard cider was the drink of choice in colonial America. The distilleries failed because of economic ups and downs. Just like today."

"Speaking of drinking, you want to come in for something to drink?" Meg asked. "Although it's a bit early in the day for whiskey."

"You're just being polite, but no thanks. I'll let you get to work. And I can't wait to hear what Seth has to say about our building plans—I really want to get started on this."

"In case he forgets, I'll remind him later. Good to see you again, Gail."

Gail pulled away with a backward wave of her hand.

Meg went inside, greeted Max and Lolly, pulled a bottle of water out of the fridge, and started up the hill to join the pickers.

By six o'clock Meg and Bree were back in the kitchen, sitting in a daze of fatigue. Meg tried not to count how many crates they'd filled with apples. It was great that they had a crew of skilled workers who made the picking go quickly. But why was it that the apples would decide to ripen all at once for a short time, and then simply stall for no particular reason? *Feast or famine in picking*, Meg thought.

Thank goodness the weather was cooperating. While it was still in the high seventies during the day, the nights cooled nicely. And after the blazing-hot days and prolonged drought in August, it was a welcome change. Still, the heat during the day took its toll on her, too.

"Do we have to cook?" Meg asked.

"Yes," Bree said reluctantly. "Where's a good genie when you need one?"

"There are still plenty of veggies in the fridge, and lots of lettuce. And we should grill while we still can."

"Ugh," Bree replied. "That means standing up and finding meat and building a fire and all that stuff. I'd rather just sit here and complain."

"About what?" Seth said, coming in the door, looking energetic. Better yet, he was carrying several supermarket bags.

"Is that food?" Meg asked.

"Yes, it's food," Seth said, smiling at her plaintive tone. "I picked up some premade stuff at the market on the way home. What are you complaining about, Bree?"

She grinned. "I was wishing for a genie to show up with

food, and bingo, here you are! Maybe I should make wishes more often."

They spent a few minutes opening containers and finding plates and cutlery and cold drinks. Meg fed her cat, Lolly; Seth fed his dog, Max. Bree bounced with impatience until they finally all sat down. There followed several silent minutes devoted to intense eating.

Finally Meg leaned back in her chair and stretched. "So much better! Thank you, Seth. So how was your day?"

"Busy, although probably less physical than yours."

"Gail told me to ask whether you've had time to look over the plans she gave you. So I am. Asking, that is. I know you probably haven't had more than three minutes of free time all day."

"What's that all about?" Bree asked.

Meg recounted the meeting at the Historical Society that morning. "So what do you think, Seth? Is it doable?"

"I think so. The engineers have declared that the building is rock-solid, even though it's over two hundred years old, and I agree—I've looked at all the supporting beams and the sill. I think the soil beneath it is stable enough to support temporary shoring. The concrete pour wouldn't take long, once the framing is in place. And as for the excavation, I talked to a couple of local contractors I've worked with before. The vacuum process is cheapest overall, and they said it was appropriate for a project of this scope, since it's a relatively small building. So I guess that's the way to go."

"Gail will be thrilled," Meg said. "What permits and approvals does her board need to move forward?"

"There's a long list that the town requires, but most of them don't apply here, like a wetlands review." He started ticking off on his fingers, "We don't need to bring in the highway department since there are no street or curb changes involved. No food service, no flammable or hazardous materials. No perc test if they're hooking into town water. They *will* need a plumbing permit, but I think I can handle that for them. The only thing I'd have to verify is whether the town has to hold a public meeting or need a site plan review. Since the footprint and the elevation of the building won't change, I think we can limit ourselves to the structural issues only. I'll talk to the building inspector about what he's looking for, but I don't think he'll stand in the way. I'll verify a few things tomorrow, and then I'll talk to Gail."

"I love it—everybody wins. Granford gets to maintain the appearance of its quaint little green, the Historical Society can finally pull all of its records and artifacts together in one place with state-of-the-art storage standards, and they'll be able to make it available to the public—plus they'll have an indoor bathroom for the first time in the history of the place. *And* heat. Any other miracles you want to work before bedtime?"

"Nah. But how about you come for a walk with me and we can let Max run a bit?"

"Sounds lovely, if I can still stand up. Bree, anything we need to go over before tomorrow?"

"Did you order those crates?"

"Oh, shoot, I forgot. Do you need me to do it right now?"

"No, but you'd better do it tomorrow, lady. I'll remind you in the morning."

"Yes, ma'am."

Meg gathered up a light jacket while Seth whistled for Max. Outside the sun had fallen below the horizon, and the

air felt deliciously cool. Meg took a deep breath. Autumn
was the time of year she liked best; warm days, cool nights,
and ripe apples. They headed out toward the Great Meadow,
which ran alongside and then back beyond her house. Some
years it was boggy, she'd been told, but this year it was lush
with tall grass. Meg checked to be sure that her goats had
enough hay and water before they turned toward the faint
path that led toward the tree line at the rear. Seth tossed a
stick for Max, which the dog fetched eagerly.

"He's full of energy, isn't he?" Meg said.

"He hasn't been outside working all day. That's why I
brought him out now, so he can burn it off."

"We need to figure out where to keep him here during
the days." Seth had put in a dog run at his own house up the
hill, so he could probably do the same down here, Meg
thought. "Maybe off to the side of the old carpenter's shop?"

"I'll put it on the list," Seth said. "I should get to it by,
oh, March. Of next year."

Meg let out a snort of laughter. "Just about the time I
build a distillery and start making apple brandy."

"Hey, that's something to think about. Maybe not
brandy, but cider could be a nice little profit center for you."

"Gail was saying the same thing to me, basically. Who
do you have in mind to run it?"

"I'll think about it. Maybe there's someone at the university that you could talk to? That could fit under either
agriculture or hospitality—maybe they could supply you
with an intern, or at least a consultant." They'd reached the
end of the open meadow, and Seth put his arm around
Meg's shoulders and turned her to face the house. "You
know, you can almost believe it hasn't changed since it was
built."

"It hasn't, really," Meg said. "Except for the heating and plumbing, which don't show."

"Do you ever feel any of those generations of Warrens who lived here before you? After all, they're your kin."

"You mean, like ghosts? I . . . I'm not sure," Meg hedged. "Don't people leave something behind, when they've lived in a house for a long time? What about at your house, or your mother's?"

"Maybe," he said, but didn't elaborate. "There must be a lot of former Chapins and Warrens running around here, then."

"Well, if there are, I hope they're friendly. I *think* they are."

"So do I," Seth said. "They must like us. Ready to turn in?" When Meg nodded, he whistled to bring Max back, and then the three of them rambled back to the house in the near-dark.

4

The next morning Meg, once again up early, was seated in front of her laptop in the dining room with a cup of coffee when Bree came down the back stairs.

"Look! I'm ordering those crates!" Meg called out.

"About time," Bree grumbled.

Meg made a rude noise. "You know, I think the reason I've been putting this off is because I think the new ones are ugly. Plastic may be lighter in weight and will last longer, but I like the old wooden ones. They seem more appropriate somehow."

"But they fall apart. You love 'em so much, make 'em into furniture or something." Bree poked around in the refrigerator in search of breakfast.

Meg hit Send to place her order, then shut down the computer. Bree's suggestion had merit—maybe Seth could find some use for the recycled apple crate boards, which were nicely weathered. The new plastic ones wouldn't look the same, but no point in buying special-order wooden crates purely for sentimental reasons. Not a wise business decision, and growing and selling apples was a business.

Meg went to the kitchen for another cup of coffee. "Bree, can I ask you something?"

Bree finished buttering her muffin, then sat down. "That always sounds ominous. There a problem?"

"No, nothing like that." Meg sat down at the kitchen table across from her. "I was just thinking that even though we're working with the same crew of pickers as last year, I don't even know their names, except for Raynard. I mean, I write the checks, but I don't know who's who."

"Why do you bring this up now?" Bree asked.

"I feel guilty about it, I guess. I mean, we work side by side all the time, and I don't even know what to call them. And to them, I'm just 'Ms. Corey.'"

"Liberal guilt, eh? What do you plan to do about it?"

"Could we set up something so we could all share a meal or something? Just talk? I don't expect us to be friends, but I'm uncomfortable with whatever we are now. Do you know what I mean?"

"Maybe. I'm not all that comfortable either," Bree said, not looking happy.

"Shoot, I didn't mean to open up a whole can of worms. You're Jamaican by origin, but you've spent most of your life here, gone to college here. You're part of both sides, aren't you?"

"Or part of neither. The pickers don't trust me automatically just because my family comes from the same island. I have to earn that trust. But I see people around here look at me funny now and then because of my skin color. Not you, Meg, or Seth, but more than one other person."

"I'm sorry to hear that. I hired you because you were qualified for the job."

"Not because I came cheap?" Bree grinned.

"Well, don't think that wasn't a factor, because you know exactly how much money we're making here. But mostly it was because Christopher vouched for you, and you've proven he was right. But to get back to my first question, are you saying I *shouldn't* try to get to know the pickers, just a little?"

"No, not exactly," Bree replied slowly. "But keep it casual, you know? What were you thinking of?"

"If the weather holds, how about we just have a barbecue? Grill something outside, use up the last of the summer veggies? That is, if you think we can spare the time, or everybody isn't too exhausted at the end of the day."

"Could work, if we can do it this week. We're kind of between varieties. Short notice okay with you?"

"Sure, as long as I have time to buy food. Should Seth come, or should we keep it just us?"

"You want them to get to know you, leave him out of it. He's a good guy and all, but throwing him into the mix would change things. In my opinion."

"Got it." *Maybe.* "Anyway, you want to ask if one day is better than another for them?"

"Fine. Now finish your coffee—we've got to get up the hill."

Seth was already outside, loading up his van for the day's round of projects, so Meg wandered out to say hello (or maybe it was good-bye). "Are you going to talk to Gail today?" she asked.

"If I can find the time. I'll double-check the permitting requirements, but I think she's okay there, and I'll get some bids from excavating companies—not that there are many who use the vacuum process and can be here on a tight schedule. Plus I have to find one or more contractors who can shore up the building and pour a foundation on that same tight schedule."

"Don't drive yourself crazy," Meg said. "After all, the Historical Society has muddled along for, what, thirty years now? They can wait another week. By the way, what exactly is your official role with them?"

"General contractor, I guess. Which if I'm lucky won't conflict with my official responsibilities to the town. I'm just overseeing it, lining up the subcontractors, things like that, so the society doesn't have to hire someone else to do it. My main goal is to get the job done quickly and save the Historical Society as much money as possible, but still get it done right."

"You mean you're not getting paid for this? It's not like you don't have enough else to do."

"Are you worried that I'm going to start mooching off of you? Look, I volunteered because I want to do this, for the town. It's one of the oldest buildings in Granford, and I want to be sure this is done right. Don't worry—it won't take long."

Meg wasn't sure she believed that last statement, but she didn't doubt that Seth was serious about caring about the building. His Granford ancestors had probably attended religious services there, since they'd been among the town's earliest settlers, after Seth's great-great-times-whatever grandfather Samuel Chapin had finished the official survey for this part of Massachusetts. Come to think of it, her

Warren ancestors had probably been there as well, in the adjoining pew or bench or whatever they used back then, so she should be interested, too. The real problem was that Seth had a tendency to bite off more than he could chew, and he had trouble saying no to anyone.

"Anyway, we'll see how it goes. I assume you'll be up the hill in the orchard?" he said.

"Of course. Dinner?"

"I'll let you know. Oh, by the way, I heard Rick Sainsbury will be coming through town. Or at least, he'll be hitting Northampton and Amherst. The places where the money is."

Rick Sainsbury was a Granford native and former high school football hero who was also a newly minted candidate for a vacant congressional seat for the district that included Granford in the coming November election. Now he was trying to capitalize on his local connections for the election, which was no surprise. He wasn't what Meg and Seth would call a friend of theirs, but it made sense to maintain a cordial relationship with the man who might be their next congressman.

"Do you think he's likely to drop in on us?" Meg asked.

Seth laughed. "I doubt his campaign staff would let him, since he's got kind of a compressed schedule until the election, but he might hit us up to volunteer for the campaign, or, heaven forbid, make a contribution."

"I think we've made all the contribution we need to," Meg replied tartly. "Not that I have any money to spare. And I thought you didn't feel warm and fuzzy enough about him to volunteer."

"Most likely I won't, but I just wanted to alert you. He's

going to be around until the election. Granford looks so good on television."

"Gosh, maybe you should worry about starting a messy construction project right on the green, if he's hoping to use it as a backdrop."

"If I know him, he'll just parlay it into a sound bite about how we 'treasure our local history.' Of course, that might be good publicity for the Historical Society. Or maybe 'providing jobs for local workers.'" Seth slammed shut the rear doors of the van. "Well, it hasn't happened yet, and who knows if it will. I'll try to make it back for dinner, and I'll let you know if anything changes." With that, he hopped into the driver's seat and pulled out with a wave.

Meg sighed. She gathered up her gear and headed up the hill to join Bree and the pickers.

Hours later, Meg's stomach was telling her it was well past lunchtime when she saw Gail Selden pull into her driveway. *Again?* Funny how someone who dealt with centuries of history could be so impatient.

"Bree?" Meg called out. "Gail Selden just arrived. I'm going to go down and see what she needs, so I'll take a break and get some lunch, okay?"

"Sure, fine. I'll be down in a bit."

Meg loped down the hill. It was only when she reached the driveway that she realized that Gail was not alone. Gail was leaning against her car, and next to her stood a kid who looked to be about fifteen—too old to be one of Gail's kids, both of whom Meg had met anyway. This boy was unfamiliar to her, though. He was conspicuously neat (not that Meg had a lot to compare teenagers to these days; she didn't see many of them in her line of work). He wore what she assumed was still the standard uniform for high school kids—T-shirt, jeans, and running shoes—but the items all looked very clean, almost new, and his hair was neatly cut.

"Hi, Gail," Meg called out.

"Sorry to barge in on you like this, but I talked to Seth this morning and he said we could go ahead, and I'm just so excited. He's so great! We couldn't do this without him." The words tumbled out of Gail's mouth.

"Hey, slow down, please. I'm glad it's working out—it sounds interesting. Did you stop by to tell me that?"

"No, it's a bit more than that. Have you eaten? I brought sandwiches and stuff. Can we go inside and sit down?"

"Of course. Come on in." Meg led the way into the kitchen, noting that the boy politely held the door for the two of them first, and when they walked into the kitchen, she saw him catch sight of her cat, Lolly, sitting on top of the refrigerator, and go over to introduce himself by offering his hand for her to sniff before scratching behind her ears.

"I didn't know what you'd want, so I got all sorts of things," Gail said as she went straight for the table in the center of the room and started laying out sandwiches and chips and napkins. "Oh, jeez, where are my manners? Meg, this lovely young man is Jeffrey Green. He's a student at the high school in Granford. And he's also a Boy Scout, which is why he came to talk to me."

Meg's stomach was growling. "Welcome, Jeffrey. Let's sit down and eat, and you can tell me why you're here."

"Thank you, ma'am." The boy waited until both Meg and Gail were seated before sitting down himself. Who had taught him his manners? Meg hadn't seen this kind of courtesy from a young person for quite a while.

Talk of anything serious was deferred until after they'd all selected sandwiches. "You live here in Granford, Jeffrey?" Meg asked between bites.

"Yes, over toward Belchertown. It's kind of a new house—not like this one."

"By new he means post–World War Two," Gail tossed in, "which I guess is new by your and my standards."

"Only by a couple of hundred years, Jeffrey," Meg said. "What brought you to Gail and the Historical Society?"

Jeffrey glanced at Gail, who nodded her encouragement. "Uh, okay. You know Rick Sainsbury?"

That wasn't what she expected to hear. "Yes, as it happens I do." Was Rick using teenagers to infiltrate local households and beg for money for his campaign?

"He's my uncle, my mother's brother. Since he won in the primary, he's been putting pressure on my family to be part of his campaign. My mom's really into it—it's her kind of thing. But I really suck—oh, sorry—I'm really bad at shaking hands and smiling at lots of people. I told my mom about six times and I guess she finally heard me, but then she started saying that I never did anything other than study, and I told her that I was in the Boy Scouts, and she said back that I didn't do anything except show up for meetings . . ."

He seemed to run out of steam, so Meg broke in gently. "I don't like political campaigns much either. But I'm still not sure I understand what this has to do with the Historical Society."

Jeffrey took a deep breath. "I figured I'd better do something that she'd actually recognize. What do you know about Scouting?"

"Not much. What should I know?"

"Well, the Boy Scouts of America is a national organization, founded to promote good character, citizenship, and personal fitness." The boy sounded as though he was reciting from a manual, Meg thought. "A lot of activities take place outdoors, like camping, and there are a lot of community service projects too, like litter cleanup in your town, or food collection. You can advance by earning merit badges. Since I was already in Scouts, my mother decided that I ought to try to make Eagle Scout before I went to college—said it would look good on my applications. I'm already a senior, so I'd need to get more badges soon. I would need twenty-one in all. There's a whole list of them to choose from, but I wanted to do something that interested me, and I figured if I took part in the Historical Society project, I could use that for my archaeology badge. I really like history, and it's also kind of a public project for the town." By the time he'd reached the last part of his explanation, Jeffrey had begun to show some enthusiasm.

"That sounds great," Meg said, upwardly revising her estimation of Jeffrey's age. If he was already a senior, he was probably closer to seventeen than fifteen. "I'm here because I'm curious, too, and I also like history."

"Let me fill in a bit," Gail broke in. "Karen Green, Jeffrey's mother, is on our board, and she's helped out with a couple of projects. She's been involved since we first started talking about our building renovations. I don't know if we'll see a contribution from her, not that it's essential. Don't worry, Jeffrey—I'm not going to make you nag your mother! But I think that may have planted a bee in her bonnet. Do you agree?"

He nodded. "Yeah. I said I was interested in archaeology, and she said right away that the Historical Society was going to be digging up its building, and maybe I should see if I could help. Of course, according to Scouting regulations there's a lot more to it than just watching, like some research and some hands-on stuff, but I thought it sounded like a good idea. And it would make both of us happy."

"Jeffrey stopped in just after I'd talked to Seth," Gail finished triumphantly. "And here we are. Is Seth around, Meg?"

"I don't know where he is at the moment—he's all over the place these days. I'll tell him what you and Jeffrey said, unless you'd rather tell him yourself. Do you know Seth Chapin, Jeffrey?"

"Don't think I've met him. He knows my uncle, though, right?"

"They knew each other slightly in high school," Meg told him. That was the simplest way to put it, and Jeffrey didn't need to know more about the history between the two men. Meg wondered briefly whether encouraging Jeffrey to take part in the Historical Society project was somehow meant to pull Seth into Rick's campaign—not that she suspected Jeffrey of any ulterior motives. She'd pass on to Seth that Rick's nephew wanted to be part of the project, and they could work it out between them.

"Anyway, I've already started some of the research," Jeffrey said. "Gail told me that the building was actually the first meetinghouse for Granford, before they built the big church. Did you know that, Miss Corey?"

"Seth just explained it to me recently."

Gail interrupted. "I'm sure you'll find some even more interesting stuff when you start looking—I can help you with that. Like who the original church members were, and who contributed the land and helped build the building. Things like that."

"Thank you—that's the kind of thing I'd like to do. There's a genealogy badge, too, so maybe I could work on the two badges at the same time."

"Sounds like a plan!" Gail said. "Meg, we won't keep you any longer. I know you have things to do. Tell Seth I stopped by. Come on, Jeffrey."

The boy stood up. "It was nice to meet you, Miss Corey."

Meg couldn't remember the last time she'd been called "miss." "Meg, please. I expect I'll be seeing more of you."

She let the two out her kitchen door, then sat for a moment to finish her drink. She knew next to nothing about the Boy Scouts—but then, why would she? She had had no brothers. She herself had been a Girl Scout for a scant year before losing interest, mainly because the troop leader insisted on doing a lot of boring things she already knew how to do anyway. Well, there were the annual cookie sales—those she remembered. She still had a few favorite kinds.

But Jeffrey seemed like a nice boy, and local history was an interesting pursuit. His participation might be a good thing all around—he'd get a badge or two, and maybe his mother would be pleased. Meg couldn't remember meeting Rick's sister when he'd last been in Granford, but now she wasn't sure she wanted to; from what her son had said or hinted about her, she sounded kind of pushy. Meg had sensed a little resentment from Gail, too.

Meg finished her drink, then went back to work. She spent the rest of the afternoon picking, and was back in the kitchen cooking dinner when Seth rolled in. He didn't look exhausted for once. She greeted him with a kiss.

"Do I smell food?" he asked, when he finally pulled away.

"You do. I decided to make something for a change. You want a beer? Wine?"

"No, I think I have to go over some invoices after dinner if I want to get paid anytime soon, so I should keep a clear head. You want to talk while you cook or should I leave you in peace?"

"Hey, I can do two things at once. Sit, have some water." He did both as Meg went on, "Gail Selden stopped in today."

Seth laughed. "Why am I not surprised? Was she looking for me?"

"In part. She said you'd given her the green light, anyway. But there was something else—she brought a kid along with her. Do you know Jeffrey Green? Sweet boy, kind of a throwback to the fifties, very neat and polite. Anyway, he wants to do a Boy Scout merit badge in archaeology or history or something based on the Historical Society excavation."

"That sounds like a good idea, as long as he doesn't get in the way."

"One more thing," Meg said, keeping her eyes on the pan on the stove. "Rick Sainsbury is his uncle."

Seth tilted the chair back. "Oh ho! The plot thickens. Of course—Jeffrey's mother must be Rick's older sister Karen."

"Do you know her? Gail says she's on the board of the Historical Society," Meg asked.

"I know who she is, but I can't say I know her or her husband well. They're a few years older than us, and we don't really move in the same circles."

"Anyway, Jeffrey seems like a nice kid. I got the feeling he's doing this badge because his mother wants him to, although he seems honestly interested in the history of the place."

"So it probably has nothing to do with Rick or his campaign. Don't worry about it, Meg. I'm pretty sure I can handle it."

"I never doubted that."

Bree came in at that point. "Food?" she asked piteously. "When?"

"Right now," Meg said. "Go wash your hands and I'll dish up."

Postdinner, Bree retired as soon as the dishes were done, before Meg remembered she hadn't asked Bree if she'd talked to the pickers. "Seth, I'll be right back. I have to go ask Bree about something."

"Don't be long," Seth said, "or I'll fall asleep waiting."

"Two minutes." Meg smiled. Then she turned and went quickly up the back stairs that led to Bree's room over the kitchen. She rapped on the door, and after a few moments Bree opened it.

"Problem?" Bree said.

"No. I only wondered if you'd asked the pickers if they'd like to come to a cookout."

"I did," Bree said, then stopped.

"And?" Meg prompted.

"They said okay. Sort of."

"What's that supposed to mean?" Meg asked.

"They seemed kind of confused about why you're doing this, but they're happy to have a free meal and some relaxed time. I know it's short notice, but is tomorrow night all right?"

"Works for me, as long as there's time to buy food. And what are we making?"

"We?" Bree arched an eyebrow.

"Yes, we. Unless you think they won't eat anything I

make? Really, I was going to keep it simple—barbecued chicken, the last of the corn, salad. You can add whatever you want."

"All right. I'll get some stuff in the morning. We gonna do this out back?"

"Yes, weather permitting."

"Okay. Was that all?"

"Yes, it was."

"Good night, then. See you in the morning." Bree shut the door, leaving Meg standing on the top stair.

Not exactly what she would have called a warm response. Was that lack of enthusiasm coming from Bree or from the pickers? Meg had no idea, but she was going to have that dinner and see what came from it. If it turned out to be a mistake, she wouldn't have to repeat it, but at least she'd know she'd tried.

5

"I can't believe this all came together so fast, Seth," Meg said the next morning, watching as heavy trucks rumbled up the church driveway and parked around the Historical Society building. "Yesterday you were just talking about it, and today it's happening. Did you have to grease any palms? Twist any arms?"

Seth laughed. "No, not really. I mean, in this business we all do favors for each other, but nothing illegal, immoral, or unethical. Mostly little stuff, like expediting paperwork. This is a relatively small project, so the contractors with a little spare time could fit it in easily. Besides, we all thought that having started the work would make it more interesting to people at the Harvest Festival."

"Oh, shoot, is that coming up again?" Meg said. The Granford Harvest Festival and Tag Sale was an annual event that took place on the green. It was an endearing

hodgepodge of local vendors, like the family who made
their own maple syrup on the north end of town—and
tapped the trees around the green as well—and people who
had decided to clear out their attics and thought they could
sell their "treasures" for a couple of bucks. In general a
good time was had by all, as neighbors stopped to chat with
each other and buy each other's junk. Since the Historical
Society was just the other side of the green, they usually
attracted a fair number of people who otherwise never set
foot in the building. This year they would certainly have an
interesting story!

"You sound so excited," Seth said, with a note of sarcasm. "Yes, it's next weekend—the one after this one, in
the middle of the month. You really didn't remember?"

"Nope. I've been kind of focused on my apples, in case
you haven't noticed, and I guess I was relying on you to
remind me. Which you just did. Or maybe I'm blocking it
out—last year my mother was here for it, if you recall."
And things had gone downhill rapidly from there, as she
remembered it. No wonder she had tried to forget, though
luckily things had all worked out in the end. Was it already
a year ago that she had brought her mother along to the
event? She made a note to talk to her mother again soon—
she'd been remarkably restrained about hounding Meg for
a wedding date. "So why do you think that if people see the
big hole in the ground, they'll be more interested in the
Historical Society?"

"Well, the kids, or at least the little boys, will probably
think the big trucks are cool—we might have to bring those
back just for the event, which would be good advertising
for them. And if this works well, it might get some people thinking about adding a basement or expanding what

they've got. Anyway, if all goes according to plan, the excavation should be done, and the foundation poured by then. Which reminds me, if we have an open construction site in the middle of the Harvest Festival, then I'd better talk to Art Preston about making sure it's safe. Speak of the devil—hi, Art."

"Hey, Seth. Hi, Meg. Long time no see," said Art Preston, Granford's chief of police, as he wandered over in their direction. "Did I hear you talking about me?"

"We were. I was just telling Meg that you'll need to staff up if we're going to have a big construction site open right here on the green during Harvest Festival."

"Way ahead of you, pal—it's all set. It's not like I haven't been doing this for a while."

"But you never had to deal with an open pit and heavy machinery before, did you?" Seth countered. Meg watched in amusement: the two had been friends for years, and it showed.

"Can't say that we have, but I'm sure we'll be able to handle it."

"What are you doing here, anyway?" Seth asked.

Art grinned. "I heard you had some big trucks coming over to suck all the dirt out from under that building there. How could I stay away?"

"This is really just the first pass—you know, to get a sense of what kind of soil is down there. And of course the crew will have to stabilize the building each step of the way. We'd look like idiots if the thing fell down while we were working on it. And, yes, the excavation contractors know all about proper fencing and safeguards. I made sure everybody had the right permits."

"I'm just here to keep an eye on 'em."

Gail came up behind them, again accompanied by Jeffrey, and greeted everyone. "I know not much is happening today, but I wanted to be here for the start. This is so exciting!"

"What are you doing here, young man?" Art said with mock severity. "Isn't this a school day?"

Jeffrey responded quickly. "It is, sir, but my mom gave me a note so I could watch, too. It's for a Boy Scout badge project, and Mrs. Selden here knows about it. I'll be going back over to the school once things get rolling."

"I'm just kidding you, son," Art said. "I don't blame you for wanting to watch."

"Just like you, eh, Art?" Meg said sweetly.

Gail said impatiently, "Tell me again what's going to happen, Seth?"

"These fine gentlemen—sorry, but they don't happen to have any female employees handling the equipment—will be using an air vacuum excavation system. Essentially they shoot air to break up the soil so it can be sucked up easily. Then they truck the soil away and use it for landfill, if it's clean enough. What you see there"—Seth pointed—"is the unit. It has a diesel-driven compressor on one end, and they attach the vacuum hose at the other. The dirt goes into a holding tank, and then gets transferred through the hatch on the bottom. They might be done by the end of the day today, or tomorrow at the latest, depending on what they find. The rest of the guys hanging out over there drinking coffee are waiting to insert the bracers and jacks, so this will go in fits and starts. Then they'll start building the forms for the foundation, starting with extra-deep pads for any support columns. That'll be done by hand."

"Do you think you'll find any artifacts?" Jeffrey spoke up.

"A very appropriate question," Seth answered him.

"Actually they've got it rigged up so that the soil that's removed gets dumped onto a screen up at the dump truck over there. That may be where you want to station yourself, so you can watch for anything interesting that may come through. Then the screen is cleared off into the truck and the process starts again."

"Is that a safe spot for him?" Art said, tilting his head toward Jeffrey.

"Sure. Eye and ear protection are required, but this isn't a very large vacuum excavator, so the pressure isn't too high. They come a lot bigger, but this is plenty for our needs here. Although, sorry, Jeffrey—you might get kind of dirty. I should have thought to warn you."

Jeffrey shrugged. "Bet it'd be a real thrill for the kids at school to see me come in looking grubby. They usually call me 'Mr. Clean.' Or sometimes 'Teflon Jeff.'"

"Can we get started?" Gail asked, bouncing with anticipation.

"Let me check in with the crew," Seth said. He walked toward a knot of people and started talking with someone who appeared to be the crew chief.

"What're you doing for the Harvest Festival, Meg?" Gail made small talk, but her eyes never left the construction workers.

"I'm supposed to do something?" Meg responded, dismayed. She had planned on merely attending—besides, this year she'd be with Seth. Since he knew everybody in town, and they all knew him, no doubt everyone would offer congratulations on their engagement, and probably want to know when the event was going to happen. The two of them really had to come up with a plan sometime soon, but they both led such busy lives, at least at the moment.

Not the best time to try to fit in a wedding. It made sense to wait until winter, maybe even early spring, when both their schedules would slow down. Seth's mother, Lydia, understood, thank goodness, but Meg wasn't as sure about her own mother.

"You don't have to, of course. It's not like you have a business to promote or anything," Gail said, the twinkle in her eye giving away that she was teasing.

"Well, it's not like I usually sell directly to the public," Meg retorted. "But I guess it might be nice to put in an appearance. Maybe I should put up a table with different apple varieties, and raffle off a basket or two."

"That's the spirit!" Gail said.

"Will the Historical Society have a table?"

"Of course. I want to show off our hole in the ground and collect contributions."

Seth returned. "Looks like we're good to go."

Gail held up a small camera. "Mind if I take some pictures? This is part of our institutional history, and I'm sure the board will want a record."

"Go right ahead," Seth said to Gail, then pointed Jeffrey to a man standing next to the dump truck a few yards away. "Ask him where you should stand. He's expecting you," Seth told the teen. "And he'll give you a pair of goggles and ear protection and some gloves, because there'll be pebbles and stuff bouncing around—make sure you wear them. You two can work out some kind of hand signal to use if you see something worth taking a look at and he can tell the guys to stop."

"How hard can I look?" Jeffrey asked.

"What do you mean?"

"I mean, how big does it have to be for them to stop?

Like, if I see a bowl land in the tray, that's pretty easy. But what if I see a one-inch shard of something?"

"Let's not get ahead of ourselves," Gail said. "Remember, there may not turn out to be anything to see. As far as we know, this was the first building on this site, so there may not be many artifacts beneath it."

"*Or* there could be a ton of Native American artifacts," Jeffrey replied cheerfully as he headed off for the dump truck.

Once the machine with the compressor started up, the noise made conversation challenging. "They're going to start at this end, in the front," Seth yelled, "and those guys over there are going to go in and check for progress every couple of feet, at least until things get rolling. And then they'll start shoring up the building."

"Right," Meg shouted back. She glanced over at Jeffrey, who waved at her. He looked excited.

One man took hold of what Meg assumed was the vacuum rod and advanced on the building. It looked heavy but not difficult to direct. Seth had told her that a water-driven system was another option, using something much like a large fire hose, but she couldn't imagine wrestling a torrent of water. Air seemed a lot less messy.

The sparse shrubbery had been cleared away from the old stone foundation, and some men had dug some preliminary holes, carefully removing the large granite foundation stones, which now lay a few feet behind the building. They didn't extend very deep, Meg noted, wondering—not for the first time—how this and buildings like it had managed to survive for so long, especially in an area where the ground froze and thawed regularly. The worker stuck the end of the hose rod into the dirt, and the sound changed. Meg thought it sounded like someone was shaking a very large jar of marbles, as dirt and pebbles and who knew what else were sucked up and transported to the waiting truck. At that end the truck driver worked to control the exit hose, directing it toward a large flat tray, which Jeffrey leaned over, oblivious to the flying pebbles hitting his protective eyewear, and sorted through with a gloved hand. He didn't find anything, so he and the other guy dumped the contents of the tray into the growing pile of excavated debris.

Every so often, the workers would stop the hose and climb into the expanding hole under the building, and then they'd call over some of the other workers, and they'd all point and poke and confer. Art was still hanging around, no doubt claiming official oversight privileges, and now and then he'd ask Seth a question. The process went on for a while, and Meg began checking her watch. Luckily, today was a light picking day, since she and her crew were waiting for the next batch of apples to ripen, so there was a little breathing room. Not that there weren't still plenty of things Bree would find for her to be doing back home. And, of course, now there was the pickers' dinner to prepare for that evening.

"Is this waiting around normal?" Meg asked Seth, during one of the lulls a while later.

"More or less. But I'd rather they were careful than fast. You really don't know what kind of shape a building is in until you get into it, or in this case, under it. You bored?"

"Not exactly, but I've been here over an hour and the hole hasn't grown a whole lot. I may have seen enough for today. Jeffrey's still hanging in there. You think he's really interested, or he's just enjoying time away from school?"

"At his age, it's hard to say. He seems like a good kid,

but I'd have to call him kind of a nerd. Although I collected
arrowheads and various odds and ends at his age, so who
am I to judge? They're probably still in a box in my attic."
Meg realized she had no idea what average young people
were interested in these days. She hadn't spent much time
around teenagers since she was one. Seth's sister Rachel's
kids were still under high school age, and they had provided most of her recent experience. She remembered her
own high school days, particularly senior year, as a messy
mixture of anxiety and boredom. She doubted that a lot of
younger people cared much about history, even if they lived
in colonial homes like hers. They probably just complained
that the ceilings were too low and that it was impossible to
air-condition them, much less add the wiring necessary for
all their electronic devices.

The hose resumed its racket again, cutting off conversation. Meg was looking away from the site, admiring the
view of the green, its stately maples just beginning to turn
color, when she heard shouting. She looked first at Jeffrey,
who was gesturing wildly and yelling, "Stop," which she
could hear even over the noise of the machinery. Someone
cut it off, and then Jeffrey beckoned to anyone and everyone to come over to the truck.

When they were only a few feet away, he said, "Is this
what I think it is?" He pointed to the tray.

Seth was the first to clamber up into the bed of the truck.
He looked down at the tray then shook his head. Then he
called over to Art Preston. "Art, I think we have a problem."

"Oh no! What is it?" Gail burst out, climbing up toward
the truck bed. Seth stopped her with a hand, and kept her
still until Art had joined him next to the tray.

"Crap," Art said. "I should have known trouble would

follow you two. Why are things never simple when you're around?"

"What is it?" Meg called out.

Gail approached tentatively. "Oh, dear. That looks like part of a skull."

"It is," Art said grimly. "Which means it's time to call in the state police. Sorry, Gail, but for the moment I have to declare this a crime scene."

6

Work came to a standstill as the news of the gruesome discovery spread among the workers and spectators around the Historical Society building. Luckily, having the chief of police on-scene meant that Art Preston had known immediately what to do. *He must have the state police on speed dial*, Meg reflected. Even to Meg's inexperienced eye, though, the chunks of skull looked like they had probably been in the ground for a very long time. She wasn't surprised when Jeffrey asked the same question of Art, who took the time to explain to him that, "Even though it's pretty likely that this body has been under the building for at least a hundred years, in Massachusetts any unexplained death must be investigated, by law."

"That's interesting," was all Jeffrey said.

When Art went off to make the call, Meg walked over to join Gail and Seth next to the truck, staring at the bone fragments. Jeffrey was still standing on the bed of the truck, looking stunned by his find. "Are you okay?" Meg asked him quietly, concerned that he might feel a bit traumatized.

But when he turned his attention to her, he looked more excited than upset. "Yeah, sure! Wow, I never expected anything like this! One minute I'm looking at dirt, the next minute I'm looking at, well, something that used to be . . . someone. Really weird."

Apparently teenagers are very resilient, Meg thought. "Do you need to call your folks?" she asked.

"Why would I do that?" He looked perplexed by her question.

"So they can pick you up?"

"Why would they need to do that? Anyway, I've got my own car," Jeffrey said. "So what happens next? Do you know?"

"As Art just said, in Massachusetts, any time a body is found—and I'm guessing we'll find the rest of the skeleton under there—if the cause of death can't be determined, the site has to be treated as a crime scene until it can be proven otherwise. Now, with a body this old, they may want a forensic anthropologist to look at it, along with the medical examiner. And then somebody is going to have to excavate the rest of the area very carefully to see if there's any evidence left after all these years."

Gail and Seth had drifted closer to the edge of the partially dug hole, deep in conversation, but now Gail came back toward Meg and Jeffrey. "Gail, how're you doing?" Meg asked.

Gail shook her head, clearly frustrated. "I'm trying to figure out how on earth I explain this to the society board. Uh, construction was delayed by the discovery of a skeleton? At least it's an old one, right?"

"I'm not the person to ask," Meg said. "Have you worked with any archaeologist types at the university or somewhere else?"

Gail shut her eyes for a moment, as if to collect her wandering thoughts, then straightened her back. "I can probably pull up a few names. But won't the state police do that?"

"I wouldn't count on it," Meg said. "Normally if this was a modern death they would have their guy take a look at the remains, and a forensic team would come in and pick up what they can from the scene, and then they'd all pack up and go their own way. If this is a really old burial, they may take a quick look and dismiss it. But for you, if this burial has any historic significance, you might want to handle it differently. This is an eighteenth-century building, right? Was the land ever a burial ground?"

"Not that I know about," Gail said. "But that's not to say there weren't family burial plots on individual properties, although often they were marked with some kind of stones, even if they weren't inscribed. Sometimes the location wasn't recorded because the family just figured they'd remember where they put great-grandmother. Sorry if that sounds kind of thoughtless, but this has me rattled. As I remember it, the land here was given to the town for the specific purpose of building a meetinghouse, back in seventeen-whatever. The sons of the original landowner donated it after he died—one of them should have known that the body was here, if it was family land. Heck, there may be more bodies under there. I bet the police are really going to love checking that out—it's not like they can just crawl under there and start digging willy-nilly because the building might fall on their heads. I'd *really* rather not have to deal with that."

"Let's take one problem at a time, Gail," Meg said, try-ing to sound reassuring. "Art was here when the body was found, and he's calling the state police. Nobody has touched anything. You're here on behalf of the Historical Society, the official owner of this property, so you can explain to the state police exactly what was going on when we found the . . . skull. Maybe you should take some pictures while you still can?"

"Oh yeah, right. Good idea. I'll do that. What've we got?" Gail confronted the bits of skull. Once Jeffrey had noticed the first piece, an unmistakable chunk of cranium, they'd cautiously gone through the rest of the dirt and found some smaller pieces as well. Meg could see Gail shifting into a more analytical mode. "I see some teeth, although I really doubt there were dentists handy when whoever-it-was died, so it's not like we can use them to match dental records. Nothing to indicate gender from this end, but there may be other bones or personal artifacts still under the building. From the size of the skull pieces, it looks like an adult, which is better than the alternative. Jeffrey, how you holding up?" The boy was still staying close to his find.

"This is so cool! I mean, it's like *CSI* meets American history."

"Speaking of history, we'll have to look into the history of this site a little more closely—maybe you can help us with that, Jeffrey."

"I'd love to help. You know, I was watching the soil as it came through the tube pretty closely, and it looked uni-form. No changes in texture or color, and I didn't see any other big pieces of bone fragments. Maybe we were lucky and started at the head end, and the rest is still in there?"

"We really shouldn't get ahead of ourselves," Gail said, "but write down what you saw, okay? It might be useful. Anyway, I'm sure the police will ask the right questions."

Meg wasn't as sure, but then she'd never seen them in action with an antique body. Would anyone be able to identify it? And whether or not they did, what did you do with a centuries-old body, with no family to claim it? Although, she reminded herself, there were a lot of families in Granford now who bore the surnames of people who had lived in the town from the beginning. Maybe it wasn't so absurd to think there might still be a local relative around.

"You guys mind if I hang around?" Jeffrey asked. "I mean, I'm kind of the one who found the body, or at least part of it. The police are going to want to talk to me, right? And I bet I'll learn a lot more here than in class today."

Oh, to be so young again, Meg thought. For him these bone fragments were an interesting puzzle, not remnants of a human being who'd lived and died here. Of course, Meg had to admit she too was curious about why a body had suddenly turned up in the middle of their routine building project. She was happily surprised not to have found any burial plots on her own property—yet—and she wasn't about to go looking for any. Besides, she could account for most of the Warrens whose genealogy she knew about, since their tombstones were all lined up in the town cemetery. She'd have to ask Seth if he knew about any Chapin plots scattered around the land he and his mother still held.

Seth made one last comment to the crew still standing around the excavation, then walked over and stood beside the truck, watching for a state police car coming from Northampton. "I told the crew to stop whatever they were doing but to stick around until they could talk to the police," he told them. "They weren't exactly happy about it, but they all understood why. You okay?"

"Oh, sure, I'm fine," Meg said with a false cheeriness. "I take a day off, and the first thing I find is a body. At least I'm just an innocent bystander."

"That you are," Seth agreed. "Gail, you holding it together?"

Gail was busy snapping pictures of the remnants of the skull. "I'm staying busy so I don't have to think about it. Won't our next newsletter be interesting?"

"This was Moody land originally, wasn't it?" Seth asked her.

Gail stopped what she was doing and faced him. "Yes, it was. Seth, you consistently embarrass me by knowing as much or more about my town than I do, and I'm the official keeper of its history. How do you do that?"

"I ask him the same question all the time, Gail," Meg said with a grin as Seth shrugged. "Seth, are there any Moodys around that we could talk to?"

"Um, excuse me," Jeffrey broke in. "Like I told you, I'm working on my Scout genealogy merit badge. Maybe I could do some research on who gave this land to the town back then? And what descendants are still around?"

"That's a great idea!" Gail said. "I'd be happy to sponsor that, or oversee it, or whatever you need. I know the town has some of the original documents right up there in the town hall," Gail said. "But I don't want it to interfere with your schoolwork. Or get you in trouble with your parents if it takes up too much of your time."

"I'm sure they'd want me to assist the police," Jeffrey said, trying to look serious. Meg suppressed a smile and avoided looking at Seth. Knowing what she did about some of Jeffrey's uncle Rick's activities, the family could hardly object to a few innocent inquiries into Granford's past. And from the way Jeffrey looked, it might be hard to stop him. He'd caught the history bug.

"I think once the state police take a look at this, they'll decide it's not a crime scene pretty fast," Seth said. "Besides, it's going to be hard to find evidence over two hundred years old."

Jeffrey looked disappointed. "Well, I'll stick around for today, anyway."

"Fair enough." Seth nodded toward the road. "Looks like the state police have arrived."

The state car pulled up alongside the green, and Meg immediately recognized Detective William Marcus, whom she'd met before. More than once. Their current relationship might best be defined as a bit prickly. But this time around, he really couldn't accuse her of any illegal involvement. Meg watched as Art went to meet him; they paused out of earshot, and Meg assumed Art was bringing him up to speed on what had been uncovered so far. Then they walked over to the truck, where the pieces of skull still lay.

"Who's this?" Detective Marcus looked at Jeffrey.

Jeffrey stepped forward quickly, his right hand outstretched. "I'm Jeffrey Green, sir. I'm working on a Scout merit badge in archaeology, so I was here to participate in the excavation of this historic building. I was the one who first saw the, uh, victim."

Detective Marcus looked taken aback by Jeffrey's speech, but he shook his hand cordially enough.

Then Gail stepped forward. "Detective, I'm Gail Selden. I'm the director of the Historical Society, and I'm representing our board at the construction process here."

"Not quite what you were expecting, was it?" Marcus said with what might be considered a smile.

"No, of course not. This building was erected sometime around 1762, before the town of Granford even officially existed. We had no reason to think there might be any kind of burial on the site."

"I see. Seth, what are you doing here?" Marcus turned his attention to Seth.

"I'm serving more or less as general contractor for the Historical Society. I brought in the excavation crew here."

"Fill me in on the project, one of you? You planning to move the building or something?"

Gail spoke quickly. "No. We need room to house our collections. We looked at our options, and digging out beneath the building and creating climate-controlled storage space there seemed to be the best solution. That way we could preserve the historic integrity of the building's profile."

"Huh. Never heard of anything like that, but it sounds interesting. How far did you get before you found . . . this?" He waved at the skull fragments.

"We'd just started. There may be more bones under there," Gail said.

"The crew stopped digging as soon as we saw the skull fragments," Seth added. "Is the ME on his way?"

"Yes, he is."

"Hey, wait a minute, please, Detective," Gail said quickly. "You can't just grab the bones and whatever else you find and haul it off to Northampton. This could yield important information about the town's earliest years."

"You have an alternate suggestion?" Marcus countered. "Because if you don't, it's the ME's call."

"Yes, I do." Gail exchanged a look with Meg. "I can

make some calls, see if I can find a forensic archaeologist nearby."

Marcus sighed. "So you're going to tell me this is an historic site and this should be treated as an archaeological dig? Good luck with that." Then he added, "Let's see if you can make that happen today, unless you want your project to stall while we analyze the, uh, remains."

"Right away," Gail said. "I know someone I can talk to right now." She pulled out her cell phone and walked to the middle of the green to call. She was back in three minutes. "Got her!" she crowed. "I've got a friend who teaches at UMass who's an archaeological anthropologist. She's on her way!"

7

As if there hadn't been enough people crowded around before—between the excavation crew, the construction crew that had planned to shore up the building, and onlookers Seth, Meg, Gail, Art, and Jeffrey—now the state police had joined the fray, soon followed by the medical examiner's van. When the ME, Dr. Elijah Bartlett, parked and climbed out, Gail set off at a brisk trot to intercept him before Detective Marcus could get there. She snagged Bartlett in conversation even as he tried to walk toward the group. When they were a few yards away, Meg could hear Gail pleading, ". . . and if you could just wait a little longer before you disturb the body . . ." Gail looked up to find Marcus blocking her path.

"Ms. Selden, let the man do his job, will you?"

"But he could be destroying valuable historic evidence!" Gail protested.

"I strongly suspect that he will concur with your preliminary assessment that the body has been in the ground for a very long time, and therefore how it got there is not a concern of ours. Although the ultimate disposal of the remains might be."

"Oh," Gail replied, losing steam. "Okay. I can live with that. But my anthropologist friend is on her way over from Amherst now. Can you wait a few minutes? Please?"

Detective Marcus looked reluctant but did not protest. Meg wondered if he had nothing more pressing to do and simply couldn't bring himself to make up an excuse. It was, in fact, only around five minutes before yet another car pulled up and a slender woman about Meg's age climbed out. If this was the expert from UMass, she must have broken a lot of speed regulations to arrive so quickly. Meg wondered if the woman hoped that there were more skeletons waiting to be uncovered.

Gail hurried over to greet, and no doubt warn, her friend about where she might find herself in the pecking order for access to the bones. But the newcomer was smiling as she approached the detective. "Well, if it isn't Bill Marcus!" she said. "I haven't seen you for a couple of years. Most of your recent cases have been far too young for me to worry about."

He smiled reluctantly. "I'm sorry that I haven't been able to entertain you lately, Miranda. But it appears there are others to do that for me."

Miranda turned to the rest of the small group. "Hi, I'm Miranda Melvin. What've we got here? Gail didn't have time to give me all the details—just told me to get my butt over here ASAP. Who are all of you?" She beamed at everyone, and Gail hurriedly made introductions, ending with Jeffrey. "And this is the young man who first spotted the skull. Maybe you should include him on your next dig. He has a sharp eye!"

Miranda looked him over. "You must, young man, if you can pick human remains out of a mass of flying dirt."

"I guess," Jeffrey said. "Can I talk with you, whenever we're done here? See, I'm working on a Boy Scout merit badge and—"

Miranda laughed, but not unkindly. "One step at a time—Jeffrey, is it? Let's figure out who our mystery guest is, and then we can make a plan. Well, well, Elijah," she said, turning to the ME, "where've you been keeping yourself?"

The medical examiner responded, "Down among the dead men, of course, Miranda. I'm glad you're here. We should have fun looking at this one."

"Then let's get started," Miranda said quickly. "Okay, what've we got? Most of one skull, in pieces, check. I see a few teeth, too, but no major bones—yet. Sucked out from under that building over there? What is this, a vacuum excavation system? I haven't seen one in action before. Of course, it would wreak havoc on any scientific dig, but you weren't expecting to find anything here, now, were you, Gail?"

Gail shook her head. "Nope. Just dirt. This was a complete surprise."

"Surprises are what make life fun. So, young Jeffrey, did you see any other bits of bone?"

"I don't think so, but we shut things down quick, and we found a few bits and pieces since. But we haven't gone near the building." That last statement was accompanied by a look at Detective Marcus.

"Is it safe to crawl under there? Is the building stabilized?" Miranda asked no one in particular.

"We'd barely started," Seth told her. "But if you want to

check with the excavation crew, they're all right over there."
He pointed.

"Mind if I join you?" Detective Marcus drawled.

Miranda swatted his arm. "Now, Bill, you know this is
your show. I'm just here to make sure you don't break anything. You other good people mind staying back here for a
bit? Because it looks pretty crowded already. Thanks!"
Without waiting for a response, Miranda set off at a brisk
clip toward the Historical Society building, and Marcus
and the ME had to hurry to keep up.

"She's a bundle of energy, isn't she?" Meg said to Gail.
"How did you happen to meet her?"

"She teaches at the university, and I attended a lecture
she gave on Indian burial grounds a couple of years ago.
Not too many of those in Granford, but you never know.
Anyway, we got talking, and now we're friends, more or
less. She's pretty well known in her field, I gather. We're
lucky that she was in the country at all—she's just back
from a sabbatical—but I guess she had classes starting up."

Seth wasn't about to leave, since he had a responsibility
to the construction crew. Meg didn't have that excuse, but
she was certainly curious. She looked at her watch and felt
a pang of guilt, and decided to call Bree.

"Where are you?" Bree demanded, and she didn't sound
happy.

"I came over to the center of town to watch a little of the
excavation under the Historical Society, but we ran into a
bit of a snag."

"What excavation? Oh, right, that thing Seth got dragged
into. What kind of snag are you talking about?"

Meg sighed. "There was a body buried under the
building."

Bree greeted that with a long moment of silence—and then she burst out laughing. "Well, of course there is! What was I thinking? If you and Seth are there, there must be a body. Anybody we know?"

"No, thank goodness. It appears to be a few centuries old, and we're pretty sure it's been there since before the building went up. All we've seen is parts of the skull so far, but the experts are on the scene. Did you know the Historical Society building used to be a church?"

Bree was still laughing. "Aw, heck, digging up bodies is a lot more interesting than picking apples any day. We'll manage without you okay, so long as you can make up for it tomorrow."

"Will do. Thanks. Are we all good with the pickers for dinner tonight?"

"Yeah, they're coming. I guess I'll do the food shopping for everyone."

"Thank you. I'll pay you back. I told you we can keep it simple. I'll be back as soon as I can. Would it be wrong to offer beer? I want them to relax."

"They'd probably appreciate it, I guess. Well, you go back to your bones and I'll head over to the supermarket. See you in a bit!"

Meg hung up to find Seth watching with a smile. "What?"

"Just noticing how you always need to get Bree's permission to stay. I know, don't bite my head off. She's on top of things, and she's doing a great job."

"I just wanted to let her know what was going on—and be sure she knew I wasn't just slacking off," Meg defended herself. "Anyway, I think I forgot to tell you that we're planning to have a cookout with the pickers tonight."

"What's that about?" Seth asked.

"Well, I'm working with these guys for a second season now, and I realized I don't really know much about them—as people, I mean. We're kind of between ripening of a couple of varieties, so I figured this might be a good time. And, um . . . do you mind not coming? Because I want this to be just about me and Bree and the crew."

"Not a problem—I'll have dinner with my mother. But see you after?"

"Of course." Meg changed the subject. "Anything new here?"

"The ME and Gail's friend have crawled under the building, or as much as we managed to clear out, hence the feet sticking out. They've been there a few minutes now. Marcus is pacing and fuming, but I'm not going to ask him how things are going. Gail is having kittens trying to keep everyone happy and take pictures. Just another normal day in Granford."

"Your crew got a lot cleared in a short time."

"It's a fast process—that's one reason why we went for it. The soil is sandy and not too compacted, so it shifted easily. The body was at least a couple of feet under."

"What about Jeffrey?" Meg nodded toward where he stood next to Gail, watching the people under the building.

"Jeffrey seems to be having the time of his life. If you're going to find a body, this is the best kind, I guess—it's clean and dry, and it's nobody you know."

"Speaking of our mystery guest, what do you think happened back then, that this poor soul ended up buried under there? You think anybody missed this person, or wondered where he—or she—went?"

"It's a little hard to say without some more information," Seth pointed out. "Maybe Jeffrey can fill in some of the blanks, if he goes forward with the research. He's a bright kid."

Finally, the ME wiggled his way backward from under the building, followed by Miranda. They both stood up and brushed damp soil off their clothes, then Elijah Bartlett gestured to the others, gathering them in.

"I don't want to repeat myself, so listen up, everyone. The skeleton appears to be that of an adult male. Looks like it's possible that the rest of him is still there under the building. It's hard to determine the cause of death, but I might—repeat, might—be able to tell you more once I get him to autopsy. But let me warn you, I have several autopsies in the queue ahead of this one, and in those cases there are grieving relatives, so they take precedence. But for your purposes, I believe I can say that he was buried where he was found, and his remains were not disturbed when the building was erected over him, so if you know that date, then you at least know how long ago he died."

"So no criminal investigation is necessary," Detective Marcus said. The ME shook his head.

Miranda was quick to speak up. "Since there's no evidence of a crime here, I can do the autopsy and report back to you. If you don't mind? And if you release the scene, Bill, I can go over it and see if there are any other artifacts that might be useful or interesting."

"Knock yourself out, Miranda," Detective Marcus said. "I hereby declare that the state police see no reason to investigate this site."

"Thanks, Bill. Hey, young Jeffrey—you want to be my assistant?"

Jeffrey's eyes lit up. "Sure, yeah, cool! I'll ask my mom."

"Tell her it will be a good educational experience and will look great on your college applications."

"Awesome, that'll help. When and where?"

"Here, and the sooner the better," Miranda said. "I assume these good people here want to move on with their construction. Tomorrow morning, say, eight o'clock?"

"I'll be here."

"And wear grubby clothes, because I expect you to do a lot of the crawling and digging. I'll bring some of my students along, as well. It's good fieldwork for them. Gail, thanks for inviting me to the party. I've got to run. Will I see you in the morning, too?"

"Of course. I'm as curious as anyone about this. The poor man—I know I'd like to know who he was and why he was there. Meg, you taking off now?"

"I'd better; I've got plans for this evening. But I'll stop by tomorrow sometime, if Bree will let me. Nice to meet you, Miranda, and happy hunting."

Seth said, "I'm going to check the timetable, and I guess I can let these guys go home for the day, since Marcus doesn't need to talk with them. And then I've got to do everything else I was supposed to be doing today. Like I said, I'll go see my mom for dinner. I don't know when I'll get home."

"Do what you have to do. I'm going back to the orchard."

"See you later," Seth said, then he and Gail walked over toward the building.

Meg wasn't sure whether to feel relieved or disappointed that her role in this investigation seemed to be ending so soon. It was good that the preliminary review of the body and the site had been carried out so quickly, and that Detective Marcus was on his way back to Northampton, after releasing the site. But Meg realized that, like Gail, she wanted to know who the bones they'd found belonged to, and why he was there.

Meg sincerely hoped that Jeffrey would find out something in his research. Assuming there was anything to be found. She knew from personal experience that eighteenth-century documents were hard to come by. Unsettling and unresolved, the whole mess.

She returned home in a somber mood; thoughts of death—and, worse than death, being forgotten by everyone—weren't exactly uplifting. She enjoyed visiting her ancestors in the nearby West Cemetery, but she viewed that more as a remembrance of them rather than mourning for them. She had never known them, nor would she, except by their works: she could run her hands over the boards and carvings that a couple of Eli Warrens, father and son, had made well over a century earlier, planed on a sawmill in the backyard, from trees cut from the family woodlot. Their work lived on in her house, and in so many other homes in Granford.

Instead of going straight inside when she arrived home, Meg walked over to the enclosed field where her two goats were grazing.

"Good afternoon, Dorcas, Isabel. You're looking well."

The goats looked up at her in unison, then returned to pulling grass. Meg leaned on a fence post and studied them. She'd ended up with them because their previous owner had threatened to sell them to a Greek restaurant to be turned into kebabs. Meg had quailed at that idea, and since she had the room to accommodate them, she'd brought them home. She hadn't really given any thought to the long-term solution, and yet, here they were still. They were quiet and reasonably friendly, but they were an obligation, and they did eat. But on the other hand, they'd provided aid and comfort to her during one unpleasant episode in midwinter, so Meg thought she had something of a moral obligation to keep them. She thought from time to time about using them to provide goat's milk for cheese, but that would require some additional work—not to mention the participation of a male goat—so she hadn't decided anything.

But she found she had succeeded in cheering herself up.

8

When Meg came in the back door, Bree was already in the kitchen, and loaded plastic bags were scattered over the table and the countertops.

"'Bout time you showed up! I think I got everything, but I still want to marinate this chicken. You get to work on the salad, okay?"

"Whatever you say, ma'am." Meg rummaged through bags and found several kinds of lettuce, some herbs, and colorful peppers. "Let me find my biggest bowl."

When she returned from her hunt with the bowl, she said, "Uh, Bree, I'm going to need your help with this dinner tonight."

"What're you talking about? What do you think I'm doing here?"

"It's not that. It's that . . . I'm just not quite sure how to talk to these guys."

"What's the problem?" Bree didn't look at Meg because she was busy whisking a marinade in a bowl.

Meg went to the sink and started rinsing lettuce. "Well, you know, I've been working with these guys since last year's harvest, and you've worked with them even longer. But I feel like I've kind of cheated: I knew that there was a system in place and that you understood it, so I just figured I'd let you carry on. Not that I'm complaining, because you've done a great job. But I write the weekly checks, and I feel that I should know more about what's going on. I know you've told me in the past that there's a long tradition of Jamaican workers picking apples around here, but what are the details? What are the rules for working around here?"

Bree gave her a sidelong glance. "So you're just now asking? Okay, I cut you some slack because you really were clueless last year, but you do need to know, because you're legally responsible for these guys, and the government is watching."

"Exactly. Is there a problem?" Meg asked, shaking water off the lettuce leaves.

"No, but you do have to keep on top of things so that there won't *be* any. Here's the short version: our workers—all six of 'em—are here under what is known as an H-2A visa, which is specifically for temporary foreign workers for seasonal agricultural work. You as the employer apply for it every year, before the season starts, and the visa is only good for one year minus one day—they can't become permanent. You've got to prove that there aren't enough other workers in the area to do the work, which isn't hard to do. You've got to pay them at least minimum wage. In theory, you've got to make sure they have a safe place to live, food, and transportation to and from work."

"Yikes! I had no idea. You've been handling all this?"

"I have, but you've signed the papers I stuck in front of your face. I guess you didn't read 'em too close, huh? Anyway, the guys more or less take care of their own housing and meals, and a couple have clunker cars to get around, although if they insisted, you'd probably be required to house and feed them. There are something like seventy thousand of this kind of visa issued each year, but Massachusetts isn't even in the top ten. Apple picking makes up only about four percent of the total, nationally."

"And you know all this why?" Meg asked, as she started slicing strips of red and yellow peppers.

"Hey, I've got a degree in agriculture, remember? This is part of the degree package. And I should warn you—Congress keeps trying to pass a new farm bill that could change a lot of these regulations."

"But you're on top of it?"

"Of course I am. What else you want to know?" Bree was sloshing chicken parts in a bowl with the marinade.

"What about health insurance? That's got to be a sore subject."

"They're covered by workers' comp. If they're injured—say they fall off a ladder, like I did that one time—and it's work-related, that covers medical care and even some wage reimbursement. And there are migrant health clinics around, and for Jamaicans, there's sometimes health insurance from the Jamaican government. Next question?"

"Now I feel guilty that I didn't know all this before. I'm overwhelmed—but listen, on a less formal level, is there anything I should avoid asking about, or anything we need to talk about?"

"Depends on what you want to know."

"At the very least I want to know who's who, to be able to put names and faces together. Are they happy working here? I know you've told me that there are other farms that pay more, but you know as well as I do that we just can't afford to go up on their salaries."

"Look, the pay is fair, and it helps that you're out there, too, working alongside them. If you're thinking you'll suddenly be all buddy-buddy with them, though, don't get your hopes up. There's an active Jamaican community around here. The workers all know each other, since they've been coming back to this area year after year, and when they have free time, they hang out together. Don't patronize them."

Meg stopped what she was doing and turned to Bree. "Is that what you think I'm doing? Playing lady of the manor to the humble servants?"

Bree shrugged. "It's happened. I'm not saying you're doing that, but don't expect the guys to be all warm and fuzzy. They respect you, and they're willing to work hard—not just for you, but because they're proud of what they do and want to do it well. I think this was a good idea, but don't expect it to be a regular thing."

"Fair enough. Maybe one more, when the harvest is over?"

"Maybe. You about done with that lettuce? Because the corn still needs shucking. They'll be here in half an hour, and I'd better go fire up the grill. They wanted to go home and shower before eating with us, and they'll be back here at seven."

"Go build the fire, then. I'll take care of the corn." Meg looked in the fridge and was relieved to find that Bree had bought a ready-made cake—and a couple of six-packs of beer, as well as a couple of gallons of iced tea. Paper plates, napkins, plastic forks—check. Why was she so nervous?

As promised, Raynard's truck pulled into the driveway just past seven, and a couple of the men tumbled out of the back, all wearing short-sleeved button-down shirts, their hair still damp from showering. They'd dressed up for her? What she wanted more than anything was for them all to feel comfortable with each other. They did do good work, and she was grateful. Without them she couldn't hope to survive.

Bree came around the building to greet everyone, and a second car pulled up behind Raynard's truck. That accounted for all five of the men—and they'd all come, which pleased Meg, though she hoped they hadn't assumed it was required. She took one last look around the kitchen: the chicken and salad were already out on the picnic table in the back; the water for the corn was boiling and it would take only a couple of minutes to cook the ears; a Styrofoam cooler filled with ice held the beer. She tucked in her shirt and went out to greet her guests.

As befit his status as unofficial foreman, Raynard Lawrence was the first person to greet her. "Thank you so much for inviting us, Meg."

"I'm glad you could all make it. I hope you didn't think it was a job requirement." Meg's small joke didn't produce any smiles. "Look, I'm not going to make any speeches. I just wanted to get together because last year was so crazy I never had a chance to really talk to any of you, we were so busy getting the apples picked, and since we had a little free time now, I thought this would be a good opportunity to get to know each other better." Even to Meg's own ears she

thought she sounded like an insincere social worker, all
sweetness and light. Maybe this was a bad idea after all.

Bree took pity on her. "Hey, guys, don't mind Meg—
she's just nervous, so I'll help her out with the formal introductions. Raynard you know, Meg, but from left to right
you've got Romano Higgins, Tiyone Palmer, Delroy Camp-
bell, Andre Morgan, and Darren Thompson. You can probably figure out the nicknames for yourself."

"Thank you, Bree. Guys, I feel like such an idiot, doing
this after a year. We should have done it last year." Meg
added quickly, "I'm sorry I couldn't increase your pay this
year, because I know how hard you all work. If we do well
this year, maybe next year will be better. If you're willing
to come back?" No comments. She swallowed a sigh. "But
tonight isn't about work. There's beer in the cooler. Bree,
why don't you start cooking the chicken? Oh, and there are
chips in the kitchen—let me go get them."

Meg fled. She was an uneasy hostess under the best of
circumstances, which this wasn't. And she sounded like
such a prissy idiot! Inside she checked to be sure that the
corn water was still simmering, then grabbed up a couple
of bags of chips and went back outside.

Bree was poking at chicken pieces on the grill, and they
smelled wonderful. Meg spied a few open beer bottles—
and better yet, a few smiles—which was encouraging. She
helped herself to a bottle of beer and sat down next to . . .
Tiyone, was it? He was one of the younger pickers. "So,
Tiyone, have you been working around here for long?"

After that, the conversations around the table warmed
up gradually, and by the time the chicken was cooked and
Meg carried a platter of steaming ears of corn from the
kitchen, everybody had finally relaxed. Meg had learned

that Delroy had two small daughters who lived with their mother near Kingston, and that Darren had been working at this orchard for fifteen years now.

"Do you guys go home to Jamaica when the apple harvest is over, or do you move on to other areas?" Meg asked.

"It depends on where the work is, and whether we have small children at home. The money we make is important, but it is hard to be away from our families for too long," Delroy volunteered.

"I can imagine," Meg said. "But you guys are really good at what you do. I mean, you pick the apples without damaging them or the branches, you handle them carefully, and at the same time, you're so fast. I feel like such a slowpoke when I work with you. I swear, you each finish three trees to my one."

"True," Raynard said, smiling. "But it's good to know you understand what we do. And why it matters. What we do *not* understand is why in this country, when there are so many people looking for jobs, including young, healthy people, none of them are willing to get their hands dirty with jobs such as these." There were murmurs of assent from some of the others.

Meg had asked herself the same question. "I wish I had an answer. You know, until about a century ago, most people in this country lived on and worked their own farms. It was good, honest work. Then industry came along and sucked everybody into the cities, and the farms got bigger and used more machines instead of people. And now look—the cities are falling apart from the inside out. And still, people don't want to work at jobs in fast-food restaurants or convenience stores, much less on farms. I agree with you—it just seems wrong."

"But," Delroy interrupted, "you went to college and you

had a good job in the city. What is it you're doing here? Is this just to fill time until something better comes around or the economy changes yet again?"

Meg wondered if his real question was whether she planned to bail on the orchard when and if she found another job in the city. "That's what I grew up thinking I was supposed to do. I don't personally know anyone who said, 'I want to be a farmer.' I know more people are turning to that now, like in Vermont, or are starting up artisanal cheese-making or organic farms, but it's still a minority. Maybe it will change. It probably should. Too many kids now don't know how to do anything that doesn't involve a keyboard or a touch pad. They have no idea where their food comes from. As for me, I can point to about ten generations of my ancestors who worked right here on this farm. They raised their families here. They were part of the town. Sure, it was hard and uncertain—we all know how fast the weather can change around here—but they weren't looking for the easy way out, and they weren't afraid of work. I can't promise I'll be doing this forever, but I'm happy to be doing this now."

The men around the table smiled, and raised their bottles to her. Meg could feel herself blushing. "Hey, I didn't plan to make a speech. Everybody ready for cake?"

Once the cake had been doled out, the gathering broke up pretty quickly. After all, they all had to be up early for work in the orchard the next morning. Meg felt cautiously pleased by the results of her dinner. She knew a little bit more about each of the men, and she hoped they felt a little more comfortable with her. One step at a time, anyway.

"You going up? Or is Seth coming over?" Bree asked, one foot on the stairs leading to her room.

"He said he'd be here eventually. You go ahead. And thanks, Bree. I think the evening went well."

"Yeah, the guys seemed to like it. The beer helped. I know it's hard to get to know people, especially under these conditions. Heck, they don't know me much better than they know you. I might have the right skin color and history, but I still have to keep fighting the image that I'm a snotty kid who went to an American college and now bosses them around."

"Well, hang in there. Good night."

Meg dropped into a chair at the kitchen table and watched Bree climb the stairs. She should go upstairs, too, but right now all she wanted to do was sit. Funny how even in a town as small as Granford there were two separate and distinct layers: the local townspeople and the itinerant pickers who worked for them. The townspeople were not notable for their ethnic diversity, but that wasn't unusual in the more rural areas of Massachusetts. But how did the pickers manage to stay so invisible? She never saw them shopping at the market or buying pizza or filling up a gas tank. She never saw them anywhere at all, other than at work, for that matter. Was that by choice? And if so, whose?

Seth came in while Meg was still thinking, or maybe dozing, upright in the chair. He helped himself to a bottle of water from the fridge before sitting in the chair across from her. "How'd it go?"

"Good, I think. Maybe I broke the ice. At least I didn't make things any worse. How about you?"

"Work starts again in the morning. I was surprised Marcus let things go so easily—he could have fouled things up for the Historical Society if he'd wanted to."

"He's a pain, but he's not a bad guy—and he doesn't

have any reason to make trouble, does he? At least he won't be back. You ready to go up to bed?"

Seth drained the bottle of water. "Now I am."

Meg held out a hand to him. "Then let's go—tomorrow will be another crazy day."

9

Meg was considering creating a little shrine to the Roman goddess Pomona, protector of orchard trees. She needed all the help she could get, and a goddess seemed like a handy ally to have. Apparently Pomona's festival day was on August 13, which corresponded neatly to when the first few of Meg's apple varieties ripened and were ready to pick. Trust a woman to look after the gritty details of day-to-day management while the male gods were off fighting huge battles somewhere else.

"How're we doing?" Meg asked Bree over a late lunch the next day.

"Overall, not bad. Yield's down about ten percent from last year, but after that spell of dry weather we had it could have been a lot worse. We're about halfway through picking the Cortlands, and I'd give the Empires another week. And we're going to be real busy in October."

"That's good news, isn't it?"

"Sure," Bree said, "and I've already told the crew. But why are you asking? Are you plotting something?"

"Me?" Meg was startled by the question. "No. It's just that Seth's flat out with about six different building projects scattered all over, and this business with the skeleton has put him behind on the Historical Society one, although not by much. Detective Marcus signed off on it in what must be record time for him, although there was no way to argue that it was a recent death. I was thinking I'd go over there this afternoon and see if they've made any progress."

"Wonder if anybody will be able to figure out who it was, this long after," Bree said.

"It's early days yet, and Gail will be looking more closely at the history of the site. But at least I have zero expectations that he'll turn out to be either a Warren or a Chapin." *Although in a town this small*, Meg reflected, *anything was possible.*

"Never say never," Bree said darkly, echoing Meg's thoughts. "Well, if you want to run over there, I give you my blessing."

Apparently Pomona was smiling upon her. "Thank you *so* much!" Meg replied sarcastically. "Hey, did I tell you about Gail's new shadow? He's a high school kid who's working on a Scout merit badge, or two, or maybe a dozen—he seems really eager—and Gail said she'd mentor him. Talking to him, I realized that I'm completely out of touch with teenagers or high school students today."

"I hope you're not asking me for advice." Bree laughed. "Meg, I haven't been in high school for years, you know. And I don't think I was exactly typical when I *was* there. Why do you even care?"

"Because Jeffrey seems like a nice boy, smart and eager to help—"

"That's what Boy Scouts are," Bree interrupted.

Meg ignored her. "But he also seems kind of, I don't know, vulnerable? Innocent?"

"You're saying he's a wimp," Bree said bluntly.

"Well, maybe. I hate to label him, and maybe I'm reading too much into what I've seen of him, but he does seem like a loner, or maybe somebody who just doesn't fit in. Maybe that's why he got into Scouts to begin with. Maybe he was looking for friends, or for a group that would welcome him, or at least accept him." *Or maybe his parents pushed him into it because they thought it would help*, Meg added to herself.

"Why is this kid your problem?" Bree asked again.

"He's not, really. It's just that I like him, and I'm worried about him, but I'm so out of touch with kids that age that I don't know what the range of normal is these days." *If there is such a thing as normal among teenagers.*

Bree stood up and took her plate over to the sink. "Meg, give it a rest. You've got plenty to worry about without looking for problems. He'll figure his life out without you sticking your nose in it."

"I hear you, o wise one." Maybe her tone was facetious, but Meg was willing to admit that Bree had her head firmly attached to her shoulders and was probably right. "Still, maybe I'll take a run over and see what's happening on the green."

"Go ahead. You cooking tonight?"

"I guess. Thanks for pitching in last night—at least the cleanup was easy. Hey, I haven't seen much of Michael lately." Meg liked Bree's activist boyfriend Michael, though like Jeffrey, he tended to be awkward in social situations.

"Michael and I aren't joined at the hip. I'm busy." Bree's tone didn't invite any further comments. "See you later." She strode out the back door.

Once again, not your business, Meg told herself. Bree and Michael's kind of offhand relationship seemed to work for them, so she had no right to comment. She decided to grab a shower and change clothes before going into town.

It was past two when Meg arrived at the town green and parked in the church parking lot on the hill. The "new" church, she reminded herself: built in 1821, to replace the "old" church, or rather, meetinghouse, now the Historical Society, built in the 1760s. Time in New England wasn't like time in most other parts of the country, where there was nothing so old. On the other hand, compared to Europe, Granford was a baby. As Meg strolled down the hill toward the Historical Society, she counted the vehicles: far fewer than the day before.

Gail was watching the lack of activity anxiously. "Oh, hi, Meg. There's not a lot to see today, if that's why you're here. Miranda is doing her thing back at the university, and she said she'd report her results to me ASAP. But she's got a couple of classes this term, so who knows when she'll have time for our poor skeleton? I wish the weekend weren't interrupting this." She waved her hand at the torn-up site.

Meg laughed. "Hey, most people are happy when the weekend rolls around. Why the rush here? Will the builders come in over the weekend?"

"You'd have to ask Seth. If they'll do it without charging triple-time or something, I'd be ecstatic, but I won't count on it. I know we've got a ridiculous timetable, but I always expect the worst, like earthquakes or a plane falling out of the sky. I didn't figure on something like a body, though, even if he is two hundred and something years old."

"I know what you mean," Meg said. "I worry about hail and hurricanes and droughts and tornadoes, none of which I can control." She looked around. "Is Jeffrey here today?"

"He was here in the morning, but he said he had some classes he couldn't miss, so he left. He'll probably be back after school lets out for the day." Gail checked her watch. "Shoot—my kids'll be home any minute now. You can hang around, Meg, but I've got to go."

"Oh, before you go, can you tell me whether I have to ask permission or get a permit or something, if I'm going to have a table at the Harvest Festival?"

"Talk to Heather Nash at the library—she's handling that. See you later!" Gail hurried off to her car.

Might as well get one small thing accomplished, Meg thought, turning toward the library at one end of the green. She'd been inside the charming neoclassical structure that housed the library maybe once or twice, looking for information on her Granford ancestors, but even upon a cursory glance it was clear that they'd outgrown their space long ago. The staff must be thrilled by the possibilities offered by a much larger new space. Meg was embarrassed that she hadn't even known that there was a new library under construction until Seth had mentioned it, nor did she know anything about when it would open. She'd have to ask Seth for more details.

She crossed the road carefully, and pulled open the main door to the current library. A pleasant-looking woman about her own age behind the desk looked up and smiled immediately. "You're Meg Corey."

"Yes, I am," said Meg, a little startled as always when the locals knew who she was. "I'm terribly sorry, but I don't know your name."

"Heather Nash, at your service. I'm the library director. What can I do for you today?"

"Oh, perfect, you're exactly the person I was looking for. I wanted to ask about reserving a table at the Harvest Festival. Gail Selden said I should talk to you. Do I need to sign up or something?"

"Sure do, but we've got plenty of space. Are you going to be selling something?"

"Uh, maybe? I thought I'd sell apples, and I can guarantee they'll be freshly picked. If that's all right? I'm sorry to be ignorant of the whole process, but I've been so busy picking, I haven't had time for much else. I hadn't even thought that far ahead."

"No problem." Heather smiled. "Mostly the event is an opportunity to chat with the neighbors and swap useless items from your garage or attic. Which then get swapped back the next year. It's fun. If you have anything you're looking to get rid of, I can tell you who to take it to."

"Okay. I'll think about it."

Heather fished through a stack of folders under the reception desk and came up with a piece of paper. "Here's the form. Just go ahead and fill it out. We'll provide the table and a canopy over it, and a chair, and you bring whatever else you want, like a table cover, and a sign if you have one. We're pretty informal. Oh, here's a pen." She handed the pen to Meg and stepped back, clearly waiting for her to fill it out, so Meg obliged.

When she handed it back, Meg said, "The plans for the new library sound great. You must be looking forward to it."

"Sure. But I'll miss this old place, even if it's too small. And impossible to wire for all the modern stuff everybody expects these days. Andrew Carnegie didn't see that coming!"

"So it's a Carnegie library?" Meg knew about the libraries funded by rich Scottish businessman Andrew Carnegie, and had in fact grown up near one, as her mother had pointed out every time they drove past it. In fact, she seemed to recall that Carnegie's money had paid for nearly half the libraries in the country at one time, so she shouldn't have been surprised to find one in Granford.

"It is. Opened November 1917, although Granford had a library even before that, up in part of town hall. The land we sit on was given by a descendant of one of Granford's earliest settlers."

"Not a Warren?" Meg asked.

"Nope. Not a Chapin either. By the way, congrats. Seth's a great guy."

"Thanks, I know." Meg grinned. "So what's going to happen with this building when you guys move out? I hope nobody's going to tear it down and build a gas station or something."

"No way! But I don't think it's been decided yet. By the way, did you hear what they found over at the Historical Society?"

"You mean under it? Yeah, I was there when they found him. How do you suppose the body ended up there?"

"Hard to say, this long after the fact," Heather commented.

"There's a student from the high school who might be looking into it. Jeffrey Green? Do you know him?"

"Jeffrey? Sure. Nice kid, real quiet. He's in here a lot. If he can't find what he needs here, he uses the college libraries."

"He's the one who first noticed the shards of skull during the excavation at the Historical Society," Meg said.

"Oh, wow. I hadn't heard that. Though Gail did tell me about the big shot anthropologist she called in—I think she's over there today."

"That's where I'm headed next. By the way, did Gail ask you to store any of the Historical Society's records here?"

Heather laughed. "Where would we put them? Maybe she's the one who should take over this place when we move—at least then all the records would be in one place. Of course, she'd have to fix the roof . . . Why?"

"Just curious. I've been working on cataloging some of them, on and off since last winter, when I have the time. Mostly whatever includes anything about my Warren family. Now she's talking about giving me some more. Since my house and the meetinghouse over there are about the same age, I'm wondering whether there's anything useful about the dead man. You know, purely local records, the sort that would never have left town. The problem is, it's hard to find those kinds of records at the moment since they're scattered all over town."

"One step at a time. If Jeffrey comes by I can help him look at what we've got, and if he comes up dry maybe we can look for the other records." A mother with a couple of young children came in. "Oops, story hour," Heather said. "Gotta go. Nice to finally meet you, Meg—I hope I'll see you at the Festival."

Outside again, Meg crossed the street and walked along the edge of the green. On the other side, there was a lot of activity, but it was different from yesterday's. Meg recognized Miranda, who appeared to be directing traffic in the form of a gaggle of college-aged kids. Even from a distance, Meg could hear her barking orders.

"Easy with that! Kaitlyn, don't dump that dirt so fast. We don't want to miss the little stuff. Dylan, watch your head. Who's doing the drawings?"

Meg smiled at Miranda's obvious enthusiasm. She crossed the green but stopped short of the building, reluctant to get in the way. However, Miranda noticed her.

"Hey—Meg, right? You come to work or to gawk?"

"A little of each, I guess. Find anything interesting?"

"Nothing incriminating. The poor guy didn't seem to be wearing anything made of metal."

"But he was wearing something?" Meg hadn't even contemplated the idea of a body being buried naked.

"Sure, but all that's left are a few scraps of fabric now."

"Anything unusual about the body itself?" Meg asked, almost in spite of herself.

"You mean like six toes or a healed fracture? I didn't see anything obvious like that, but I haven't had time to really study the bones. I can tell you that it was an older man, kinda short—but so was everyone back then—and it looks like he died from natural causes. Advanced tuberculosis. I'll know more when I've completed the autopsy, but I thought it was more important to finish up here first."

"You can identify tuberculosis in a skeleton?" Meg asked. "I've never heard of that."

"Consider yourself lucky. TB can spread to both the bones and the bone marrow, and it ain't pretty," Miranda said. "Sorry to cut this short, Meg, but the diggers want to get back to digging with something larger than a teaspoon, so I need to finish up here. Shouldn't really be a problem, since there's so little here. A very clean grave, if you will."

"What happens next?"

"The bones are back to the university waiting for me. I'll

do a more thorough autopsy when I can find the time, but it's not a top priority. If nobody can identify him, I guess we either cremate him or stick the remains into storage. I don't suppose they have potter's fields in Granford these days."

The idea that the unknown man would be consigned to anonymity saddened Meg. It was possible that he had relatives buried only a mile or two away. If so, didn't he belong with them? But how was anybody going to spend the time and energy to find out? "I don't know, but you could ask Jeffrey to look into it."

Miranda broke into a smile. "What a treasure he is! Bright kid, and careful—puts some of my other students to shame. He's really into this. He was here first thing this morning, and he said he'd be back later today. Oh, there he is now." She pointed.

Meg followed Miranda's finger. Yes, that was Jeffrey, driving a relatively recent, conservative sedan—just the kind of car Mom and Dad would have picked for him. He parked at the far end of the green and climbed out of the car, but before he could come any closer, another car—what Meg would describe as a middle-aged rust bucket—pulled in behind the sedan and slammed to a stop. The door opened and a young guy jumped out and stalked toward Jeffrey, who turned to face him. Then the passenger side of Jeffrey's car opened and a girl emerged and hurried over to the two boys.

It was impossible to hear what any of them were saying, but their emotions were clear even from a distance. The newcomer was mad. Jeffrey was cautious and defensive. The girl seemed caught between the two, trying to placate both of them—and failing. After some posturing by the second boy, the girl got into the passenger side of his car, and once she was seated, the driver made a U-turn that left gouges on the grass at the edge of the green, and sped off the way he had come. It was a troubling scene, although the girl seemed to have gone willingly.

"Quite the drama, eh?" Meg was startled by Miranda's comment when the other woman came up behind her. "Wonder what that was all about."

"I have no idea," Meg said. "I don't know many kids around here, and I don't suppose you do either." Jeffrey probably hadn't realized that he'd had an audience.

"Only college age, and I don't live in town here," Miranda said cheerfully.

After watching the other car disappear, Jeffrey turned and plodded to where they were standing. "Hey, Miranda. Hi, Meg."

"Is everything all right?" Meg asked. "What was that about?"

"No big deal—some guy's been hassling a friend of mine from school. It's okay. What can I do now, Miranda?"

"Come on and I'll show you. Meg, either you get your hands dirty or stay out of our way. No offense, but we've got only a few hours of daylight left."

"I understand. I'll leave you to it, then. But I hope I'll see you again."

Miranda had already turned back to the dig and didn't appear to hear her.

10

Dinner finally came together after eight, thanks to a Crock-Pot meal Meg had somehow managed to throw together earlier in the day, containing whatever she could find in her refrigerator that wasn't too shriveled or sporting green mold. Seth was late, as he had expected, no doubt still tied up at the green in town. Bree seemed distracted. Meg was just tired, which was her steady state these days. When they finally all sat down, conversation was patchy.

"I signed up for the Harvest Festival," Meg told Seth midmeal. "What do I need to do for it?"

"I hope you don't expect me to make a dozen apple pies," Bree muttered.

"Of course not. I don't expect *anyone* to make a dozen of anything. I was thinking more along the lines of selling a few handsome bushel baskets of apples. Which varieties will be ripe by next weekend?"

"I'll check and let you know. How many different ones do you want?"

"Four or five?" Meg suggested. "Whatever a six-foot table could hold. I could make up little cards about the history of each variety. I'm thinking I should get some bags, so people can take their apples home, and maybe I'll look for a piece of oilcloth or something to cover the table. And I'll need to make a sign, like that old crate label I found. Anything else?"

"I'll think about it," Seth said. "I have to get my head back into it, try to remember what I've seen at earlier festivals. But don't go overboard—remember, it's pretty low-key. I mean, there won't be hordes of people clogging Route 202 for miles."

"The leaf-peepers will be out," Bree reminded him.

"That they will," Meg agreed. "And Granford does have some leaves, not that they're very far along. Seth, is your sister's B and B fully booked?"

"Rachel's cut way back because of her pregnancy," Seth said. "Maybe some regulars, who booked a year ago. The foliage lovers sometimes plan years ahead."

Meg shook her head silently, trying to imagine driving across states just to look at dying leaves. But hey, tourism brought in good money for the region.

A couple of more minutes passed as they ate. "I stopped and talked to Miranda when I was in town," Meg said finally. "She's doing the autopsy on that skeleton from under the church, since the state has no further interest in him, but she doesn't know when she'll be finished."

"Who's Miranda?" Bree asked.

"Oh, right, you haven't met her. Miranda Melvin—she's an archaeologist at UMass, specializing in old burials. When Jeffrey saw the bones, Gail asked for her help. She managed to shortcut the usual autopsy procedure. Even made Bill Marcus smile. She is a force to be reckoned with," Meg said with a smile.

"Her I've got to meet," Bree replied.

"I doubt she'll find anything useful," Seth said.

Meg turned back to Seth. "Why not? She's already figured out that the body is of an older man who died of TB. Maybe she can tell what his diet was like and correlate it to local crops or something, although I suppose it's likely that most people grew the same things. Maybe she'll find the eighteenth-century version of industrial pollution, like sawdust if he worked at a sawmill, or a lot of smoke residue if he was a blacksmith."

Seth tried to get into the spirit of the discussion. "If the man worked at an iron forge, there might be some residue."

"Was there an iron forge in Granford?"

"Not then. How about pollen on his clothes? That might at least indicate what time of year he died."

"No clothes, or at least, only a few shreds," Meg said. "No metal—so no buckles or jewelry or coins."

"Well, maybe there'll be something in the written records," Seth said. "You know, 'Hezekiah went to town to sell the cow and failed to return—ever.'"

"Would DNA evidence help?" Bree asked suddenly.

"Possibly, together with some genealogy," Seth replied thoughtfully. "If there's any DNA to be found, say in teeth or the bigger bones, then that could be compared with DNA from families that we know have been living here since the 1790 census—there are still a few of those in Granford, like the Chapins. Of course, the families would have to be willing to give a sample."

"Why wouldn't they?" Meg asked.

"Paranoia, maybe," Seth said. "Like they're afraid their DNA profile will end up in some secret government database." When Meg rolled her eyes, he added, "Before you jump all over me, I didn't say I believed it, but that some people might."

"Got it. Gail says Miranda is a renowned expert at what she does, so if there's anything to be found, she may be our best bet, and she certainly seemed eager to try. Oh, and I saw Jeffrey there again. Apparently he showed up early to help Miranda, then went to school for a while, then came back when school let out. He really seems excited about this project. Anyway, Miranda said she'd be wrapping up her end of things on the green by the end of today, so the construction crew can get back to work. Will they be working this weekend?"

"They said they would. They wanted extra for overtime, but I persuaded them that this was a public service. Assuming they don't uncover more bones, it shouldn't take them long to finish digging, in any case. Then they'll build the concrete forms, but they probably won't pour before Monday."

"Do you have to oversee them tomorrow?" Meg asked.

"Yes. Why, did we have plans?"

"Nope. We'll be picking. Right, Bree?"

Bree gave a start. "Huh? Oh, right, we are. Look, guys, I'm falling asleep at the table. I think I'll go up now."

"See you in the morning," Meg said. When Bree was gone, Meg turned to Seth. "Looks like it'll be an early night all around. I'm having trouble keeping my eyes open, too."

Meg stood up to take their plates over to the sink and

heard Seth's cell phone ring. He glanced at it, then walked into the dining room to talk. He was back within a minute.

Meg glanced at him, and then looked more closely: his expression was grim. "What?"

"That was Art. A body was just found behind the feed store on the highway, with serious head injuries, clearly not accidental."

"Oh my God! Who is it?" Violent crime was pretty rare in Granford, or so Meg had thought.

"Art doesn't know all the details yet—he just arrived. Marcus was on his way. All Art said was that the victim was a young African-American male, between sixteen and twenty."

"Why did Art call you? Are you supposed to go over and do something?"

"He just wanted me to know what was going on, in case there's any interest from the press. I'm a selectman, remember? So I guess I represent the town." Seth hesitated, looking at Meg with an odd expression she couldn't read.

"What is it? Do you know who the victim might be?" she asked. As she'd noted before. There weren't many African-Americans in Granford—except, she reminded herself, the apple pickers, who were almost exclusively dark-skinned Jamaicans. But none of the ones she knew were that young. She realized with a pang that the victim could be a friend or relative of any one of the local pickers, even one of the ones she worked with. But who would have attacked him? She'd have to ask Bree to keep her ears open tomorrow. "It's not that. But the person who found the body and reported it was Jeffrey Green."

"What?" That was the last thing Meg had expected to hear. "What was Jeffrey doing at the feed store? It's not even open this late, is it? I thought they closed at five. And why would this other boy be there?"

"Meg, all I know is what Art just told me. I don't have any details, and I'm not going to guess," Seth said. "I'm too tired to try to make sense of it now in any case."

"I'll clean up the kitchen, but I promise not to use up all the hot water if you want to shower first."

"Deal. See you upstairs."

When Seth headed upstairs, Meg carried their few plates and glasses to the dishwasher. She'd seen Jeffrey only a few hours earlier—how had he ended up at a crime scene? What was he doing at the feed store so late? She'd seen him at the green earlier in the afternoon when he'd been helping Miranda. Which in turn reminded her of the odd confrontation she'd witnessed between Jeffrey and that boy and girl when he arrived. But the other boy had been white, she thought. How long had Miranda kept everyone on the green at work?

Well, she'd just have to wait until she got the full story. Which Seth would probably hear from Art in the morning. The village grapevine at its finest. She wiped out the sink and the counters, made sure that Max and Lolly had enough food and water, turned off the lights, and went to join Seth upstairs.

The next morning Meg was up with the sun. She made coffee and settled at the kitchen table to read the daily paper and enjoy a few minutes of peace before she went up the hill. Lolly sat on the windowsill, taking advantage of the sun as well.

Meg was startled when someone knocked on her front

door. That was unusual, since most people in Granford came to the kitchen door, and it was too early in the day for a solicitor. For some people, Saturday was a day off—but not for apple farmers in September. If it was a pollster or campaign worker, she'd tell him that it was kind of rude to bother anyone this early on a Saturday morning, and he probably wouldn't get the support or the contribution he wanted.

Meg checked to see that she was wearing presentable clothes—they appeared to be marginal but okay—then went to open the door and found herself face-to-face with Rick Sainsbury.

"It's too early for door-to-door campaigning, you know," she said a little flippantly. But she did notice that he looked worried, not in campaign mode.

"Sorry to disturb you so early," he apologized, "but this isn't about the political race. It's something personal. May we come in?"

We? It wasn't until then that Meg realized Rick was accompanied by Jeffrey Green and a woman she didn't recognize, but who bore an unmistakable resemblance to Rick. *Rick's sister Karen, Jeffrey's mother*, Meg deduced.

"Sure." Meg stepped back and let them pass. No one looked happy to be there. She greeted Jeffrey first. "Good to see you, Jeffrey. How're you doing?"

"Okay," he mumbled.

His mother prodded him. "Speak up, Jeffrey."

Which in turn moved Rick to say, "Lighten up, Karen, and leave the kid alone." He turned to Meg, and Seth who had now come up behind her. "We need to talk. Seth, I'm glad I found you—I tried your house first."

"In case you haven't heard, Meg and I are getting married," Seth said levelly.

Rick looked momentarily startled, then said, "Hey, great. Congratulations. When did that happen?"

"Last month," Seth said. "What's this about?"

"Introductions first. Seth, Meg, I believe you both know my nephew Jeffrey. This is my sister Karen Green, his mother. I thought it was important that we all talk now, as soon as it was possible. I apologize again for the early intrusion."

"Please, sit down, everybody," Meg said. "You want coffee? Because I know I do."

Karen maintained her stony silence, and her body language as she perched on the edge of a chair made it clear she would rather be anywhere else. Her brother Rick was trying his best to compensate. "That would be very kind of you, Meg. This may take some time. Have you and Karen met before?"

"No, I don't think we have," Meg replied, wondering how one family could have produced both the gregarious Rick Sainsbury and this stiff sister of his. Karen alternated between glaring at Meg and Seth and ignoring both her brother and her son. Jeffrey looked miserable. Whatever this discussion was about, it would not be pleasant, Meg guessed.

"I'll go get that coffee," Meg said to no one in particular, and turned and headed for the kitchen. She busied herself with the coffee-pouring as Bree tiptoed down the back stairs.

"What's up? Whose car is that?"

"Rick Sainsbury's, and he's brought his sister and nephew along, to talk with Seth and me."

"And why does he need to do that right now?"

"Because someone was killed in Granford last night behind the feed store, and Jeffrey found the body."

Bree gave her a long, silent stare. "Who?" she said finally.

"As of last night, Art didn't know. I'll find out if there's any more news."

"And you're hiding in here pouring coffee," Bree said. "I get it. I think I'll go find something very important to do upstairs in my room, which will last until they're gone. You can fill me in then."

"I left Seth in there to handle them, so I suppose I'd better go rescue him." Meg found a tray, stacked mugs and coffee needs on it, and headed for the parlor. At least everyone had found a seat by the time she arrived. "Oh, Jeffrey, I'm sorry—do you drink coffee, or would you like something else?"

He shook his head. "No, I'm good. Don't go to any trouble."

Karen finally spoke. "Meg, I apologize for barging in on you at home, but my brother seemed to think you can help us."

Rick looked down at his hands for a moment. "Look, I won't keep you any longer than necessary. Here's the problem. It appears that Jeffrey was involved in an incident last night."

"I know," Seth said. "Art Preston called me as soon as he heard about what happened. He told me that Jeffrey called 911 about a fatal assault."

Rick avoided looking at either of them. "It's a bit more complicated than that. Jeffrey found the boy and he called the police, and he stayed with the victim until the police arrived. It was a fluke that Jeffrey happened to stumble over the boy the way he did. He was just there for some bags of fertilizer Karen ordered, which had been left out back for him to pick up." Rick stopped, wrestling with his next words. "I'm in a difficult position here. You know the election's less than two months off, and I'm a political newcomer and I'm supposed to be running all over campaigning. Before you slam me for being insensitive, I'm not thinking about me or the campaign, I'm thinking about Jeffrey here. But because I'm a candidate, and because of what happened here last spring, I'm concerned that there will be media attention."

"What do you think we can do?" Seth asked noncommittally.

"I'm trying to be proactive here. I know how plugged in you are to the local community, and I know you both have some experience with criminal investigations. I also think you're both smart and fair. Obviously the state police will be involved, but if this situation . . . gets worse, I think you're the best people to find out what really happened, from a local perspective. I know Art will do his best, but you two come at things from a different direction."

Meg and Seth exchanged a glance. Seth had a long history with Rick Sainsbury, going back to high school; Meg had met him only earlier in the year, and they had gotten off to a rocky start, before he had won the spring primary. She hadn't seen him since. He appeared to be sincere, but Meg still had reservations. "Why do you think this will get worse?" Meg asked.

"Because a boy is dead, they don't know who he is, and the police don't have any suspects. I'm afraid they'll focus on Jeffrey, for the wrong reasons."

"Detective Marcus doesn't railroad people, even if they are related to political candidates," Seth said tersely.

"I'm not saying he would. I just want to find out as much as possible before this escalates. I've told Karen how helpful both of you were when I had that trouble back in the spring, and that she can trust you. I'm committed to sticking close to Granford until we can get this mess with Jeffrey sorted out."

"Rick, you don't have to jeopardize your campaign over this," Karen snapped. "I can handle Jeffrey's problems."

"Karen, forgive me, but I don't think you're doing such a great job of that," Rick shot back.

"Hey, guys, I'm in the room, you know," Jeffrey protested. "And I'm not a problem to be handled, by either one of you. I'm not a child."

"I'm sorry, Jeffrey. You're right," Rick said, and he sounded like he meant it. But Meg wasn't sure Karen was as happy with that situation.

Meg turned to Jeffrey. "You know, we're kind of in the dark here about the details. Can you at least run through the outline of what happened for us?"

Jeffrey spoke before anyone else could interrupt him. "I went to pick up Mom's fertilizer order at the feed store. I found this guy lying behind the store. I didn't know him. He was either dead or pretty close to it. I tried to stop the bleeding and I called 911. That's what I told the police about eighty times. What else can I say?"

"Jeffrey!" his mother burst out. "You're being rude."

Jeffrey turned toward her. "Mom, I think the fact that I found a bloody body and was questioned by the police for like three hours is enough of an excuse to be rude. I know they're really interested in how I got his blood on me, but that only happened when I was trying to help him, to stop the bleeding. It was everywhere."

"Jeffrey, how old are you?" Seth asked suddenly.

Once again Rick cut Jeffrey off. "He's seventeen. In Massachusetts that means he can be tried as an adult. And he can make his own decisions."

"The police still haven't identified the victim?" Meg asked.

"No. The only thing they'll say is that he isn't a local high school student—they checked with someone at the school."

"Hello?" Jeffrey interrupted. "Does anyone want to listen to me? Like I keep telling everyone, I did not know this person. Not from school, not from Scouts, and not from any extracurricular activity, all right? Why would I want to harm him? Or anybody, for that matter?" Jeffrey said in a tone that seemed to Meg to be quite reasonable under the circumstances. "When I left the dig at the green last night, I drove over to the feed store and parked in the back, and that's when I found the guy. He was on the ground, on his back. It was getting dark, so I couldn't tell for sure if he was still alive. I knelt down and looked for a pulse, and I thought I found one. That's probably when I got the blood on me. I know you're not supposed to move anyone with a head injury, so I called 911 and just tried to keep him warm. And stayed there waiting for the police and the ambulance. That's all."

Everything Jeffrey said made sense to Meg, and she wasn't sure how anyone could suspect him based on that. He'd done things by the book, and acted quickly and appropriately. So why were they all here talking about it?

"Do you believe him?" Rick asked Meg and Seth.

"I do," Meg said, and Seth nodded in agreement.

"No ID on him?" Seth commented. "Isn't that odd?"

"Yes, most kids these days carry something—student ID, driver's license, debit card. No phone, either. All of those could have been taken if this was a mugging or . . . something else."

"What about asking around the colleges, to see if the victim was a student?" Seth asked.

"They'll get to those if need be, but we're talking thousands of students, and it's Saturday, so the administrative staff isn't there."

Meg realized that there was one significant omission in their conversation. "Jeffrey, where's your father?" she asked. "Nobody's mentioned him."

"He's not really in the picture," Rick said, answering before Jeffrey could.

"What's that supposed to mean?" Meg demanded. "Divorced? Separated? Deceased?"

"My husband and I are separated," Karen said stiffly.

"Come on, Karen," Rick said, "it's more serious than that." He turned to Meg and Seth. "Sam moved out a few months ago and took a job in another state. Before you slam him for abandoning Jeffrey, it was the only job he could find, and he needs to work since Karen doesn't. It was Jeffrey who chose to stay behind, to finish high school. He's an only child. I'm his only other relative. I should warn you, I'm afraid Karen's main concern here will be how it impacts her public image." The contempt in his tone was clear.

"Rick!" Karen hissed at him.

"Oh, cut the crap, Karen," Rick said impatiently. "Jeffrey, when was the last time you saw your dad?"

Jeffrey glanced at his mother before answering. "Uh, June? He took me out to lunch. He was in Boston for something—he lives in Ohio now."

Meg noted Jeffrey's use of the word "lives," like he knew his dad wasn't coming back. "Karen, have you told Jeffrey's father what's going on here?" Meg demanded.

"Do you even have his current phone number, Karen?" Rick demanded.

"Stop it, both of you!" Jeffrey burst out. "There's nothing

he can do about it. He's not here. This is *my* problem, and I have to deal with it."

"And you've been doing it so well, since the police still seem to think you're a suspect," Karen said, her voice sharp with sarcasm.

Meg watched Jeffrey react. For a moment she thought he was going to lash out at his mother, but then he got himself under control. He stood up and stalked into the kitchen without saying a word. The adults in the room—Meg amended that to "so-called adults"—were left in uncomfortable silence. She waited for Karen to go after her son, and so did Rick, apparently. When that didn't happen, Meg stood up herself and followed Jeffrey.

She found him standing in front of the sink, drinking a glass of water and staring out the window. When Meg walked in, he turned toward her. "Sorry, that was rude of me."

"I don't blame you, Jeffrey. Is your mother always so, uh, supportive?"

He shrugged. "She hasn't been the same since Dad left, although they weren't getting along for a long time before that. But I guess now that he's out of the picture, she's been alternating between lashing out at me and ignoring me."

"I'm sorry. It must be hard for you, even without . . . what's happened." From the little she'd seen of the woman, Meg had a feeling that Karen would see herself as the victim in this drama, watching her social standing in Granford go down the drain. Her son couldn't expect much help from that quarter. And whether Rick's motives were sincere or merely practical, the fact remained that he didn't live in Granford and wasn't a full-time part of the family—and now he was a public figure. Jeffrey was legally and effectively an adult, and very much on his own.

Her heart ached for him. He was trying so hard to be adult about what was happening to him. "Jeffrey, I think you're doing a great job holding together. But if there's anything you know about the boy you found, you need to tell Art or the state police."

"You think I'm hiding something?" He sounded honestly curious.

"No, not really. Look, just tough it out. But please let me know if there's anything I can do to help you," Meg said softly.

Jeffrey looked surprised. "Help *me*? Not Mom or 'the candidate'?" He made air quotes when he referred to his uncle. It sounded as though Jeffrey didn't think very highly of either of them.

"Yes," Meg said. "I've got a feeling those two have their own agendas. What are *you* going to do?"

"Thank you for taking me seriously, Meg. To tell the truth, I don't know what I'm supposed to do. All I can say is that I did not assault that guy. I had no reason to kill him. I told you how and why I got the blood on me. I was trying to help. Won't people believe that?"

Meg looked at Jeffrey, the sweet, smart, eager Boy Scout who looked very young at the moment, and whose family seemed unable to provide any meaningful support. "Let's hope so." She took a deep breath. "It seems to me that the only way to prove that you *didn't* injure the boy is to figure out who did."

"Isn't that what the police are doing?" he asked.

"It's what they *should* be doing. It doesn't always work out that way. That's why people like Seth and me try to do what we can, without getting in the way. Most of what we can contribute comes because Seth is so connected to this town, on a lot of levels. We'll try our best to sort this out. Does that work for you? I won't make any promises I don't think I can keep."

Finally Jeffrey smiled. "Yes, it does. I can't ask you for anything more. And thank you."

Meg looked up to see Karen standing in the doorway. Meg wondered how much she had heard, or if it mattered.

"Jeffrey, we're going now," Karen said, her tone brittle. "Thank you for your hospitality, Meg. We won't be bothering you again." She turned her gaze to her son. "Jeffrey? Now."

Jeffrey looked at Meg and shrugged, then followed his mother out. Meg trailed behind and said good-bye to Rick. She and Seth watched the family drive away together.

Meg leaned against Seth and said, "Leave Jeffrey out of the equation and tell me why a black kid was hit over the head behind the feed store."

"I can't answer that."

"I need to talk to the pickers, don't I? Because they're the only black faces I see around here."

"Statistically that's true. But you don't suspect the pickers, do you?"

"No, I don't. But someone is likely to." She sighed. "You know, I never suspected there were such dark doings in Granford. It looks so peaceful."

"I'd say we're about average. Messy divorces, kids with problems—that's pretty ordinary. Still, overall it's always been a peaceful place. At least, it was until you came to town."

11

"I'm going over to the Historical Society now," Seth said. "I'll let you know if I find out anything new."

"Are you taking Max with you?"

"Sure. I'll take a long lead and let him stretch his legs on the green."

"Sounds good. For him, I mean." Meg crossed the room to kiss him good-bye, although it was more for reassurance than anything else. "Poor Jeffrey," she said into Seth's chest.

"What about the poor victim?" Seth responded.

"Well, of course it's terrible for him, but I don't know him. And I do know Jeffrey, a little." Was he capable of being violent, and then lying to conceal it? She didn't think so. Could her judgment of his character be that far wrong? "I'm not convinced that Jeffrey was involved in any way, other than being unlucky enough to find the victim. But

I've been wrong before, so I'll keep an open mind, if Art or the state police come up with something substantial. Let's hope he finds out who the boy is." She gave Seth another quick squeeze. "Now, go."

As soon as Seth had gone out the door, Bree sneaked down the back stairs. "Is the coast clear?"

"Yes, they're all gone, but I can't tell you a lot more. Jeffrey called the police when he found a teenager behind the feed store who'd been fatally injured. The police questioned him, but he said he'd never met the boy and they let him go home with his mother, so maybe there's nothing to it."

"No way!" Bree exclaimed as she helped herself to coffee. "Is this the same Jeffrey who found the skeleton at the Historical Society the other day?"

"It is, and Rick Sainsbury is his uncle." Meg hesitated before plunging on, "Bree, because this dead boy was black, I think the police are going to want to talk to the pickers."

Bree turned to face Meg, but her expression was hard to read.

Meg went on, cautiously, "You know as well as I do how few people of color there are in Granford."

"So, because they're black and he's black, you think they know this dead guy?"

"Well . . . possibly. There are quite a few pickers around here this time of year, and most people in town don't know them. I thought maybe you or we could ask our crew, see if anybody knows the victim."

Bree sat down with her muffin and coffee. "You want me to pump our crew for information?"

"No! Just find out if they know who he might be. I gather he's younger than most of the guys here, but he could still be a relative. It's worth asking, isn't it?"

Bree gave her a look of contempt. "Hell, they probably wouldn't know anything yet. This happened, what, last night? You know how these guys live—their families are usually somewhere else, they come here and camp out wherever they can find a room, sometimes lots of guys in a room. So even if he was a picker, nobody's likely to be keeping track of this guy. Anyway, he could have been a student at UMass, or could have come from Holyoke or Chicopee or Springfield, right? You don't have to jump to the conclusion that he's Jamaican."

"But it's possible," Meg said, surprised by her own stubbornness. Of course she didn't *assume* the boy was Jamaican, but in Granford it was clearly a possibility. "Look, Bree, if you're uncomfortable with this, you don't have to say or do anything. As you say, it may have nothing to do with the Jamaicans here, or even with Granford."

"But Candidate Sainsbury wants to be sure his shiny Boy Scout nephew doesn't mess up his campaign, right?"

"Maybe," Meg admitted. "To be honest, it crossed my mind. But at least he's not asking us to make this go away quietly, or to pin this on someone else. He said that he just wants to get the facts straight—and, I assume, to keep Jeffrey out of it if possible. The fact that Jeffrey found the body and that he had the guy's blood on him means he's already got two strikes against him."

Bree made a huffing noise and turned away, looking out the window and avoiding Meg's eyes. She was silent for several moments. "I'm not going to badger the people I work with. And I'm not going to snoop. If they know something, they're bound to talk about it. Although maybe not always in front of me, because I'm not one of them—I'm management and I'm a woman. But if they say something,

I'll ask them what they know, and I'll tell you and Seth what I find out. Is that good enough?"

"That's all I'm asking, Bree. I just want to know if they know who the boy is." And who might have reason to attack him, but that question could wait for later, if Bree heard anything.

"Yeah, sure." Bree stood up abruptly, ending the conversation. "I'm going up the hill. You coming?"

"I've got a couple of phone calls to make, and then I'll be up."

"Giving me some alone time with the pickers, are you?"

"Bree, it's not like that!" Meg protested. "If I'm going to help Jeffrey, I want to talk to Gail, to get her take on him, and to get Miranda Melvin's number from her, because Miranda has spent some time with Jeffrey now. If she saw him pitch a temper tantrum at the dig site or something, we need to know that. That's all."

"Fine." Bree stood up abruptly, her chair screeching across the floor, startling Lolly, who'd been sleeping on top of the refrigerator. "See you later."

She stalked out, leaving Meg wondering if she had mishandled the situation. She didn't see how. She'd thought it would be better that Bree ask the pickers a few questions than to have the police tramping all over the place questioning the men in the midst of their busiest season.

With a sigh, Meg picked up her cell phone. Gail had young children, so Meg knew she'd be up, possibly even already out and about, on this Saturday morning.

Gail picked up on the second ring. "Hi, Meg," she said cheerily, then added in a lower voice, "you heard about, uh, Jeffrey's latest find?"

"I did. Art called Seth last night. Where are you?"

"At the Historical Society, of course. My husband is watching the kids. Were you looking for Seth? He's around here somewhere. You want me to find him?"

"No, I wanted a phone number for Miranda. Is she there, too?"

"No. She wrapped up the archaeology part yesterday, but said she wasn't sure when she could get to the autopsy. I told you, she was on sabbatical last year, so she's playing catch-up now, getting her classes sorted out. I suppose if that poor man has been dead for two hundred and fifty years, a couple more weeks won't matter much. Why do you need her?"

Meg laughed. "Let me know what she finds about the skeleton, whenever it is, will you? But right now I just wanted her take on Jeffrey."

"Of course," Gail answered. "Hang on a sec, and I'll get the number off my phone." Meg waited until Gail retrieved the information and read her the number. "Thanks. I can wait until Monday to call her. Have you heard anything else?"

Gail laughed. "You're asking me? You practically live with the point man for anything relating to Granford."

"Just wondering. Oh, by any chance, is Jeffrey there?"

"He is, much to my surprise. Of course, it *is* Saturday, so no school. Not that Jeffrey would be likely to tell me what's going on, and I'm not about to ask him. And I don't know his mother well enough to ask her. She'd probably think it was kind of weird if I called. I'd guess they're both going to put on a stiff upper lip and pretend it's business as usual. And to be fair, from what I hear, Jeffrey did exactly what the first aid manual says, and we don't know anything more than that." Gail sighed, then perked up as she said, "Oops, the foreman wants me—gotta go!" She hung up.

The examination of the old skeleton would be nice and clean compared to last night's discovery, Meg reflected. It was reasonable that Jeffrey had been bloodied, if he had been trying to help the victim, right? Head wounds were bloody, or so she had heard. Jeffrey, on an errand for his mother, had found someone in distress and had done all the right things. End of story. She hoped.

Seth would no doubt know more when he came home. Now she had to get back to work—which she found she was reluctant to do, since apparently she'd ticked off Bree without meaning to. Still, wasn't it a reasonable assumption to make, that if an unknown African-American teenager was found dead in this town, that he might be somehow connected to the only group of local black males—the itinerant pickers? And Meg wasn't the only orchard owner in the area who employed them; Jamaican workers had been coming to Massachusetts to pick fruit for decades. Which also reinforced the assumption that they might know something about the young dead man. It was a question that needed to be asked, even if it made Bree uncomfortable.

Meg squared her shoulders, went out the back door, and headed up the hill to the orchard.

When she arrived, Bree sent her a warning look and shook her head quickly. Meg took that to mean either Bree hadn't asked, or that she'd asked and nobody knew anything—or that no one was willing to talk about it. Whatever the case, Meg decided not to push it: she needed the goodwill of the workers to get her crop in, and she didn't want to antagonize them, especially now, after they'd spent some pleasant time together. "Where do you want me, Raynard?" she called out. He pointed toward a tree with a waiting ladder farther down the row. Meg pulled on her bag and got to work.

A couple of hours later her cell phone rang: Gail. Meg answered, "Hi, Gail. What's up?"

"The excavation is done, and the forms are in place. But they won't pour concrete until Monday, Seth said."

"Wow, that was fast!"

"Heck, they said this was small potatoes for them. I'm just glad it's moving forward again. And I talked to Miranda—she said she was going to be in Granford to drop off her official reports on our skeleton, just to dot the *I*s for Art, and said she could stop by late in the day and update me on what she'd found. I kind of offered your place, since I figured you'd want to hear what she had to say. Do you mind?"

"Well, she's a woman who's used to dirt, so it shouldn't be a problem. Did she tell you if she'd found anything interesting?"

"She said she's just got the bare outlines so far, and there's more to be done. So I'll see you at five? Oh, any word on Jeffrey?"

"You're more likely to know than I am—I've been up in the orchard all morning, and I'm headed back there now. I'll expect you at five." With a sigh, Meg turned off her phone and went back to work.

At four, as she was walking slowly down the hill, feeling every muscle, Raynard fell into step beside her. "Bree told me what you asked," he said quietly, when he was sure they couldn't be overheard.

"I didn't mean to imply that any of your men had anything to do with . . ." Meg began to protest, but Raynard held up a hand.

"I took no offense. None of the men here know anything about that young man, but I will talk to some other people working around here, see what they might know. They are more likely to talk to me than to you, or to the police, I think."

"Thank you," Meg said, relieved. "I didn't mean to put anyone in a difficult position. I mean, we don't even know if the boy is from around Granford—he could be from anywhere. But if he's got relatives or friends around here, they deserve to know."

"Please don't trouble yourself. If he is one of ours, we will find out."

Meg decided this was a good time to change the subject. "Did Bree talk to you about which apples would be ready for the Harvest Festival?"

"She did. I will be sure we set aside some fine ones for you."

They'd reached the bottom of the hill. "Thanks again, Raynard. This will be my first time there as a vendor, and I'd like to put my best foot forward."

"Of course. I'll speak with you tomorrow." He made his way over to his faded pickup truck, opening the doors to cool the interior, and waited for a few of the other pickers to reach the driveway—he always provided rides for some of them.

Bree was the last one down, after all of the pickers had left. Meg said, looking after the departing vehicles, "Do you know, I never did find out where they're living."

"Wherever they can. They're here for only a few months each year, and it's almost all guys, so they don't care much."

"Still, I kind of feel I should know things like that."

"Whatever makes you happy." Bree shrugged.

"By the way, Miranda Melvin is coming over to report

on what she's got so far on that skeleton from the green, any minute now."

"That's the anthropologist lady? Do you need me to be there?"

"Of course not. Oh, right—it's Saturday. Do you and Michael have plans?"

"Nothing specific. He's got some new roomies, now that the term has started at the university, so things are a little crowded at his place."

"You know you can bring him here."

Bree shrugged again. "He feels funny about that, and I guess I do, too. Don't worry—we'll work it out. I'll meet him in Amherst, and you and Seth can have some alone time."

"Thanks, I think."

12

Bree had left by the time Miranda arrived a few minutes after five, still full of energy despite putting in a full workday examining an old corpse. As Meg went out to greet her, Gail also pulled into the driveway and parked behind Miranda's car.

"Welcome, both of you," Meg said, when they were both out of their cars. "Come on inside."

"Is Seth joining us?" Gail called out.

"No, last time we talked he wasn't sure when he'd be home. He's been supervising your crew *and* trying to keep up with his other projects."

"Poor lamb. Don't think we don't appreciate it. Maybe we'll inscribe a brick in his honor."

Once they were settled in the kitchen with iced drinks, Meg told Miranda, "I'm surprised you've had any time to look at our old bones already. Gail said you'd been away for a year and were trying to catch up for your classes this term."

Miranda laughed. "September's always crazy at the university—I'm used to it. Besides, I can recycle a lot of earlier course notes, and then I throw in some juicy bits about what I've found recently and everybody's happy. Besides, I'm kind of intrigued by your man. I haven't gotten into any detailed analyses yet—I'm going to let my seminar class observe the procedures—but I thought you'd like to hear my preliminary findings."

"We're all ears," Meg said.

Miranda began rather formally, "As you know, I told the state police that this body was not the result of a recent crime, so they gave permission for me to take it back to the university and examine it. In addition, I brought some of my students over to the burial site the next day to see if we could find the rest of the bones. I thought it would be a good opportunity for them to participate in a real dig. We found all the major bones and quite a few of the smaller ones— luckily the soil there allowed for good drainage, so the bones were well preserved. Back in my lab, I had the students lay out the bones in the appropriate distribution. As an aside, I have given my preliminary findings to the chief of police here in Granford, and sent a copy to the state police. I like to keep the professional lines of communication open, so that if they find something really interesting and old, they'll call me in. This one is in fact very interesting, at least for New England."

"Come on, Miranda," Gail said, "you're teasing us. What did you find?"

"The body was that of an older male, in his sixties, I'd guess. Teeth were better than I'd have expected. No broken bones in his lifetime. I guessed earlier that he died from TB—which they would have called consumption back then. So it was a natural death, and the evidence of the bones proves it."

"Well, that's good news. I really didn't want to hear about another murder in Granford, even if it happened a couple of centuries ago," Meg said.

"Well, this poor fellow wasn't killed, although consumption wasn't a particularly nice way to die. Anyway, the burial was what I guess I'd call semiformal: no sign of a coffin, but he was buried well below the surface, not just thrown in a shallow pit. That would have taken a little time—he was interred, not hidden. But on the other hand, there were no mementoes left with him. From the few fragments we found, I'd say he was buried in a shroud, not in his clothes, and that's why there are no buttons or buckles and such."

Meg interrupted, "What were the standards for burials in the eighteenth century around here? How many people were buried without a stone? I know I've looked for several of my ancestors and they're nowhere to be found, although their parents and siblings are buried together not far from here. Or the husband will be there but not the wife."

"Good questions, Meg. I'll see if I can track down some articles for you, since that's not my area of expertise."

"And he's always been where he was found?" Gail asked.

"I'd say so," Miranda replied. "My students and I looked at the soil, and there was no other sign of disturbance, apart from the shallow grave. I'd have to do a closer analysis of the soil on the bones, but my guess is that he was not moved from another location. He was buried where you found him. From what little I've seen, it doesn't look like that location was a cemetery. If it was, we should have stumbled across at least a couple more burials in that area. I can't see a family scattering burials around the property with no order. And often such family plots mark the burials with large rocks or boulders, even if they aren't inscribed. Of course, those might have been displaced when the building was erected. But there's one more thing . . ." She gave them a wicked grin.

"What?" Meg and Gail said in near-unison.

"The man was African."

It took Meg a few moments to process the implications of that fact. "An African man, here in Granford? In 1760-whatever? Or even earlier?"

Miranda nodded. "That's what I mean. I couldn't tell until I had reassembled the skull, but the characteristics were undeniable once I put it back together. And given the way he was laid out, I'm thinking he wasn't just someone passing through."

Gail looked uncomfortable. "Oh goodness, are you saying—"

"Yup," said Miranda. "He was probably a slave. As you probably know, there were slave owners even up here in Massachusetts during the early colonial days."

"Hold on a minute." Meg went into the dining room, where she kept her laptop and most of her research materials in less than perfect order. She grabbed her laptop and rejoined the others in the kitchen. As she turned it on she said to the other two women, "I have an idea that may support that theory." She clicked on a website, clicked a few more times, then turned it so the screen faced Gail and Miranda. "U.S. censuses are available online, even old ones. Here's the 1790 census for Granford. Look at the column on the right."

Historian Gail got it first. "Slaves," she said almost to herself. "And there were only two in the town then—and they both belonged to the same person, John Moody. Whose family gave the land for the church!" she finished triumphantly. "It fits!"

Too bad Jeffrey isn't here to see this, Meg thought. Maybe he could help do some more digging into the local Moodys, if he wanted to follow through on this project. Maybe there were documents available that would include the dead man, put a name to him, and Jeffrey could hunt them down. Maybe there was a Boy Scout history badge in it for him. "So why was this man buried all by himself? You didn't find any other burials nearby, right?" Meg asked.

"Not directly under the building," Gail answered before Miranda could. "But it's not like anyone has explored every inch of the land there, and it's not in the society's budget to do it now. Of course, if we found out it actually was a cemetery, I'm not sure what we'd do."

"Don't panic—we didn't find anybody else under the building. But when you're ready, there's GPR," Miranda said promptly. When Meg and Gail looked blankly at her, she went on to explain, "Ground-penetrating radar. You can see if there are burials under the surface without disturbing the soil. There's a group that's been doing that in Old Deerfield, not far from here, and they've had good results. There are companies that do that kind of thing these days."

"Well, there you go," Meg said. "Can you rent a GPR unit?"

"Sure. It might cost you a couple of hundred bucks a day. But you'd need somebody to interpret the results. An amateur like you could probably distinguish between disturbed and undisturbed ground, but an expert would be able to tell you whether you've got a casket or an open burial, and roughly how long the body had been there based on the deterioration of the grave itself. Hey, if you're really interested, let me know and I can set you up with someone."

Meg and Gail exchanged a glance. "That sounds like a great idea—once we get through rebuilding our building and getting all the records moved and sorted," Gail answered. "Maybe in the spring? As long as you're sure there's nobody else under the building."

"Don't worry about that," Miranda reassured Gail. "We looked very carefully. But if it was the original town meetinghouse, it would be logical that there could be other burials nearby. Like I said, let me know if you want to find out more."

"This is so interesting," Meg said. "Technology meets history. I wonder if Seth would have any use for one of those GPR things." Meg imagined how enthusiastic Jeffrey would probably be about this GPR project. Well, maybe he would be soon again, if things worked out.

"Sure," Miranda replied. "You can use them to find conduit, underground wires, pipes, maybe even rocks that'll mess up your excavation. Or if a builder has dumped rubble and old tree trunks just to get them out of the way—and they could shift and settle if you build on them. It's easy to check if there are any hidden items like that where you want to build."

"I'll talk to him about it," Meg said—adding to herself, *And then I could borrow it to look at some old cemeteries.*

"Thanks for the suggestion, Miranda," Gail said. "We'll definitely think about it."

"Glad to help. Was there anything else you needed? Because otherwise I should get going. I've got to prep for a lab next week."

"That should do it for now," Gail said. "I can't thank you enough for helping us out here."

"Hey, that's my job. And I'm glad it turned out to be something interesting. Do you still want me to do a DNA analysis?"

"Is that hard to do? Or expensive?" Gail asked.

"No, not if you do the most simple tests. I've got all the samples I need."

"Then do it," Gail said. "You never know what might turn out to be important."

"You're right," Miranda said. "Oh, and I was thinking— that Jeffrey kid seems smart and eager, and I know he was looking for projects. If he could find out more about the history of the Moody family, and of the land, or even of the church, it might help us fill in some blanks and figure out why this man ended up where he did. Think he'll be interested?"

"I'm pretty sure he would be. I'll ask him, the next time I see him," Gail said. Meg noticed that she didn't mention the recent assault in town and Jeffrey's role in it, but Miranda didn't need to know that.

Miranda stood up. "Okay, I'll go ahead with the DNA. But remember, it's only useful if you have someone else's DNA to compare it to."

Meg and Gail stood up, too. "I know," Gail said, "but who knows what we might find? Thanks again, Miranda."

"I'll get back to you with the results," Miranda said. Once she had pulled out of the driveway, Meg and Gail looked at each other.

"Well, that was unexpected," Meg said.

"You didn't know there were slaves in Granford?"

"Maybe in the back of my head, but I never gave it much thought. I've probably seen those slaves mentioned on the census at some point—I mean, there are only two pages for all of Granford in 1790—but it didn't sink in. I certainly never expected to come face-to-face with one, dead or alive."

"Well, don't jump to any conclusions yet," Gail cautioned her. "I'd like to know more about slavery in that era. And weren't there freed slaves as well? The man could have been a local freeman that the Moodys allowed to be buried there, or a slave that they owned, or someone just passing through."

"I'd like to see what Jeffrey can turn up, if he gets a chance to do the research, and I hope he will," Meg added.

"If he can find the original documents," Gail said with a sigh. "I so wish the Society had the funding to hire a cataloger, part-time at least. Maybe after we get the new space built out and all the records together again, we could scrape together funds for a short-term position for that. Or maybe Miranda could find some sort of intern at the university. And if the records were better organized, then I might have a little more time to work on things like lectures for the schools, or displays in the building."

"Can the library help?"

"They've got a lot on their plate at the moment, with the new building, but maybe down the line. I need to look into grant funding, too, if I ever find the time. Listen, I'd better get home and feed the family. Thanks for having us, Meg. Talk soon!" Gail went out the back door, leaving Meg sitting alone at the table.

She continued to sit for a while, turning over what she had just learned. The man buried under the former church had been African. That idea took some getting used to, especially given that she now knew the Moodys had been slave owners and it was likely that the skeleton was that of a slave, since slavery was still legal in Massachusetts in the middle of the eighteenth century. He'd been buried with some dignity. The land had been donated for the purpose of building a church in the 1760s—or, no, she amended, a meetinghouse. A multiuse building. The need for a church had prompted it, but it had also been sort of a town hall. In any case, this so-far-nameless slave must have died before that date—but by how much?

Her tired mind skipped to a different track. Gail could certainly use some help at the Historical Society. Now *all* the records would be coming home to roost, but who was going to deal with them? If everything went according to plan, the building would be ready before winter, and after the harvest. Meg would have more free time then, so she could help out. After this renovation, it would even have heat, so it would be possible to work in the building during cold weather, which hadn't been the case before. Assuming Jeffrey was available, Meg wondered if he'd like to help out as well, sort of as an unpaid intern? If he really did like history, he might enjoy it. And it would look good to any colleges he was applying for.

Was there a chance he wouldn't be available? She still couldn't visualize the possibility that he'd had anything to do with that unknown boy's death, but she had to keep reminding himself that she didn't know Jeffrey well. She'd only met him a couple of times and never had a significant conversation with him. Bree, who'd never even met him, had written Jeffrey off as a wimp, based solely on Meg's description. Maybe there *was* something dark beneath his surface. Would his teachers at the high school know? Was that what Rick Sainsbury was worried about?

But she hadn't sensed any violence in Jeffrey. What she had seen was a lonely boy who'd seemed kind of lost in the world of high school. He was clearly intelligent, but out of step with a lot of his peers. He'd probably fit better in college—if he went to the right school, not a huge university that specialized in parties and football games like UMass, but one where he could find like-minded people. There were good classes and faculty at UMass, but it didn't strike her as the best place for someone like Jeffrey. Amherst College might be better, if he wanted to stay close; any of the Ivies, too. But first he had to avoid being arrested.

Meg was still sitting and thinking when Seth came in a little after six, followed by Max. "Hey," he greeted her as Max went to his water bowl. "You okay?"

She smiled. "I'm fine. I'm just thinking. Does it look like it hurts?"

Seth found a bottle of water in the refrigerator and downed half of it. "I don't know—I don't remember what it's like to have time for it."

"Any word on Jeffrey?"

"I assume that's what you were thinking about? He's at home. Jeffrey keeps saying he has nothing to hide. He found the boy, he called the police, period. But his family arranged for a good lawyer, in case he needs one, and he told Jeffrey to keep quiet."

"I asked Bree to see if our pickers knew or had heard anything about the dead boy. The dead man? I don't know how to refer to him. When does a boy become a man?"

"Now, there's a loaded question. But I know what you mean. What did Bree say?"

"She wasn't happy I asked. She accused me of implying that all people with black skin around here all knew each other. That certainly was not what I intended. But as far as I can recall, there simply aren't any other black residents in Granford. Am I wrong?"

"Not according to the census," Seth told her. "That's not to say that there aren't blacks in any other nearby communities—in Holyoke that group makes up closer to five percent. But practically speaking, yes, the Jamaicans are the only likely candidates here in town."

Meg nodded. "That's what I thought. I asked Bree because I figured that the local Jamaican community would be more willing to talk to one of their own than to me—an employer—or the police." She sighed.

"They should know you're just trying to help. You get along well with them, don't you?"

"I think so, but it looks like I'm trying to help a local white boy who may have killed a black boy. I think it's a no-win situation."

"Where is Bree?"

"With Michael. She said she was giving us a little space."

"Ah. How does pizza sound?"

"If I don't have to cook it, it sounds wonderful. Remind me to put the pizza place on speed dial."

13

Meg refused to open her eyes the next morning. "They tell me that there are places where Sunday is a day of rest."

"Not for farmers," Seth replied. "Be thankful you don't have to go out and milk a herd of cows before breakfast."

"You may notice that I vetoed that idea a long time ago. At least when apples have to wait, they don't bellow at me. In chorus."

"Still picking today? Sorry, stupid question."

"Yes, dear, we're still picking today," Meg said, with exaggerated patience. "And tomorrow, and next week, and next month. And then I will hibernate for three months, work on my family history, and balance the books. Sounds exciting, doesn't it?"

"Isn't there supposed to be a wedding in there somewhere?"

"So I'm told. You're sure we can't elope?"

"There are a lot of people around here who would be disappointed."

"Including you?" Meg asked, suddenly serious.

He looked at her steadily. "Yes. I don't want to just run off. I want to stand up with you in front of my family and friends and declare that I love you and that I want to make a life with you."

Meg burrowed against his chest. "Oh, Seth—I want that, too, but everything I read or hear about planning the event makes it seem so complicated. You know: booking the church a year ahead, finding a reception hall, ordering doves with our initials on them." When he looked confused at that last comment, she laughed. "I'm kidding. About the doves, at least. But society has made this so difficult, not to mention expensive. Can't we do it like they did in the nineteenth century? Find a preacher, put on clean clothes, and get married in the parlor?"

"Only if we can still have a party for the rest of the town afterward. Besides, do you know a preacher?"

"Not exactly." Meg rolled onto her back and leaned against the pillows. "You don't feel strongly about getting married in a church, do you? Because I did have one idea . . ." She wasn't sure how good an idea it was, though.

"Yes?" Seth prompted.

"According to my research, in Massachusetts it is possible for an individual to obtain a short-term license from the state enabling him or her to perform marriage ceremonies."

"And you have someone in mind?"

"I was thinking of Christopher. He's been so important in helping me keep the orchard going, even though he's been busy with teaching and overseeing the new construction at the university. He's already blessed the orchard, sort of. He's been involved with some of the other troubles we've had here"—that was an understatement, Meg reflected—"and I count him as a friend. What do you think?"

Seth rolled over so his position mirrored hers, and he put his arms behind his head. "Interesting idea. He's a great guy. Have you talked to him about it?"

"No, because I thought I should run it by you first, to see if you hated the idea. Would you prefer a man of the cloth?"

"Not necessarily. I'm not close to one, and I guess I'd prefer to be married by someone I know, rather than someone picked at random. Let me think about it, but I like the concept. And if we go ahead with this, I think we should ask him together."

"Deal." Meg felt obscurely comforted. They had moved the wedding glacier an inch or two forward.

She could hear Bree clattering around down the hall. "I guess we should get up. What are you planning for today? The concrete pour is tomorrow, right? That's what Gail told me."

"Yes. Today is for catch-up. Paperwork, like invoices, if I want an income. Doing some inventory and probably placing some orders online. I'll probably be around most of the day, but in and out."

"Oh, you want to hear something interesting? Miranda and Gail were here yesterday, and I never told you what we talked about. Miranda said that the body they found under the Historical Society was African. Which means he was almost certainly a slave, and probably belonged to the Moody family, because they show up on the 1790 census as slave owners."

"Now, *that* I didn't expect to hear! How did he die?"

"Consumption, apparently."

"I'd never thought of that—that he could be African, I mean, not the consumption. There was plenty of consumption around. I don't recall anyone mentioning slaves in Granford."

"Well, in 1790 John Moody was the only one with slaves. But since it was his family that gave the land under the Historical Society, it kind of fits neatly, don't you think?"

"And I assume people will be looking into the history?" Seth asked.

"Once Gail gets all the local documents assembled in this wonderful new space you're building for her, and confers with the library, and I finish harvesting so I have time to help. And maybe Jeffrey will want to finish his badges. If he can. No news on that front?" A question she was getting rather tired of asking.

Seth, now dressed, sat on the bed to lace up his work boots. "As of last night, Jeffrey had not been arrested, and no one had yet come forward to identify the dead boy. And that's all I know. See you downstairs."

Seth disappeared into his office at the end of the driveway after breakfast, and Bree and Meg were lingering awhile in the kitchen talking about plans for the day when there was a rapping at the door. Meg opened it to find Raynard there.

"Good morning, Raynard. Is there a problem?" Meg felt a moment of panic: had she inadvertently insulted the pickers and they'd all walked off on strike this morning?

"Not with the orchard, no, ma'am. It's about that dead boy."

That sounded like trouble. "Please, come in. Would you like some coffee?" Meg stepped back to let him enter.

"A glass of water would be good, thank you." He dipped his head at Bree, who didn't say anything.

"Coming up. Please, sit down." Although Meg was itching to know what he had to say, she carefully filled a glass with water and set it in front of Raynard, then resumed her seat. "What did you want to tell us?"

Raynard looked down at his hands, which were wrapped around the glass. Meg looked at them, too, noting that they were rough and scarred from years of pulling apples off trees. "I asked around a bit. Have the police said anything to you about who the boy might be?"

"Not lately. The last I heard, they still didn't know his name. Do you have any idea who it is?"

"I think I do. You know, those of us who come here for the harvest, we're scattered all over the area, and we don't often gather. But last night was Saturday night, so we met in this place we go, in Holyoke. I happened to run into Hector Dixon—you remember him?"

When Meg looked blank, Bree volunteered, "He worked here last harvest, remember, Meg? Middle-aged guy, mustache, not too tall? But he didn't come back this year because he was offered more money at another orchard. Right, Raynard?"

Raynard nodded. "Yes, that is the man. We fell to talking, and he told me that he left us not only because of the money, but also because this year he wanted to bring over his nephew Novaro. He knew you did not need any extra help here, Meg, so he found someone who could take on the boy as well as himself. This nephew, he's eighteen this year, and his uncle thought it was time he started to work. The boy was finished with school, and there were no jobs for him in Jamaica. His mother was tired of feeding him. So Hector fixed up a visa for him and Novaro joined the crew where his uncle was working, but he didn't last long—he thought he was too good for this kind of farmwork. His uncle was not happy with him, but in the end the boy just stopped coming. Which was bad, because if you leave the employer that brought you here, you lose your right to stay in this country. Now he is here illegally, and he knows it. And of course, when he left the job, he had to find a different place to stay, who knows where. This was maybe two weeks ago? After he quit he didn't come around to talk to his uncle, and Hector worried that he might be going around with the wrong people."

"And you think this boy who died could be the nephew Novaro?" Bree demanded.

"The boy's age is right, and Hector does not know how to find him. Hector did not know who to talk to, and is reluctant to go to his new employer, but he has decided that if Novaro is indeed this dead boy, he should be sure so that he can tell the boy's mother. So he has asked me to find out what I can."

"Why not tell Hector to go to the police? They're going to need an official identification," Bree told him.

"We don't like to mess in police business. We're legal, but it doesn't pay to go looking for trouble."

Meg couldn't entirely disagree. "All right. What do you want me to do, Raynard?"

"Ask your police friends if they have found out who the dead boy is," Raynard said. "And if they have not, ask them if he had a gold cross on a chain around his neck. If there is such a cross, tell me, and I'll have his uncle come forward."

It seemed to Meg like a reasonable request, given the Jamaicans' distrust of police in general. "All right, I can do that." She stood up. "I'll go call the police chief now." She took her cell phone into the front parlor for privacy, and punched in Art Preston's home number. The case would be the state's jurisdiction, but she'd rather ask Art about this cross than wade through the bureaucracy of the state police phone system.

"Yo, Meg, it's Sunday morning, isn't it?" Art answered after four rings, his voice still rough with sleep. "Or did I sleep through a day?" He paused a second or two. "Don't tell me you have another body."

Meg laughed briefly. "No, not that. And it *is* Sunday. I apologize for butting in on your day off, but I have a question about the boy found at the feed store. Have you identified him yet?"

"No," Art said. "If you have a possible line on him, I'm listening."

"One of my pickers just came to me and Bree and told us he talked to a friend last night who works at a different orchard, and whose nephew was here for his first picking season, except he didn't like the work and dropped out. The uncle hasn't heard from him recently, but he was worried. If the boy's not working, his visa's no good."

"Does the nephew have a name?"

"I'm sure he does," Meg hedged, "but the pickers are all kind of cautious around police. But there's one thing I was told to ask you: was the boy wearing a gold cross?"

"He was." Art sighed. "That wasn't made public. Can you put me in touch with this uncle?"

"I'll send him to talk to you, and you can decide how to handle it with the state people. I can promise him that nobody's going to get into any trouble about this, right?"

"All we want right now is an ID for the victim. Tell your contact guy I'll be in my office in town by noon, okay? I'll be pretending to be doing paperwork."

"Yeah, that paperwork does pile up, doesn't it?"

"It does. Thanks, Meg. I'd rather not be working today,

but if it moves this case forward, I can deal with it. Talk to you later." Art rang off.

Meg returned to the kitchen, where Raynard and Bree were deep in conversation. They fell silent when she walked in, and looked at her expectantly.

Meg sat down and said gently, "I talked to the police chief, Art Preston, and there is a cross. I told Art that you could tell Hector to go talk to him at the station here in Granford—he'll be there by noon. Can you do that?"

Raynard sat up straighter in his chair. "Thank you, Meg. If you don't mind, I will go look for my friend now. Bree, you can manage the men, right?"

"Of course I can, Raynard. I'm sorry about all this, but thanks for coming to us about it."

Meg saw him out, and shut the screen door behind him. As he walked toward his truck in the driveway, she saw his shoulders sag lower than they had when he arrived.

Meg went back to her seat at the table. "I guess it's good news in a way—isn't it better to know who the boy is?"

"It's better to settle this fast," Bree said sharply. "The pickers don't like trouble, and this kid sounds like trouble. Raynard and I were talking about it while you were on the phone. The guy came over because his family made him, but he was never happy about it, even though his uncle did all the paperwork and stuff. But he didn't make much of an effort here, and he quit pretty fast. That's going to be a problem for him, because he loses his visa—unless he's the dead kid, and then it's kinda moot. Oh, and bigger picture, it's a problem for us, down the line."

"I don't follow. What do you mean?"

"Haven't you looked at the guys we have working here? Most of them aren't young, and their kids don't want to do farmwork. The U.S. government doesn't want to make it any easier for migrant workers from anywhere, not just Jamaica, to get into the country to work, but there aren't many Americans who want to do this kind of work either. So who's going to pick the apples, huh?"

"Bree, I don't know," Meg told her. "Heck, aren't you the one who took classes on the economics and politics of farming in this country? I sure never did. You should know more than I do."

"I know what the problems are, but I don't see any easy solutions. And Congress isn't being much help either. They want more jobs for Americans, and that's good, but the jobs they're messing with, Americans don't want."

"Well, as for staffing needs in the future, we've been planting the new trees on dwarf rootstock, and closer together than in the past. Does that make a difference?"

"It means that the apples will be easier to pick. But you still need *some* people to do it. There's no way to mechanize the fruit picking, because you lose too many apples when they're damaged."

Meg sat back in her chair, feeling depressed. "And here I hoped today might be a nice day. Well, let's go."

They spent a busy few hours in the orchard, breaking only for sandwiches and drinks up the hill with the workers. Meg watched the men for any signs of hostility, but saw none.

Mid-afternoon, her cell phone rang: Art. She was far enough away from any of the men that they couldn't overhear, so she answered.

"You were right. Your guy Dixon just ID'd the kid as his nephew Novaro Miller, from Jamaica. Only been in the country for a few weeks."

"What a shame. How'd the uncle take it?"

"He's sad. I don't know if they were close, but from what I gather he was trying to help the kid, bring him along. Apparently Novaro just wasn't interested."

"You sound tired, Art."

"It's never easy when you're dealing with families. Dixon told me on the way over that his nephew Novaro had been acting out ever since his father died back in Jamaica. The uncle thought a real job might help straighten the kid out and fixed him up over here, but Novaro didn't want any part of it and kind of dropped off the radar. Now the next thing Dixon knows, his nephew is dead. And he feels responsible, all for trying to give a family member a chance. It's too bad."

"So now that you know who the victim is, does that make a difference?"

"Some. At least Marcus can put some guys onto tracking down the boy's known associates and seeing if they can tell him anything. The pickers in the area probably don't know much about him because he was new, but there are some kids who squat in Holyoke who might. If they'll talk." Art paused. "Please don't tell me you're going to start trying to interview street kids in the city."

"Of course I won't go looking for this Novaro's friends. I'm not stupid. Marcus is much better equipped to handle that."

Art was still talking, almost as if to himself. "It doesn't seem like a mugging—at least, whoever killed him didn't take the cash in his pocket or that gold cross. We still don't know why he was at the feed store. Maybe he was thinking of robbing the place—it's pretty isolated."

"Art! Suddenly he's gone from victim to potential criminal? Do you have any reason to believe he was thinking of breaking in?" Meg protested.

"I'm not assuming anything, Meg. I'm just trying to find

a reason why Novaro was where he was when he died. From what his uncle said, the kid's recent activities seem kind of sketchy—no known address, no known income, and he blew off a regular job and dropped off the radar. Marcus will have to consider it. Look, I've gotta go. You going to tell the pickers about the ID?"

"I guess so. The uncle worked here at my orchard last year, so my crew knows him, and Raynard helped track him down. They deserve to hear it from me," she said. "Hey, is Raynard still there with Hector?"

"They left together, but neither said where he was going. Talk to you later." He hung up.

Bree had approached while Meg was on the phone, and was watching her expectantly.

"Yes. It's confirmed," Meg told her. "The dead boy was Hector Dixon's eighteen-year-old nephew, Novaro Miller. I should tell the rest of the guys."

Bree shook her head, and pointed down the hill to where Raynard's truck was pulling into the driveway. "Raynard's back—let him do it."

Meg was embarrassed by the relief she felt. "I'll go down and talk to him. You don't need me back up here, do you?"

"No, you go. I'll finish up."

Meg went slowly down the hill to intercept Raynard. "I heard from Art, Raynard. Is there anything I can do?"

He regarded her steadily. "I appreciated your counsel earlier. I only wish the outcome could have been different."

"Well, let me know if you need anything," Meg said. It felt like a stupid response—what could they need? But she did feel bad that the victim had proved to be related to one of the pickers—one she had known herself, however slightly.

Meg continued down the hill, while Raynard went in the opposite direction.

She reached the driveway and waved to Seth, just emerging from the shop at the rear. When he was near enough to read her expression, he said quickly, "What's wrong?"

"We know who the dead boy was—Novaro Miller. He's the nephew of one of the guys who worked here last year, Hector Dixon. Hector and Raynard just identified the body."

Seth folded her into his arms. "I'm sorry."

"He was just a kid!" Meg said into his chest. "What a waste."

"I know. It always is."

When Meg and Seth returned to the kitchen, Bree was cooking something that Meg couldn't identify but which smelled good. Meg was startled to realize that most of the afternoon had evaporated. Since neither Lolly nor Max budged from their usual places, Meg assumed Bree had fed them.

"Anything new?" Bree asked, without turning away from the stove.

Meg sighed. "No. Look, Bree, we told Rick Sainsbury and Karen Green that we'd help Jeffrey, if it turned out he needed help. It's still not clear whether he's a suspect, but he may be. So Seth and I are still going to try to sort this out—for Jeffrey's sake. I'm really sorry that the dead boy turned out to be Jamaican, and related to someone we know. I feel like I'm caught in the middle."

"It's okay, Meg. I get it. Jeffrey's an only child, right?" Bree asked.

"I think so. Why does that matter?"

"Well, maybe that's why he joined the Boy Scouts—he's looking for a family."

"Maybe," Meg said dubiously. "Seth, were you ever a Scout?"

"Nope. No time, what with school and sports and helping my dad out with the business."

"And plenty of friends, I'm sure," Meg said. "Poor Jeffrey—no siblings, and we haven't heard anything about friends, although we haven't seen him at school. But we should stick to the basic problem: if Jeffrey didn't do it, who attacked the boy? Why there? Why then? And what do we do now?" Meg asked.

"We could use some more picking bags," Bree said.

"What's that got to do with anything?" Meg asked, startled by the abrupt change of subject.

"You can get them at the feed store," Bree added.

Light dawned slowly. "So maybe I should stop by the feed store in the morning and pick up a few? And maybe talk with the owner?"

"Bingo," Bree said, filling three plates.

"Are those things heavy?" Seth asked. "Because maybe I should come along and help you load up the truck."

"Lunchtime?" Meg said.

"Works for me," Seth replied.

14

The sun continued to shine, for which Meg was grateful. A couple of months earlier, drought had been a real concern and rain welcome; now she wanted the wet weather to hold off so that she could keep picking and get her crop in. Unfortunately there was no way to rush ripening apples. Bree tested them daily for sugar levels, and she made the final decisions about what to pick and when. Maybe it was a good thing that there were fewer pickers this year—at least she didn't have to pay them to sit around and wait for the apples.

When Meg came down for breakfast Monday morning, Seth was already cleaning up his dishes, and Max was standing by the back door, quivering with anticipation. Bree was seated at the table, looking at some sort of spreadsheets.

Meg helped herself to coffee, then asked Seth, "Where are you off to today?"

"We're pouring concrete, remember?"

"Oh, right. I'd love to see that. Bree, may I go watch the concrete pour?"

"I guess. We're pretty much caught up, but check back with me this afternoon, okay? With this sunny weather, things can change fast."

"Yes, ma'am. Seth, are we still going over to the feed store later or will you be too busy?"

"It's right down the road from the green, so I can get away, I think. Why don't you meet me at the Historical Society around noon and we can go over together."

"That works for me," Meg answered. "Bree, anything else I need to pick up or order while I'm there?"

"Goat food," Bree said, without looking up.

"Oh, right. Seth, I'll walk you out." Seth went out the back door, Max dancing around his ankles, and Meg followed. "You think Jeffrey's back in school today?"

"Maybe. Who knows, maybe he'd score points with his peers for being suspected of beating someone up—how often can you do that? Or maybe he's just conscientious. He's got to be thinking about college applications."

"He could have a really unusual essay for those applications, depending on how this plays out. Tell me, do you think he's given us—or anyone else—the whole story?"

Seth walked over to his work van and was sorting through some of his equipment in the back, so he didn't answer right away. Meg had followed and stood waiting to see what he would say. Finally he turned to face her.

"Do I think he got into a fight with an unemployed Jamaican kid he didn't know? I can't see why—if this Novaro jumped him, or Jeffrey interrupted him trying to break in the back, Jeffrey would have told that to the police, because it would put him in a better light. Do I think he's told us everything? No, I don't. But I don't know what he's *not* saying, and I don't know him or his family well enough to guess."

"You think there's any chance Marcus could arrest him?"

"I doubt it. He doesn't have anything like real evidence as far as we know, and he'll be fair. Jeffrey's story hangs together, more or less. And the fact that he's Rick Sainbury's nephew will come into play, one way or another. I don't think he's a flight risk or likely to do harm to anyone, so I'd guess that Marcus will tread lightly. For now."

"Understood."

Seth came over to her, took her face in his hands, and kissed her. "I'll see you at noon, in town."

Meg, rendered momentarily speechless by the kiss, stepped back to let him pull out of the driveway and watched him go.

Bree came out the back door, the screen slapping shut behind her. "Yo, Meg—I'm going up the hill. You coming?"

"In a couple of minutes," Meg called back. "You go ahead."

Bree left, and Meg went slowly inside, reviewing her plans for the day. She wanted to talk to the pickers about Novaro Miller, especially now that she knew his uncle had worked in her orchard, but she'd been through only one season with these men, and she still didn't know all the ins and outs of their local culture. Heck, they'd all been around the area far longer than she had. She knew they were proud of their skills with the orchards, and proud of their reliability, returning year after year. But she wasn't sure how they would react to a crime among their own—and how they would feel about her getting involved. She'd been glad to help discover the identity of the dead boy, but she wasn't sure how far she could push her advantage. Maybe she should ask Art about any other crimes involving the local immigrant population. She hadn't heard of any.

Not that it was her business anyway—except that she wanted to help Jeffrey. He seemed like such a good kid. If she was honest, he probably reminded her of herself at his age. Decent, hardworking, earnest—and nerdy and forgettable to all the "cool" kids at school. Did Jeffrey have any friends? Had he joined the Scouts in order to find some? Was the fact that his uncle was a public figure making it better or worse for him?

Meg drained the last of her coffee and put the cup in the sink, patted Lolly, who was perched on the refrigerator, made sure she had her cell phone, and headed up to the orchard. Three hours of picking, then back to get her car and meet Seth over at the green, and then they'd talk with the guy at the feed store and she would buy goat feed. Then back for some more picking, and dinner, and bed. What an exciting life she was leading! What would her former banking colleagues in Boston think? But she was pretty sure they didn't think about her at all. Not that that bothered her. That had been another life, one she'd left behind, and she had a new life here in Granford, one she was happy with.

She headed up the hill, and by the time she reached the orchard, the pickers were scattered among the trees, doing their jobs. Meg made a mental note to find a quiet moment to talk to Raynard, to see if he'd heard anything new. Then she checked in with Bree, who handed her a picking bag and pointed to a row, and Meg went to work. Shortly before noon she transferred her latest bagful into one of the big apple crates and told Bree by way of hand signals that she was going to go down the hill and leave. Bree nodded and kept right on working.

Meg stopped at the house long enough to wash her face and hands, and decided her clothes were clean enough to visit a construction site and an agricultural supply store. She'd look like she fit in. She drank a glass of water, found her car keys, and drove the couple of miles to the town green.

Seth was not the only observer there when she arrived. There was a small crowd watching the massive concrete truck at work. It took a couple of men to position the chute from the truck to the forms under the Historical Society building, which looked rather precarious perched on a scaffolding of large beams. A few other men were stirring the already-poured concrete, releasing any bubbles and settling it. Meg parked and walked over to where Gail Selden was standing.

"So it's not only guys who like watching the big machines?" Meg asked.

"Hi, Meg. Hey, this is fun! And I keep getting excited about how much more space we're going to have underneath."

"What's the timeline, overall?"

"I'm told we'll have it sealed up in a week or two," Gail said, "and then there will be finish work, plumbing and heating—all that good stuff. And then I'll start assembling all the scattered collections—I'm really looking forward to that! You know there's stuff here in town that I've never even seen? I know about it only from some old handwritten inventories. I just hope nobody has thrown any of it out, thinking it was old trash. Hey, you don't have anything interesting lurking in your attic, do you?"

Meg laughed. "I think you've asked me that before, and

I still haven't been up there to poke in all the corners. Maybe when the harvest is done."

"And you're going to help me inventory what comes in, aren't you? Over the winter, that is. After all, we'll have heat! Is it silly to be so excited about things that most people take for granted?"

"It just shows you care about what you're doing, Gail. I get it."

Seth strolled over to join them. "How's it going?" Meg asked.

"Good. We're on schedule, and these guys know what they're doing. You want to head over to the feed store now?"

"Sure," Meg said.

"What's that about?" Gail asked. "Are you two visiting the scene of the crime?"

"I'm buying food for my goats," Meg said. When Gail looked disappointed, she added, "And the other thing, too. We're trying to help Jeffrey, whose family is . . . How can I put this? A bit at odds?"

"I'd go with dysfunctional," Gail said briskly. "Have you met Karen yet?"

"Yes, on Saturday," Meg answered.

"Oh, good," Gail said, relieved. "So you'll know what I mean. I've worked with Karen on committees for a few years, and she is a piece of work. Do you know, I don't think she has anything like a friend in this town? I can understand why her husband decided he'd had enough, although it's too bad that Jeffrey had to bear the brunt of that."

"So you know about the split?" Meg asked. "Does everybody?"

"Most of us in town saw it coming a long time ago. But

things must have gotten really bad for Sam to bail when Jeffrey was so close to being out of the house."

"Both Sam and Karen grew up around here?" Meg asked.

"Sure did. Except Karen went off to some fancy girls' school."

"I didn't know them," Seth volunteered. "Rick and I were in high school at the same time, but barely, so I wouldn't have overlapped with Karen—she was a couple of years ahead."

"Well, from what I hear," Gail said, "Karen decided she was better than the rabble from Granford, and Sam had the biggest house and the cleanest fingernails in town, so she set her sights on him. It worked for close to twenty years, I guess. Listen to me, gossiping! Whatever his family situation, Jeffrey Green is a good kid, and I refuse to believe he could be involved in the death of a stranger. Or even *hit* anyone, in self-defense or otherwise. The police had better keep looking."

The three of them fell silent, watching the concrete flow into the forms. Then the truck shut down, and one of the workmen near the foundation gave Seth a thumbs-up sign. He nodded back. "Well, Gail, it looks like you've got yourself a new foundation, once it sets up."

"Oh, goody! Can I put my initials on it somewhere?"

"Just don't fall in. Meg, you ready?"

"Lead the way," she said.

As they drove the short distance to the feed store, Meg said, "You know, I've been in this place plenty of times, but I don't think I've met the owner, although I've probably seen him. Who is he?"

"Jake Stebbins. Grew up in Granford, went to New Hampshire and worked there for a while, then he came back here a decade or more ago and took over the feed store—only one in town. Good guy, works hard, and his prices are fair."

"Got it. How big is his operation?"

"Didn't you say you'd been there?"

"Yes, but I never spent much time there, and I didn't count employees. All I buy is the goat feed."

"Well, Jake works in the store, and he's got maybe five employees? During busy seasons he hires part-timers to fill in, mostly high school kids, including his daughter."

"Maybe Novaro was there looking for work? Though his work visa is specific to one employer and can't be transferred. So he couldn't just pick up another job."

"Maybe Novaro didn't understand that. But since Jeffrey found him after closing, we don't know how long he may have been lying there."

"Will the police have talked to Jake?"

"I assume, since that's where Novaro was found. We'll find out." Seth pulled into a parking space in front of a long low building with stacks of brightly colored plastic containers lined up along the perimeter, and large signs advertising feed products on the wall above. They climbed out of the car, and Meg followed Seth into the building.

She watched as a thickset fifty-something man emerged from an office at the back and walked toward them. "Hey, Seth, how you doing? I see you've dug up the town green."

"Hey, Jake. Yeah, it seems like Granford can't leave well enough alone. You heard about what we found under the building?"

"Yeah, I did. Weird, isn't it? Poor guy." Jake turned to Meg. "Meg Corey, right? How're those goats of yours doing?"

"I'm surprised that you recognize me—I don't think we've met officially."

"I like to know who my customers are." The man held out his hand. "Jake Stebbins, at your service. Besides, there aren't that many goats around here, and you're buying the most feed for 'em."

"Well, my goats are fine, as far as I can tell. Do you know, I kind of like having them around? They're very undemanding, and they look so intelligent when I talk with them. Plus they don't talk back. They seem happy. Though I need another bag of that pelleted grain."

"No problem."

"I hear you had some trouble here last week," Seth said.

Jake's expression turned somber. "Awful thing, that. Poor kid. They figure out who he is?"

"His name was Novaro Miller, age eighteen," Meg replied after glancing at Seth. "It turns out he's the nephew of one of the Jamaican pickers who used to work at my orchard. This was his first year working as a picker in an orchard, but he decided he didn't like the work and quit after a couple of weeks. Any chance he applied for a job here?"

"Come on back into the office and I'll check, but I doubt it—mostly I hire kids from the school when I need help. Yo, Billy?" Jake shouted.

A teenage kid appeared from the far end of the building. "Yeah, Mr. Stebbins?"

"I'm going to be in the office with these folks for a few minutes. Cover the floor, will you?"

"Sure thing."

15

 Jake led Meg and Seth back to his office. He waited until they found chairs—dusty from the inevitable grain chaff—and began, "Why are you two so interested, anyway?"

"Well, like I said, he's related to a former employee of mine. Plus, we'd just met Jeffrey Green right before all this happened, and he seemed like a good kid," Meg said. "I'm hoping he doesn't get labeled a suspect just because he was the one who found the boy." She wasn't sure how to appeal to Jake, and she and Seth hadn't discussed any sort of strategy. "And Jeffrey's family asked us to help if we could." She shot a quick glance again at Seth, who didn't interrupt her. "You must know we've been involved in a few problems here in the past. It's not that we don't trust state police to do their job, but we might have a different perspective."

Jake nodded. "It's good of you to try, Meg, but I don't

know what I can tell you that I haven't told the police. I didn't know Jeffrey."

"Jeffrey told us that he came by here to pick up an order his mother had placed?"

"Yeah, that's right. She wanted to fertilize her lawn before winter. But she didn't want to come pick it up herself—might mess with her manicure."

One more person who doesn't like Karen, Meg thought.

Jake apologized immediately. "Sorry, that was kinda rude. I don't think she could lift a full bag of fertilizer anyway, so she sent her son over."

"But you didn't see Jeffrey?" Meg asked.

"No, she told me over the phone that he'd be over late—something going on at school, or maybe that stuff going on at the green. I said I'd leave the bags out back so he could swing by and pick them up whenever. It's not like anybody's going to make off with bags of lawn fertilizer—I figured they were safe enough out there. I stuck a label with his name on it so he'd know what to look for. I went home about five thirty, like always, and an hour after that I got a call saying there's been some trouble at the store. I don't live far away—maybe half a mile past your place, Meg, so I came right over."

"Did you see the victim?" Seth asked.

"Yes and no," Jake said. "He was still there when I got back, but the police had him covered up. Some cop showed me a picture of the boy's face on his tablet, but I didn't recognize him."

"You're sure he never came here looking for work?"

"If he did, I never talked to him, although he might have left an application. But I'm not hiring at the moment anyway." Meg thought Jake looked suddenly uncomfortable. Was there something there he was keeping from them?

"Who else works here?" Seth asked.

"Me, of course," Jake said. "I've got a couple of full-time employees, and some high school kids who work here after school, like my daughter, Emma, but most kids are so dang busy with sports and programs nowadays, it's hard to find anybody. And the money's not great, I'll admit."

"Did you ever meet Jeffrey Green?"

"Not to speak to. This was the first time he'd made a pickup. Mostly Karen asks me to have the stuff dropped off at her place."

"Does she have a lot of lawn?" Meg asked, mildly curious. She wasn't familiar with Karen's neighborhood.

"Not huge, I'd have to say, but she's one of those people who thinks it has to be perfect, so she's always fiddling with it. I'm not going to tell her to stop, since she's buying all the lawn stuff from me."

"So who applies it? I can't see Karen out there with a fertilizer spreader."

"Don't know, and I didn't ask. She never asked me to recommend someone to do it for her. If I had to guess, I'd bet her son takes care of it. From what I hear, her husband's not in the picture anymore."

Interesting that Karen was still trying to keep up appearances while cutting corners now that her husband was gone. Not that asking Jeffrey to help out with some chores would be wrong.

"Okay," Seth said, "just to sum it up—you hadn't met Jeffrey, and you'd never seen Novaro until this incident."

"Yup, that's about it. You working for the cops now, Seth?"

"No, just trying to get it straight in my head. And I do have a responsibility to the town. So there was nobody in the store because it was past closing."

"Right. Emma locked up, and she said she hadn't seen anyone hanging around. That's what I told the cops."

"You have any security cameras?" Seth asked.

"Sure, but they're pointed at the register inside, not at the parking lot. I can't afford more, and who the heck wants to steal ag products?"

"You ever work with any of the Jamaican pickers?" Seth pressed on.

Jake shrugged. "Can't say that I have. I deal mostly with the orchard owners—either they come in to place any big orders, or they just call them in. One of these picker crew guys might drop by to get up some work gloves or something, but that's about it. Anything else you folks want?" Jake asked. "'Cause if not, I've got a business to run."

"Wait," Meg said, "there was one other thing I've been wondering about: how did Novaro get here? Did he drive, do you know?"

"Yeah, he did, or that's my guess. There was a crappy old car sitting in the corner of the lot—didn't belong to anybody I know. I noticed it the next day, Saturday, and I told the cops. They came and took it away."

"And you have no idea why Novaro was here?"

Jake shook his head. "Not a clue."

Seth stood up. "I think that about covers it. Thanks for taking the time to talk to us, Jake. We'd really like to clear this up sooner rather than later, and we appreciate your help."

"Glad to be of assistance, Seth. I'll see you out."

"Before we go, can you order some new apple bags for me? The old ones are getting pretty ragged," Meg said.

"Let me check what we have in stock. If I've got any out back, I'll drop 'em off at your place on the way home. How many you need? Six enough?" When Meg nodded, Jake added, "I'll make sure Billy takes that feed you wanted out to your car now."

Meg paid at the register, then Jake accompanied them out to the parking lot, where they saw that the sack of feed had been deposited against the back door of Seth's van. Seth opened the door and hoisted it in easily.

"Thanks again, Jake," Seth said.

"Good to meet you at last, Jake," Meg said. The feed store owner raised a hand in good-bye, then turned and went back inside.

Meg and Seth climbed back into Seth's van.

"I'm going back to work," Seth said. "You headed home? I'll drop you at your car."

"Fine. You can unload the goat feed later—I think Dorcas and Isabel will survive until tonight."

Two minutes later they arrived at the green and found Art watching the cement mixer pull away. "I missed all the fun," he complained when Meg and Seth approached.

"There will be other pours, Art." Seth laughed. "Hey, can we ask you a question?"

"About Novaro Miller?"

"How'd you guess?"

"Why else would you two be running around town in the middle of the day? Don't you have work to do?"

"We're on our way back. We had an errand at the feed store. Listen, did you talk to Jake Stebbins about Novaro Miller?"

"We didn't know he was Novaro Miller then, remember. But, sure, the state police talked to Jake the next morning. He said he'd never seen the kid before, and he had no idea what he was doing behind the feed store. He suggested maybe it was some kind of gang thing, and Miller was dumped there because the place was close to the road but out of sight, if you know what I mean."

"Gangs?" Meg said, surprised.

Art sighed. "Yes, gangs. Not in Granford, but around— and this is a main highway here."

"Have any of the Jamaican pickers gotten mixed up with the gangs?" Seth asked.

"Not that I can recall. It would be quite the stretch, I agree. You know they're here only for a short while, for the harvest, and then they move on. Plus most of them are kind of on the old side to be caught up in that kind of thing. Besides, I think any involvement in a crime, even a minor one, might cancel out their visas. Not that I've ever had to check. You happen to know anything, Meg?"

She shook her head. "I've never even heard a rumor of any criminal activity. I've let Bree handle all the hiring, including the visa applications. I promise I'll pay closer attention in the future. But I do have to wonder: if this Novaro quit the job he signed up for to get here, I gather that means he'd have to go back?"

"That's my understanding, and I'm sure the state people have checked. Like I said, it's never come up before."

Meg went on, "But that kind of raises another question: if Novaro quit work after only a couple of weeks, how had he been supporting himself? I hate to ask this, but *could* he have been involved in something, uh, criminal?"

"Maybe," Art replied. "I won't pretend there's no crime around here. Heck, it's everywhere. But I haven't had to arrest anybody in town. I will say I've broken up a couple of small gatherings of young guys from out of town who might have been looking for trouble, but I just asked them to move on, and they did. So to answer your question, maybe Novaro could have connected with someone, but there's no evidence of anything. Maybe the state police will find something."

Meg hesitated a moment before asking, "Art, this may be a stupid question, but has Jeffrey Green ever been any kind of trouble?"

"With the law?" Art said, swallowing a laugh. "He doesn't even jaywalk. I swear. He'd stop traffic on 202 to let a bunch of ducklings cross the street."

"I know what you mean," Meg said. She could just about see that scene. Art had confirmed her overall impression of Jeffrey, but deep inside she kind of wished he would cut loose, just a little. Rebellion—within limits—was a healthy part of teenage life, or so she remembered.

"Oh, one more thing, Art," Meg began.

Art started laughing. "Only one?"

"I hope so! While we were at the feed store, we started wondering how Novaro had gotten there. Jake said there was an old car left in the lot, and that the state police took it away. Do you know if that was Novaro's?"

"Not officially, if you know what I mean. But they did a quick fingerprint check and found Novaro's prints inside the car. Also a couple of empty beer cans, though the kid was underage."

"So he did drive himself there," Meg said slowly. "But why?"

"No idea. If the staties know, they haven't told me," Art replied.

"Thanks, Art," Seth said. "Let us know when you hear anything more, will you? I'd better get back to work. Meg, you headed home?"

"I am. There are apples waiting for me." She watched

Seth leave. "Art, there's something else I think I need to tell you."

He looked her in the face and realized she was serious. "What?"

"I don't know if this is important, but I guess it might be. When Jeffrey came over here after school last Friday, I saw him kind of get into it with another boy, somebody about his own age. And there was a girl involved."

"You want to tell me what you mean by 'into it'?"

"Nothing physical, but they kind of faced off. It might have gotten physical if the girl hadn't gotten between them. And then she went off with the other guy, and that seemed to be the end of it."

"Why do you think this matters?" Art asked.

"Like I said, it may not. And that guy was white. Which might suggest that Jeffrey's had issues with at least one other person in town. When I asked Jeffrey about what I'd seen, he said it wasn't important. And then he went back to the dig."

"Would you know the boy again if you saw him?"

Meg shook her head. "They pulled in at the far end of the green. I recognized Jeffrey when he got closer, but I didn't know the other boy. Of course, I don't know *any* other teenage boys in Granford, so I'm not saying he was from out of town."

"And you didn't happen to overhear what they were arguing about?"

"No—too far away. But I got the impression that it involved the girl."

"Thanks for letting me know, Meg," Art said. "I don't know if it's important, but you never know. How're the wedding plans coming along?" he asked, clearly closing the other subject.

"We haven't had time to make any plans yet," Meg replied. "This is a busy season for both of us. Don't worry—you'll be invited whenever it happens."

Art's cell phone rang, and he held up a finger to Meg while he responded. "Where? Okay, I'm close. Be there in five." He turned back to Meg. "Gotta go. Look, if I hear anything, I'll let you know, promise." He turned to hurry back to his squad car, leaving Meg alone on the green.

16

A few hours later Seth arrived home with two pizzas, to Bree's applause. He set them down on the kitchen table, distributed plates and napkins, and they settled around it. "I thought I'd change things up a little—one's a white pizza with veggies," Seth said.

"Interesting comment Art made earlier about gangs in the area," Meg said, after they had consumed their initial slices.

"Didn't he say there aren't any in Granford?" Seth protested.

"Yes, but that doesn't mean they're not around."

"Hang on, guys—now you're saying that Novaro Miller was part of a gang?" Bree said indignantly.

"No, I'm not saying that," Meg said sharply. "We were only trying to figure out why he was found where he was, because he had no known reason to be there. We do know now that he drove there, so he had use of a car. But it wasn't his."

They were all startled when the front doorbell rang.

"Who's that going to be?" Meg asked. "Most people who know us come around to the kitchen door. It's only strangers who use the front."

Seth stood up. "I'll go see who it is."

"Please. I want to get in at least three bites of dinner before I have to face anyone else."

Seth disappeared toward the front of the house. Reluctantly Meg listened to the sound of the door opening, the rumble of unfamiliar male voices—and the absence of anyone leaving. She sighed.

Seth returned with another man in tow. "Meg, this is Sam Green, Jeffrey's father."

Meg swiveled in her chair to take in the newcomer. The father who lived in Ohio? What was he doing here? He was nothing like what she had expected, after meeting Karen: he was tall and rangy, with an open face and a worried expression. She could see the resemblance to Jeffrey.

"Oh, I'm sorry. I didn't stop to think you might be eating," he said, contrite. "I can come back later . . ."

Meg summoned up a smile. "Hey, there's plenty, and you're here. Sit down and help yourself. Can we get you something to drink?"

"Is it too much to hope for cider?" Sam smiled, and his face lit up—definitely like Jeffrey, or at least the Jeffrey she'd met a few days ago, before the trouble started.

"Sure. It's not from my orchard, but it is local. Seth, would you do the honors?"

Sam sat down, looking sheepish, and Meg introduced herself and Bree. "Didn't Jeffrey say you lived in Ohio? Did he call you?"

The light in Sam's face faded again. "Yes to Ohio, no to the call. Someone I know in town called to let me know what was going on. I started driving as soon as I heard, but it took me until now to get here."

It must really hurt when your own son doesn't reach out when he's in trouble, Meg thought. "How did you end up at my house?"

Seth set a glass of cold cider in front of Sam, who drank down half of it at once, then inhaled a slice of pizza. "Sorry, I didn't stop to eat," he mumbled around a full mouth. "I started calling the house, and Karen's cell, and then Jeffrey's cell, before I left, and all I got was a 'not in service' message— I'm thinking maybe Karen changed them all recently. I went by the house when I arrived and there was nobody there. So I went into town and talked to someone at the police department, who sent me to you. And that's the sum total of what I know. Do you have any clue where my son is?"

"I'm sorry, no. But he was here last night, with his mother and her brother, so I doubt they've gone far—I think they're staying in Northampton. You know Rick is running for Congress?"

For a moment Meg wondered if Sam was going to choke on his pizza. "It doesn't surprise me," Sam said after he recovered. "He's still a resident of this congressional district?"

"He is," Seth said. "When our last congressman decided to retire, Rick kind of jumped on the opportunity."

"Again, I'm not surprised. May I?" Sam gestured toward the remaining pieces of pizza.

"Please," Meg said.

Bree stood up. "I'll get out of your way—I know most of the story anyway."

"Okay," Meg said. "Same routine tomorrow?"

"Yup. Bright and early. Night, all." She went up the back stairs to her room.

Sam sat back in his chair, looking marginally better after having inhaled some food. "Seth Chapin—didn't your father have a plumbing business near here?"

"Right over the hill. He's gone now, and I inherited it. My mother still lives in the house."

Sam turned to Meg. "I remember this house, but not you."

"I've lived here less than two years," Meg said. "My mother inherited the house, but it was in the family for generations before that. I've been so busy trying to learn orchard management that I haven't gotten involved in too many other things around here, which is probably why we've never met."

"Got it. Okay, what the hell is going on here?"

Seth, with a few assists from Meg, outlined the events of the past week, starting with Jeffrey's volunteering to help with the Historical Society excavation through the discovery of Novaro Miller's body and the state of the investigation, or as much as they knew of it.

When they were done, Sam looked drained. Then he said, "I refuse to believe that my boy would hurt anyone, much less someone he doesn't know."

"We agree," Meg said gently.

"So, what are we going to do about it?" Sam said firmly. Meg was relieved when her cell phone rang, giving her an excuse not to answer Sam. She didn't recognize the number, but with all that was going on, she thought she should answer it. "Hello?"

"Meg? It's Jeffrey." He sounded young, and not very sure of his welcome.

"Jeffrey, where are you?"

"We're staying at the hotel in Northampton with my uncle right now. Mom wanted to get out of the house—I think she expected nosy reporters to show up, not that I've seen any, but she was worried anyway. Listen, I really need to get out of here and talk to somebody. Can I come over?"

"Of course. Go ahead. I'll be here." Meg guessed his request was more about getting away from his family than talking to her, but she didn't mind either way.

"I'll be there in twenty. Thank you." He hung up abruptly.

Meg looked up to see Sam staring at her. "You didn't tell him I was here," he said.

Meg looked at him levelly. "He'll find out soon enough. I thought maybe Jeffrey wouldn't come if he knew you were here, and he sounds like he really needs a friendly face right now. I wasn't sure how he'd react to seeing you—after all, he didn't call you when all this happened, did he?"

Sam looked at the ceiling, clearly frustrated. "No. But he's always had my cell number, and I always answer if he calls. I bet this is Karen's doing—she's done everything she could to turn Jeffrey against me. Or maybe he's trying to prove he can handle this himself, without help."

"Maybe he didn't want to upset Karen by keeping in touch with you. You were the one who left, and she's the one Jeffrey has to live with day to day."

"I know, and I'm not proud of it. But I figured if I stayed with Karen, one of us would do something we'd regret, and that wouldn't do Jeffrey any good. And he had only this last year of school left—if he'd gone with me he'd have been starting his senior year in a whole new place, with no friends."

Meg refrained from saying that from what she'd seen, Jeffrey didn't have a lot of friends in Granford, either. "When did you leave?"

"Spring sometime—I don't remember the exact date. But I've been back a couple of times, to see Jeffrey. I guess I hoped that he could handle it, and that he'd escape when he went to college. That doesn't reflect very well on me."

"I know it's not my business, but what happened between you and Karen? I understand you don't know me, but I'm trying to figure out what's best for your son."

"We both are, Sam," Seth added.

Sam faced Meg. "I can't tell you because I don't really know. You live with someone, you lose objectivity, and Karen and I spent close to twenty years together. If that person is smart, he or she can sound very convincing and make you doubt yourself. And, of course, they don't believe there's anything wrong with them—it's everyone else who's at fault. And nobody appreciates them. Karen doesn't open up much. Since I've put some space between us, I think I've come to see her more clearly. She was demanding, self-centered, and unreasonable—and as we got older, she got madder."

"Why?"

"Don't ask me. I didn't make enough money. The house wasn't big enough. The local organizations didn't make her head of everything. When we were younger I thought she was just ambitious. Once she passed forty, it looked more like frustration to me. But she never figured out how to fix it, so she took it out on me."

"Not on Jeffrey?" Seth asked.

"Emotionally, maybe. I mean, if I was a disappointment to her, she was going to do everything she could to make sure Jeffrey didn't repeat my mistakes, or whatever she thought they were. She expected him to get top grades and take part in every sport on the calendar, and then she was disappointed when he wasn't made team captain in his junior year. I tried to tell her he just wasn't that into sports, but she didn't want to hear it."

"Sam, I know you haven't seen much of him lately, but do you think Jeffrey's okay?" Meg asked. "I mean, he's under a lot of pressure—your leaving, finishing his last year of school, the whole college application thing, and trying to keep his mother happy. That's a lot for any kid to deal with."

"Are you suggesting that all that pressure would make him snap and take it out on some stranger?" Sam sounded angry.

Seth stood up, then leaned against the kitchen counter. "Sam, that's not what Meg's saying. I don't see that kind of violence in him, not that I'm an expert. What I do see is a kid who's dealing with a lot of stress, and it's hard to say what outlets he's got for it. It is possible that Jeffrey may have gotten mixed up in some things that somehow brought him into contact with Novaro, even if he wasn't directly involved."

"Like gangs or something? I'm not ready to believe that. But more important, what can I do to help him?" Sam asked simply.

Right question, Sam! Meg cheered silently. She was beginning to like the man—and she was looking forward to seeing him and Jeffrey together, which promised to be revealing.

She heard a car pull up, followed shortly by a knocking at the front door. "That should be Jeffrey. I'll go get him." Meg stood up and went to the front of the house, wondering what to say to the troubled young man, and whether she should warn him that his father was in the kitchen, assuming he hadn't already recognized Sam's car.

When she opened the door, her first reaction was that this was a boy who needed a hug, badly. The poor kid looked like he was trying hard to keep everything under control, but rapidly fraying around the edges. She settled for squeezing his shoulder. "Come on in, Jeffrey. Did you tell anyone you were coming?"

He walked into the hallway, shaking his head. "Nope. Uncle Rick and Mom were arguing—what else is new?—so I just left. But then I couldn't figure out where to go. It's not like I can go to some bar and sit in a corner and brood."

Meg smiled. "No, you can't, and you shouldn't. I'm glad you came to us. Come on back—we're in the kitchen."

She led the way, then waited for father and son to greet each other. Sam stood up quickly and faced Jeffrey. Jeffrey stopped suddenly at the sight of him, and Meg could watch the play of expressions over his face. So much for self-control. It took only seconds before they were hugging—man-hugging, with lots of back-slapping and throaty rumbling. Meg felt tears starting, and glanced at Seth, who was smiling. She decided she definitely liked Sam.

After a few more moments, Meg thought it was time to move things forward. It was getting late, for all of them. She and Seth had work stacked up for the next day, Sam had just driven more than five hundred miles to get here and must be exhausted, and it was a school night for Jeffrey, although that seemed the least of anyone's worries. "Sit down, everyone. Jeffrey, have you eaten?"

He shrugged, which she took as a no.

"Sorry all the pizza's gone, but I can make you a

sandwich." When Jeffrey started to protest, Meg held up a hand. "Don't say no. You'll think better with some food in you. We can clear out and let you and your father talk, if you'd rather."

"No, please stay," Sam said, then turned to his son. "If that's all right with you?"

"Yeah, sure. Thank you, Meg—I'd like a sandwich, if it's no trouble."

He'd lapsed back into polite mode, but at least he seemed calmer. "Coming up. Seth, get Jeffrey some cider, will you?"

While Meg was assembling a sandwich, she tried not to listen in on the conversation going on between father and son, although if it had been truly private they could have gone into another room or left altogether. As it was, mostly what she heard was normal catching up, with no discussion of the death yet. She set the sandwich on the table in front of Jeffrey and sat down, as did Seth.

"Sam, do you have a place to stay?" Seth asked.

Sam shook his head. "I hadn't thought that far. I just started driving. I'll find a motel."

"You can stay at my place—it's just up the hill, and no one's there," Seth said. "Well, my clothes are, and I stop by now and then." He smiled at Meg.

"Can I stay there, too?" Jeffrey asked.

Sam looked simultaneously pleased and alarmed. "You'll have to tell your mother," he said. "You can't just disappear on her."

"I know," Jeffrey said. "I wouldn't do that. But she's driving me nuts. And there are all these newspeople at the house. They wouldn't know where to find me if I stayed at your place, Seth."

"Why are there newspeople hanging around?" Sam asked, looking confused.

"Because Uncle Rick is running for Congress and there's not much else going on in the world. Having a nephew suspected of murder is news. So they're following him, and he's trying to avoid them, and the whole thing is ridiculous."

"What about school?" Meg asked.

"I don't want to miss any school, if I don't have to. The television people would have to leave me alone there."

Meg wondered what kind of response he'd gotten from his peers at the school, but that was a question for another time.

"Then you can stay, too, as long as you tell your mother where you are," Seth said.

"I'll talk to Karen," Sam said. "It's not going to be pleasant, but she needs to know I'm here."

"Dad!" Jeffrey protested. "I should talk to her."

"Jeffrey, I think your mom needs to hear it from me. I don't want her to think I've kidnapped you, or brainwashed you. I need to talk to her."

Jeffrey's mouth twitched in what might have been a smile. "Okay, go ahead."

Sam stood up. "I'll take care of it now. You have her new cell number, Jeffrey?"

Jeffrey pulled out his phone and called up Karen's number, then showed it to his father. Sam stalked into the front parlor to make the call.

"Thank you for offering us your house, Seth," Jeffrey said politely. He tried to ignore the sound of his father's raised voice, audible from two rooms away, but it wasn't working. "I'm sorry about . . ." He waved vaguely toward the front of the house. "And I'm sorry you got dragged into this whole mess. It's not your problem."

Seth looked down at the table and smiled. "Well, Meg tells me I *am* Granford, so that makes it my problem. But I'm glad your dad's here for you."

"Me, too," Jeffrey said, and fell silent.

It was another two or three minutes before Sam came back. "She always manages to remind me why I left. Okay, Jeffrey my lad, we have your mother's permission to bunk at Seth's house. I doubt we could have achieved that much without the intervention of Uncle Rick, but he seems to have her under control, which is something. Do you need to stop by the hotel and get anything?"

"Will you write me a note for school and explain why my homework isn't done?"

Sam stared at him for a moment, then burst out laughing. "Kid, you are something else. In the middle of a criminal investigation you're worried about your assignments?"

"And don't forget Scouts," Jeffrey added, though Meg wondered if there was a sly gleam in his eye. Was he making fun of himself? If so, that was a good sign.

"Sure, why not? Anything else you want to throw in?" Having faced his ex-wife and won, Sam now seemed in a giddy mood. Or maybe his exhaustion was catching up with him.

Seth stood up. "Okay, guys—you go over and pick up whatever you need. I'll go to my place and make sure there are sheets on the beds and towels and that kind of stuff. I'll meet you back here and show you the way, all right?"

"But I want to hear the details of this murder business," Sam said.

"Nothing's going to change before tomorrow morning,"

Seth told him. "You all can join us for breakfast here and we'll give you the outline and tell you what we know. Right now you need some rest, and a chance to talk to your son. Deal?"

Sam nodded reluctantly. "Okay. Jeffrey, you ready to go?"

"Sure, Dad. I'll drive. It'll be faster." Jeffrey grinned. "Mom let me get a car, a used one, after you left. So I could get to school—and run errands for her."

"Fine by me—I've had enough driving for one day. We'll be back, Seth. Thanks for the food, Meg."

Meg took them back to the front door and let them out, then returned to the kitchen. "Well, that was interesting. What do you think of Sam?"

"I like him a lot better than I do Karen, I can tell you that."

"I agree. Poor Jeffrey, stuck between the two of them. I can understand why he decided to stay with his mother, but it can't have been easy for him. I hope she'll loosen the reins when it comes time for him to go to college."

Seth stood up again, reluctantly. "Well, I'd better check those sheets, and Max needs a walk."

"Can I come along?" Meg asked. "I love this time of day, or evening, or whatever it is."

"Glad to have you. Come on, Max!"

Outside the sun was all but gone below the horizon, and there was a nip in the air. Meg was glad she'd thrown on a sweater before leaving.

"Do you think anyone at Jeffrey's school would know anything?" she said, as she and Seth climbed the slight rise behind her house.

"About Novaro's death? Are you thinking faculty or students?"

"Either. Seems like Jeffrey is the type who would be more likely to talk to a teacher than a buddy. If he *has* any buddies."

"He does seem to be a loner. Maybe his Scoutmaster would have a handle on him?"

"Possibly. But how do we find a way to talk to those people? We're not actually part of this investigation."

"I can find out from Art if he has already. Beyond that, we just approach them—teachers, principal, Scoutmaster, whoever—as friends of Jeffrey's, nothing more. We're trying to help. If they say no, or they won't speak to us, so be it. We will have tried."

"I like the way you think, Seth Chapin."

17

Get up. Eat breakfast. Pick apples. Eat lunch. Pick apples. Eat dinner. Fall into bed. That was Meg's daily routine, and would be, until there were no apples left on her trees. There was precious little time for anything practical like shopping for food, which was kind of necessary. Or doing laundry or cleaning house. Or visiting with friends. Or planning a wedding.

Or solving a crime.

When she'd fallen into the farmer's way of life, Meg hadn't realized how all-consuming it was for most of the year. The only exception was the middle of winter, but some things couldn't be put off until then. She had to prioritize somehow. Getting her harvest in was high on the list. Getting married should be, too, but at least Seth understood the other demands on her time and attention, and he was as busy as she was. Finding whoever had attacked Novaro

Miller so that Jeffrey Green could get on with his life? It shouldn't be important to her personally—but it was. She knew too well how events over which you had no control could suck you in and toss you around, and from what she'd seen, Jeffrey didn't deserve that. So Meg had to bump that up the list, alongside apples and Seth.

"Good morning," Seth said, kissing her behind her ear. "What's on your calendar for today?"

She rolled over to face him. "Picking apples. Finding Novaro's killer. You?"

"The MacPhersons' kitchen project—they have no running water at the moment, since we tore the place apart yesterday. Helping Jeffrey somehow."

"At least we're on the same page. I know what to do with the apples, but how do we help Jeffrey?" Meg said.

"We were talking about getting in touch with some of his teachers, and his Scoutmaster," Seth said.

"I remember. But how do we do that? I don't know anyone at the high school, and I certainly don't know anything about local Scouting. Do you?"

"There are teachers at the high school who have been there since I was in school, although they must be getting pretty close to retirement. I did the principal a favor when they had some burst pipes over the winter break a couple of years ago, so the school owes me. I'm thinking of one teacher in particular—and as it happens, he teaches history. He's a good guy, and I think he'd talk to us. I'll give him a call later."

"Sounds perfect. Do we need to tell Karen, or Rick, or Sam, or Jeffrey what we seem to be doing?"

"I wouldn't worry about it. If we don't learn anything, it's moot."

"Okay. What's the next thing to happen with the Historical Society building?"

"We'll check the concrete footings and make sure everything came out right, then we'll settle the building back down, with new sills all around. Then we can start the build-out. You know the clock is ticking, because Gail and the board want it done by winter, so they can move all their collections back in."

"So Gail told me, but is that really doable?"

"It's tight, but I think we can manage, if everything works the way it should."

"Then I'll try to call Gail this morning, after her kids are off to school, and see if I can wangle some time with Karen. It seems only fair to try to talk with her." Meg sat up and swung her legs over the edge of the bed. "Time to face the day."

"I seem to remember we invited Sam and Jeffrey over for breakfast," Seth said. "Does that ring a bell?"

"Shoot, you're right. And there's really no food over at your house. I guess I'd better go down and get things started."

Fifteen minutes later, Bree, Seth, and Meg were gathered in the kitchen. Coffee had been brewed, and Meg had thawed some frozen muffins, when Sam and Jeffrey appeared at the back door. "Is this okay?" Sam said. "I hope we're not too early. Your pantry is kind of bare, Seth, and Jeffrey here has to get to school."

"Yes, of course—we invited you. Come on in," Meg said warmly. "There's coffee and muffins. I could make eggs if anybody wants any."

"Don't go to any trouble," Jeffrey said. "I don't want to be late."

"Then sit down and help yourselves," Meg said. She

thought both Sam and Jeffrey looked more relaxed than
they had the night before. They seemed to be good for each
other. Meg filled her own coffee mug. "Jeffrey, did you tell
your dad about the skeleton you found?"

"What?" Sam said. "A skeleton? Where?"

"Under an old building on the green. It was really cool,
Dad." Jeffrey went on to give Sam the whole story behind
the excavation and how he had become involved, with Seth
throwing in the occasional comment about the construction
aspects. Meg had never seen Jeffrey so animated, and Sam
listened eagerly.

When he stopped to take a break, Meg said to Sam,
"That's how Seth and I first met your son. By the way, Jef-
frey, did you hear about Miranda's preliminary findings?
She stopped by here on Saturday with Gail."

Jeffrey shook his head. "I've been kind of, uh, distracted. What did she say?"

"For a start, it turns out that the man was African—she
had to reassemble the skull to figure that out. She says he
died in his sixties, from a rather nasty-sounding form of TB."

"Wow!" Jeffrey said. "African? That is really interesting."

"The 1790 census shows that the Moodys, who gave
that land, still had slaves then. And he was given a decent
burial, too."

"Is she going to be doing more with the bones?"

"She said she would when she had the time. She was
going to enlist some of her students to help, I think, at least
with the technical analyses. But we were thinking that you
could work on the local history angle—who the Moodys
were, the history of slaveholding in early New England,
that kind of thing. If you're interested."

"Absolutely! I should talk to Gail again, right?"

"I'm sure she could tell you where to look for more information."

"Then I will. Dad, I'd better move fast if I'm going to get to school on time."

"Right. Give me a call when you know your plans for the rest of the day."

"Gotcha. Bye, Meg, Seth, Bree. And thanks." Jeffrey slammed out the back door like any normal teenager, headed for his car.

"I shouldn't keep you any longer," Sam said to the others. "I'm sure you have your own plans."

Bree snorted. "I'm headed up the hill. See you there, Meg. Bye, Sam." She got up, took her mug and plate to the sink, grabbed her jacket, and went out the door.

"What exactly does she do?" Sam asked.

"Bree? She's the orchard manager. I just inherited the orchard, and I didn't have any idea what to do with it. She'd already worked here, while she was in college, so I hired her. I couldn't do this without her. And she lives here as well—I can't afford to pay her what she's worth, so I throw in free living space."

"Okay, now I get it. So she was hinting that you'd better get to work fast, right?"

"Exactly." Meg glanced at Seth. "Do you know any of Jeffrey's teachers, Sam? Or his Scoutmaster?"

Sam shook his head. "Not really. Last year I might have known his teachers, but not this year. And we've had very little interaction with his principal, other than at public events. Jeffrey decided to join Scouts on his own, but I'm guessing that once he did, Karen started pushing him to stand out after I left. Not that it's a bad idea—I'm just saying I don't know anyone on that front. Why do you ask?"

"We're trying to get a handle on Jeffrey. We only met him a week ago, so we don't know much about him."

Sam finished the unstated thought. "And you want to know if he's capable of violence?"

"Please don't be offended—we're trying to help."

"I know. And of course you can't just ask Karen or me, because we're biased, to say the least. I understand."

"Has he ever done anything violent?"

"No, he's practically too restrained," Sam said slowly. "It's actually always kind of worried me. Not that I want him to lash out at anyone or anything, but he's always been so . . . controlled, I guess, ever since he was a kid. I wish he'd cut loose, just a little, you know? That's one thing Karen and I almost agreed on. He's trying too hard to be perfect, and it kind of makes me want to mess up his hair or something. Maybe Karen and I were responsible for it— maybe he thought that if he did everything right, we'd stay together. Isn't that a sad thing? Like any of our problems were his fault."

"I'm sorry," Meg said, laying her hand over Sam's. "But he is a good kid. Let's hope the police get to the bottom of this soon, so we can all move on."

"Thanks, you two. I appreciate everything you're doing for him." Sam stood up. "Well, I should let you all get to work. Seth, I'll go pick up some supplies for the house, so we won't be bothering you for meals. And thanks again for letting us use the place. I'll give you a call if anything changes."

When Meg and Seth were alone in the kitchen, Meg said, "It's all so sad. Sam and Karen must have been happy once, don't you think? And they have a great son. Seth, how do we know we won't go off the rails the way they did?"

"There are no guarantees, Meg. Nancy and I split up for

some of the same reasons, mostly about what we wanted from our lives. At least we didn't harm anyone else along the way."

Back in the orchard Meg worked for a couple of hours alongside Delroy, one of the pickers who had always seemed shy around her. They fell into an easy rhythm, and after a while Delroy started a conversation about the weather, to which Meg responded with enthusiasm. Meg managed to steer the talk toward other orchards Delroy had worked at, and the time passed quickly. Maybe her barbecue had actually paid off. She was a little surprised when she found herself next to Raynard, and it looked as though he had taken that spot deliberately. She waited for him to say something, and it didn't take long.

"That boy Novaro—he wasn't always a bad one," Raynard began slowly, keeping his eyes on the tree in front of him. "But young men these days, they don't know how to work. They expect things to be easy, you know? And they want money in their pockets and a pretty girl on their arm. He didn't understand. His uncle tried to set him straight, but he was busy working himself. And Novaro was young, but he wasn't a child. It was time he started working."

"That seems fair," Meg agreed. "Do you or any of your friends have an idea what happened? Why someone would have attacked him?"

"You don't believe that boy Jeffrey did it?"

Meg stopped picking apples and turned to face Raynard. "No, I don't. And I can't for the life of me see why Novaro would have been behind the feed store after it closed. Do you have any idea?"

Raynard had stopped working as well and was regarding her with his usual reserve. "Those are the questions we have been asking among ourselves. But only Hector knew Novaro well at all."

"Do you think Hector would talk to me?"

Raynard cocked his head at her, as if considering her request. "Why would you wish to do that?"

"Because I don't understand, and I want to. I'm not trying to pin blame on anyone here. I just want to know why Novaro was there." *And why he's dead*, Meg added to herself. "Do you know where I can find him? And if he can take time off from work?"

"I will talk to him. Perhaps I can bring him by later."

"I would really appreciate that, Raynard. And if you hear anything about what happened, even if it doesn't seem important, will you tell me? Please? I can take it to the police if you aren't comfortable doing it."

"I will keep my ears open." He paused to survey the next row of trees. "I think the Baldwins will be ready soon."

Apparently the conversation about Novaro was closed, Meg realized. "How do you think this year's crop compares to last year's?" she asked, and their talk turned to practical orchard matters.

An hour or so later, Meg pulled out her cell phone and called Gail. "Where are you?"

Gail laughed. "Where do you think? Standing on the green, staring at the Historical Society building. It's so exciting to see a plan actually come to life. And I love seeing all the gritty details of building construction, now that the underside is revealed. Seth came by and said everything looked good. Did you need me for something?"

"I wanted to ask a favor. Has Karen Green come by to check out the progress?"

"She's been, uh, kind of busy over the last few days, as you can imagine."

"I can. But I want a chance to talk with her, and I figured if I called her directly she'd blow me off. You know her from a different angle."

"You want to talk with her about Jeffrey and that Jamaican boy?" Gail asked. "What good will that do?"

"Don't tell me you believe Jeffrey did it!"

"No, of course I don't," Gail replied promptly. "But I don't have the time or the skills to get involved. Do you?"

A fair question. "Not the time, no, but you know I've got some experience with how local investigations work. And if the local grapevine hasn't reported in yet, Jeffrey's father arrived in town last night, and he asked us to help."

"Sam's here?" Gail sounded delighted. "He was always the better half of that couple. I'm so glad, for Jeffrey's sake—he needs someone in his family to watch his back, and Karen's too self-involved to fill the slot."

"So can you get us together?"

Gail was silent for a few moments. "Let me give her a call. I'll tell her that in her capacity as a board member of the Historical Society, she has a responsibility to keep tabs on the construction project. I'll tell her it won't take long, but she should see the process in each stage. You think that will work?"

"It would with me, but I'm not Karen. Go ahead and try, and let me know what she says."

Meg hung up and went back to picking apples.

Fifteen minutes later her phone rang. "Gail?"

"I talked to Karen, and she promised to stop by here between her other terribly important appointments. Why don't you grab us some sandwiches and come over so we can wait for her together?"

"Sounds good. I'll be there in half an hour. If Karen shows up before I get there, sit on her."

"I wish!" Gail said. "See you soon."

Meg sought out Bree. "I'm going into town, to try to talk with Jeffrey's mother. Oh, and in case you haven't already figured it out, Jeffrey and his dad are staying in Seth's house for the moment."

"Yeah, I kind of put two and two together about that. Are they in hiding or something?"

"Not exactly. Sam needed a place to stay, so Seth offered him the use of the house, and Jeffrey said he'd rather stay with his dad than with his mother in a hotel. He claims she's hiding from reporters."

"I'm glad you told me—if I saw people lurking around Seth's house I might have worried. What did you think of the dad?"

"Nice, I think. He showed up after driving all day and he was exhausted, but Jeffrey was really glad to see him. Nicer than Jeffrey's mother, Karen, anyway."

"So why do you think you need to talk to her?"

"I want to learn more about Jeffrey, maybe figure out who he knew or hung out with. Karen's view of her son may be skewed, but even that would tell me something. I'll be back after lunch."

"All right. We'll still be here."

Meg headed out and picked up sandwiches and drinks on her way to the green in town. She spotted Gail standing near the building, which was still on its scaffolding. Meg parked on the lane next to it.

"At least the building survived the jacking up," Meg said as she approached.

"Of course it did! This was built to last. Let's eat—all this staring at construction makes me hungry."

They strolled toward the nearest bench, under one of the large maples that ringed the green. "No sign of Karen yet?"

"Nope," Gail said, pulling food out of the bag Meg had brought. "You know, I keep trying to feel sorry for her—I wouldn't wish this kind of mess on anyone—but I've never seen her show much warmth toward anyone. I can't say I've seen her with Jeffrey much, but based on what I've seen of her with other people, it's him I feel sorry for right now. I can't imagine treating my kids that way."

"I hope Sam can balance that out—he seems a lot warmer. I wonder how long he'll be able to stay. Do you know what he does professionally?"

"Not offhand. Something with numbers, I think. He made enough to pay for that big house, anyway. Karen has never worked, at least not for a salary."

"Hasn't she done a lot of volunteer stuff?"

"Sure," Gail said, between bites of her sandwich. "But not the messy stuff, you know? She never pitched in at the child care center or the PTA, only the more high-end things. Like us." Gail grinned. "It's a small town, remember? There's the library, and us, and some town committees, but that's about it."

Maybe someday I'll have time to participate in some of those things, Meg thought. At least she'd tried to help out with the cataloging for the Historical Society, but part of that was for herself, to learn as much as she could about her house and her family history. Still, it was a start, and she'd promised herself she would do better as soon as the harvest was in.

They'd finished eating and collected their trash by the time a shiny black Lexus pulled into the lane and parked behind Meg's car. Karen Green emerged, wearing dark glasses and a fancy scarf that looked like silk. In fact, to Meg's eye she looked like she was dressed up as Jackie Kennedy, although in a town the size of Granford her disguise—if that's what it was—wouldn't fool anyone. Gail stood up and walked over to greet her, while Meg followed more slowly.

"Hey, Karen, thanks for coming! I know you must have a lot on your mind, but I thought you should see the progress we've made. It's moving really fast. We've already taken pictures. Come on and take a look."

Karen glanced briefly at Meg, hovering nearby, but didn't greet her. "Let's get this over with. Is the project on schedule?"

"Sure is. Seth Chapin pulled together a good crew . . ." Gail's voice faded out as she led Karen over toward the building. Karen moved stiffly, as if reluctant to be there— or afraid of dirtying her delicate shoes—but Gail more than made up for it, gesturing broadly as she pointed out details. Even if she hadn't known already, Meg could see clearly how much Gail cared about this whole project, while Karen was just going through the motions. Had Karen always been like this? Or was it the events of the past week that had sapped her attention and enthusiasm?

Finally Gail wound down, and turned and pointed toward Meg. From what Meg could see of Karen's expression as she looked her way, she did not look happy. Meg decided to approach quickly before the other woman could bolt.

"Hello, Karen," Meg said. "Can we talk?"

"Why should I talk to you? I gather your . . . fiancé is harboring my ex-husband, and he's made off with my son."

"Seth offered Sam a place to stay, and Jeffrey chose to stay with him, that's all."

"What do you think you and I have to say to each other?"

"Sit down and I'll tell you."

After wavering for a long moment, Karen sat on the bench.

"Uh, I have to go get something at the store," Gail broke in. "I'll be back in a bit."

Meg recognized that as a lame excuse, but Karen didn't seem to notice.

"So, talk," Karen said.

18

Since Meg hadn't had much time to formulate a plan, she wasn't sure how to start. She didn't know Karen, and nothing that she'd seen of her offered an easy lead-in to what promised to be a difficult discussion. She decided she might as well get to the point.

"Karen, I only met your son Jeffrey for the first time last week. But what matters now is that I have some personal experience with police investigations, and how the local police work. I don't think your son has done anything wrong, but so far he's the only suspect they have."

"Surely the state police will find a more appropriate suspect," Karen said stiffly.

"Well, of course we hope so. But Seth and I want to help him get out from under this, and in order to do that, we need to know more about Jeffrey. Can you help us with that?"

Karen didn't respond immediately. She was still wearing her oversized sunglasses, so Meg couldn't see her eyes, but up close she could see a few lines and creases, a softening of the jawline. Karen sat stiffly, as if she was afraid she would break, and she was painfully thin; it had taken more than a week of worry to reach that condition.

Finally Karen shook her head. "There's no one else to talk to," she said softly, to no one in particular. Then she turned sharply toward Meg. "Do you want to know how many of my so-called friends have called me this past week? None. None at all. I grew up in this town, and I've lived here all my life. My son goes to school here. And nobody cares enough to check in and see how I'm doing. Do you have any idea how that feels? Do you?"

Meg wasn't sure how to respond to that. Clearly Karen was in pain, but she apparently had no idea that she was the one who had brought that on herself. And, worse, once again she was making it about her, not Jeffrey. The woman apparently didn't have a maternal bone in her body—and most of her bones were visible.

"Actually, Karen, I do. When I first moved here, I was accused of murder. I didn't know a soul in town. The man who died was someone I knew and he was found on my property, so it was no surprise that everyone suspected me. I didn't have anyone to turn to, and nobody offered to help me. But I didn't do it, and I proved it. Don't you want to clear Jeffrey's name? If this attack is never solved, it will hang over him for years."

"Of course I want to clear him," she snapped. "This can't be allowed to drag on. But what are you suggesting? My brother Rick has already talked to the police, and he's monitoring the situation closely."

Of course he was, even if Meg still wasn't sure she trusted his motives. "Karen, I'm sure that's helpful, and I'm not criticizing the police, but what I think Seth and I can bring to this is the human factor, if you will. Look, I helped the police to identify the dead boy, Novaro Miller, who is related to one of my former employees. So that's one plus."

Karen didn't say anything, and being unable to see her eyes behind the glasses was unnerving to Meg, but she decided to push on anyway. "As you probably know from your brother, I've only lived in Granford for the past two years, but I'm going to marry Seth Chapin, who has a very long history with the town. Seth and I know people around here, and we can talk to them—and, more important, they'll talk to us. As neighbors and as friends. I think that the more we know about Jeffrey, the better we'll be able to help him—to ask the right questions, to look in the right direction. And obviously you know him better than anyone else. Tell me about him."

Karen still didn't speak, and Meg held her breath. Finally Karen's shoulders slumped. "Jeffrey was always such a good child," she said softly. "I had an easy delivery, and he met or surpassed all of the tests. Apgar, is it?" She didn't seem to expect an answer. "He never had colic. He slept through the night quite early. He did everything right, according to all the baby books. And he was sweet and thoughtful, which is rare in a small child. He could always tell when I was upset. He'd even bring me his favorite bunny to comfort me." Karen smiled, but there was a tear or two emerging from under those dark glasses, and she wiped them away impatiently. "He always did well in school, and he never got into trouble."

"What about extracurricular activities?" Meg asked.

"He tried a lot of things. Sports—but he wasn't big enough for football, and he wasn't quick enough for basketball. He took music lessons, on several instruments, and he practiced diligently, but he didn't really have a musical ear. He likes to read. I was happy when he joined the Boy Scouts, because I thought he'd meet boys there who were more like him."

From what she knew of Boy Scouts, Meg thought Jeffrey fit the image well. She seemed to remember terms like "honor," "duty," "obedience," and "helpfulness" in the motto. "Is he happy with Scouting?"

Karen shrugged. "He hasn't made a lot of friends, if that's what you're asking. He's more interested in the badges, and the challenge of collecting them and moving up. He's very goal-oriented. Competitive."

Meg wondered whether it was Jeffrey who was competitive, or if Karen had been the one pushing him to stand out—but now was not the time to find out. Since Karen had opened the door, Meg felt compelled to ask, "Did he have friends at school?"

"No one he talked about. No one he brought home. Sometimes I worried about that . . ." Karen trailed off. "But he was so *good*. Always polite, thoughtful, considerate. He even kept his room clean, for God's sake!" Now her voice was shrill. "What was I supposed to do about a boy who's too good?"

"How did he take your split with your husband?" Meg asked.

"He was quiet. He was even more polite. He treated me like I was made of china. Do you know, I really did wish he'd yell at me, or show some sort of emotion? He almost scared me, he was so calm. Of course, he's intelligent, so it probably wasn't a surprise to him when Sam and I split up—he would have seen it coming."

Karen's description troubled Meg. Was Jeffrey really so devoid of emotion? What was the term—"affectless"? Jeffrey appeared to have few or no friends, and he'd navigated through his parents' divorce without any obvious reaction. Maybe there was both more and less to Jeffrey Green than she had thought.

"Did Jeffrey ever get any counseling?" Meg asked. *Did you, Karen?*

"You mean a psychologist? A therapist?"

"Yes."

"I never thought he needed one," Karen snapped. "I'm supposed to tell a therapist that I think my son needs help because he's too *good*?"

Meg resisted the urge to shake the cold woman in front of her. Karen had no idea what was going on in her son's mind, and apparently no interest in finding out. And she wasn't about to send him to someone who might be able to help him. Why not? Was she afraid of what she and Jeffrey might find out? Concerned that it would reflect badly on her parenting skills and upset her perfectly structured little world?

Time to switch to a more neutral topic, before Meg said something unforgivable and shut down any hope of getting some insights from Karen. "Is Jeffrey close to any of his other relatives?"

Karen shook her head several times. "Maybe he used to be, with his father. Sam is so much more . . . open than I am. He and Jeffrey had fun together. He made Jeffrey laugh. They even got dirty together. So when we separated, I knew that Jeffrey would lose all that."

"What about with your brother?"

"You've met Rick—he's been too busy building his career, and now running for office, to spend much time with Jeffrey, and his children are much younger. I'd say they have a cordial relationship, but not a particularly warm one. I had hoped that Rick might bring Jeffrey into his campaign, but Jeffrey declined—he said what Rick needed was a staff that was good with people, and Jeffrey couldn't see himself in that role. He was right, of course, but I thought it would have been good for him. And Sam's an only child, so there aren't many relatives on that side."

"Is Jeffrey dating anyone?" Meg asked.

"Jeffrey's too young to get involved with anyone," Karen said stiffly. "He'll be going to college next year, where he's more likely to meet someone appropriate."

Was it true that Jeffrey had never found himself a girlfriend, or was that just Karen's wishful thinking? Meg had no way of knowing. And if Jeffrey was really so disengaged from the world around him, or at least the people in it, then maybe he really did need psychological help, and it was pretty clear that Karen wasn't about to provide it. Maybe she or Seth needed to talk to Sam about all this.

Then she stopped herself. *Meg, this is not your problem! Right now you want to know who killed Novaro, period.*

Karen stood up abruptly, startling Meg. "I have another meeting to go to. Was there anything else you wanted?"

Meg stood up as well. "I think that's enough for now. Thank you, Karen. You've been very helpful." *More than you know, and probably more than you intended, although it doesn't get us any closer to solving the murder.* "Will you be seeing Jeffrey today?"

"I . . . don't know." Karen seemed at a loss. "I'll call him when he gets out of school. I'm glad you found our

conversation helpful. And . . . thank you for being a friend
to Jeffrey." She turned and marched off to her car without
a backward look, her back straight.

Karen had barely pulled away when Gail emerged from
the store across the green and trotted over to the bench
where Meg was sitting. "I've been watching," Gail said.
"Karen actually stayed quite a while—I don't think I've
ever had that long a conversation with the woman. What
did she say, or can't you talk about it?"

"Well, I don't think I have any right to claim confidenti-
ality, but I'm not sure where this lapses into gossip. You can
be discreet about it, can't you?"

"Of course," Gail said.

"The whole thing makes me sad, and it worries me. I
don't know that I've ever met a colder person. She seems
totally lacking in empathy. And she accuses Jeffrey of
being "too good"—though she may be on to something
there. If Jeffrey had been a more challenging child, if he'd
pushed her boundaries a bit, Karen might have been a different person. Too late for that."

"But what did she say about the assault on that kid?"

Meg sighed. "We didn't really get into that. I was taking
it slow, trying to get a sense of Jeffrey as a person, and what
Karen was saying really bothers me. I mean, the kid has
virtually no friends and doesn't seem to be dating anyone.
He's either completely shut down emotionally, or he doesn't
feel anything anyway. And his mother sees nothing wrong
with that. He's a kid who gives her no trouble, and if he
seems a little isolated, well, she thinks that will work itself
out in college. Although her description of her son makes
him sound a lot like her, so it's not surprising that she
doesn't see much wrong with that. The saving factor is that

she says he had a much more open relationship with his father—they had fun together when he was around. I'm going to have to see them together for more than five minutes to get any sense of where they are now."

"How does all this fit with whatever happened behind the feed store?" Gail pressed again.

"I really don't know. Jeffrey seems like a really nice kid. But that's based on my long and close relationship of one week with the boy." Meg looked Gail in the eye. "Maybe he's a psychopath and I can't see it. But I think it's more likely that he's a sad and lonely kid who's very tightly wound, and he's juggling a lot of stress. There's something else going on here."

"Is he dating with anyone?"

"I asked the same question, and Karen brushed it off—said he didn't need that in his life now."

"Wow!" Gail responded. "Has she visited the high school lately? You can cut the hormones in the air with a knife."

"I'll believe it. But if Jeff was involved with anyone, I doubt he'd tell his mother."

"I agree!" Gail replied, grinning.

Meg looked at her watch. "Shoot, Bree is going to have my hide if I don't get back and get some work done. Thanks for setting this up, Gail. I think I learned a lot from Karen, even if I don't like much of it. At least I don't think I've made anything worse, and Karen knows there are other people who are trying to help."

"There is that. Good luck."

19

As Meg drove back to her orchard, she decided to invite Sam and Jeffrey over to dinner, but her plans to call them were scotched when as soon as she parked in her driveway she found Raynard Lawrence, accompanied by another Jamaican man she found vaguely familiar-looking, who had to be Hector Dixon. So Raynard had succeeded in finding him so they could talk, and maybe she'd find out something useful about Novaro.

"Meg, I told Hector that you wished to speak to him, to learn more about his nephew, and as it happened he had finished for the day," Raynard said as Meg got out of her car. "I hope this is a convenient time for you."

"Of course!" Meg said quickly. "Do you want to come in?"

"I am more comfortable outside," Hector said, "if you don't mind. May we walk?"

"You two talk, then. Hector," Raynard said, "I will wait here to give you a ride home, but there's no need to hurry."

Meg mouthed a thank-you to Raynard, and she and Hector set off across the meadow, rather than toward the orchard. After they had walked perhaps fifty feet in silence, Meg asked, "Novaro was your sister's son?"

"He was. She has several younger ones at home. She lost her husband some years ago, and the rest of our family tries to help her out. That is why I found the position for Novaro. I hope you did not think that I left your employ because of how I was treated here. It was that I knew you could not take on an extra worker, and this other man could."

"You don't need to apologize to me, Hector—I understand the problem. So you and Novaro came over together?"

"We did. At first he stayed with me and some others, older men like me, but he wasn't interested in our activities. Nor was he very happy with the work, even though he had grown up listening to the family talk about it and knew what to expect." Hector's pace slowed, but he did not look at Meg but at the distant row of trees instead. "There are some things I have not told the police, Meg."

Meg all but held her breath, waiting. *Let him tell his story at his own pace.*

"You see, I was the one who filled out the visa application forms for Novaro, and there were certain facts that I feared would disqualify him, so I did not include them. He had had some small problems with the law back home—he had fallen in with a bad crowd, and as he had nothing better to do with his time there, he got into trouble. I had hoped—as did my sister—that getting him away from certain friends would set him back on the right path, but it did not turn out that way."

Hector fudging Novaro's visa application might explain his earlier reluctance to go to the police. "What happened next?"

"Novaro quit the job, then came to me and said he would no longer be staying where we stayed. I told the boy that without a job he could not remain in the country, but he did not seem concerned."

"Did he ask you for money?"

"I had nothing to give him. We had just begun the season, so we had little. And what I earn, I send back to Jamaica."

"Do you know how he was supporting himself, in that case?"

Hector stopped then and turned to Meg. "I do not. I lost sight of him after he quit, and as I told the police, I did not even know where to look for him. Meg, please do not think badly of the rest of us because of the thoughtless acts of one young man. It may be that he found another bad crowd here, but he did not tell me. His mother had not heard anything of this, until I called to tell her that he was dead. I suppose that cross she gave him was of little use to him—I was surprised he even kept it."

"And you told the police that you didn't know who his current friends were?"

"That was the truth, and that was what I told them. I kept silent only about the troubles he had before he came over—it seemed wrong to speak ill of the dead, and he was my blood."

"I'm so sorry this happened, Hector. I think you did your best for him. I'd be happy to have you back here, if you're looking for a place."

"You are kind to offer. Perhaps next year, but I am set for now, and my employer is also a fair man. But he grows vegetables, and I do prefer the apples." Hector smiled, although it took an effort. "I should let you return to your dinner preparations. And thank you for trying to find out what happened to Novaro. My sister will be grateful as well."

"I only want to help, Hector."

They found themselves back at Meg's back door, where Raynard was leaning against his dusty truck, his eyes on the orchard. He straightened up when Hector and Meg returned, and as Hector climbed into the passenger side, Raynard took Meg aside. "Is everything all right?"

Meg nodded. "I think so. I feel so sorry for Hector—he thought he was doing the right thing, and then this happens. I'll let you know if I hear anything new. Thanks for bringing him over." She watched the truck pull away before going back to the kitchen.

"What was that all about?" Bree asked when Meg walked in. "I saw you and Hector out in the meadow."

"I asked Raynard if he could get me together with Hector—I wanted to find out more about Novaro. Raynard brought him over."

"Did you learn much?"

"Not a lot. Mainly that he'd had some trouble back home, and that he seemed totally ungrateful once he got here—blew off the job and the lodging and went his own way. Hector doesn't seem to know where he went. Maybe the police will have better luck."

"Don't count on it. Anyway, what are the plans for dinner?"

"I'm going to call and invite Sam and Jeffrey over. Stay and eat with us? You're closer in age to Jeffrey than either Seth or me, and it might help Jeffrey feel more comfortable with us all."

"At least you didn't put us at the kiddie table," Bree said, grinning to offset her sarcasm. Meg quickly dialed Sam and settled the details, then came back to where Bree was laying out cutlery and plates on the hastily cleared dining room table.

"You know what I mean," Meg said, picking up the thread of conversation. "Sometimes I think I was never young. That's one reason I sympathize with Jeffrey. I was always the serious, studious, completely boring kid in my high school. Anything I belonged to, I was always vice president, never president, because I was responsible, but nobody ever saw me as leadership material." *If they saw me at all*, she added to herself. Sometimes she'd wondered if she was invisible. Yet she had had more friends than Jeffrey seemed to—hadn't she?

"Stop apologizing, Meg. I get it. I don't want to see this get pinned on him any more than you do. Unless, of course, he actually did kill the guy."

"I don't think the police have enough real evidence to pin this on anyone yet." Meg still couldn't point to anyone else, but she didn't see Jeffrey as guilty, although she had no right to claim to know him well, just because she thought she recognized something of her long-ago self in him. Still, he was innocent until proven guilty, right?

It had been nearly a week now since Novaro's death. If no one was ever charged, would the suspicion forever hang over Jeffrey? Somehow they all needed resolution—which meant finding who had killed Novaro.

Sam and Jeffrey came down the hill on foot from Seth's house shortly before seven. "Thanks a lot for inviting us for dinner, Meg," Sam said. "You know, there never were many restaurants in Granford. I was glad to see the new pizza place, but I'm not looking forward to eating there twice a day."

Seth came into the kitchen. "Sorry, I haven't kept the fridge stocked up at the house."

"Hey, don't apologize! We're grateful for the beds." Sam turned to Meg. "I was looking at your land as we walked over, Meg. How large is your orchard?"

Meg dished vegetables and rice into serving bowls, then handed them off to Bree to take to the dining table. "The place came with fifteen acres, right up the hill. I also lease another three from Seth, and this past year we planted those with a mix of steady producers and heirloom varieties. You must have walked past those."

"Those trees are tiny!" Jeffrey said. "How long before they produce apples?"

"It'll be a couple of years, but at the moment I'm just happy they've settled in well."

"Did you always want to be a farmer . . . Meg?" Jeffrey asked. Meg found his hesitation to use her first name endearing.

"Not at all! I used to be a financial analyst for a bank, until I lost my job. My mom owned this place but hadn't seen it in years, so she thought it would be a good idea to send me here to fix things up. I didn't even know there was an orchard until I arrived. How about you, Jeffrey? Do you know what you want to do?"

He shrugged. "I haven't really decided."

Meg hurried to reassure him. "That's fine—you're not supposed to have all the answers at your age. But if you want to know more about farming or orchards, you should ask Bree. She got her degree from UMass not too long ago, and she knows a whole lot more than I do." Meg handed

Seth a platter of chicken. "Dinner's ready. This is a treat for us—we don't get to use the dining room all that often. If you look carefully, you'll notice that most of the woodwork in the room is original to the house."

"That's cool," Jeffrey said. "When was it built?"

"I think around 1760, although I'm still looking for documents to prove that, but the town didn't officially exist then—it was still part of South Hadley. Gail at the Historical Society has been a big help finding things for me. She's going to be thrilled to have all her records in one place."

Jeffrey turned to Bree. "I don't mean to be rude, but you're not from around here, are you?"

Bree bobbed her head. "I was born in Massachusetts, but my parents were both from Jamaica. I spent most of my life here in the state, living with my aunt."

Dinner was a surprisingly comfortable and normal event. There was plenty of food, and both Jeffrey and Sam relaxed. They even managed to joke with each other, which Meg found an encouraging sign. Once again she reminded herself that she shouldn't take Karen's rather grim view of her son as the only one; from what Meg was seeing now, Jeffrey did have a lighter side, and even a sense of humor. It was clear how much he cared for his dad. She felt a surge of pity for Karen, for what she was missing.

When they'd finished eating, Bree said, "I'll clean up. Is there dessert?"

"I cheated and bought cupcakes on the way home," Seth said. "You can turn up your noses if you want."

"I never turn down dessert," Jeffrey said happily.

"You must get that from me," Sam added. He sat back in his chair and stretched. "I can't tell you how great this was,

Meg. Not only that you fed us, but that you welcomed us into your home."

The cupcakes disappeared quickly. Bree loaded the dishwasher and disappeared discreetly up the back stairs after saying good night.

Sam waited until she was gone, then said, "And now, I think, we've really got to talk."

Jeff's expression shut down again. "You mean me, too?"

"Yes, you, too," Sam said. "You're the one stuck in the middle of this. We need to hear your side of things."

Meg hesitated a moment, reluctant to disturb the ease they'd achieved over dinner, but it was important. "Jeffrey, I know you've said this all before, more than once, but can we go over this one more time?" Seth signaled his agreement.

"What, finding Novaro? Sure, I guess."

"Let me start with what we know." Seth ticked off the main points on his fingers. "You were at the feed store to pick up your mother's order, right?"

Jeffrey nodded.

"You drove around back," Seth continued, "where Jake Stebbins said he'd leave the order for you. Was it dark?"

"Maybe halfway—it was around seven, I think. There aren't any lights back there, but I could still see pretty well."

"And you found Novaro Miller lying outside the building?"

"That's right."

"You didn't see anyone else there? Anyone running away?"

"Nope. And it looked like he'd been lying there for a while, because there was a lot of blood."

"You checked to see if he was alive?"

"Yeah. I thought maybe he had a pulse, so I checked but

wasn't sure, then I called 911 and just waited there. Oh, and I put my jacket over him—I thought he might be in shock or something and I figured he should be kept warm."

"You'd never seen Novaro before?"

"I never met the guy," Jeffrey replied.

"Did you see his car?" Meg asked.

"Uh, maybe?" Jeffrey looked at Meg. "I think there was one parked in front when I pulled in, but I wasn't paying attention to it."

"There was no one in the store?"

"Not that I noticed," Jeffrey said. "The lights inside were turned off."

"Was the back door open or unlocked?"

"I didn't check. I pulled in, looking for some big bags of fertilizer. And then I saw the kid, all bloody. I didn't need to go inside—I had my cell, so I used that to call the police. And I figured the less I messed with stuff, the better it would be. I touched him just to see if he was still alive. I might have gotten blood on my hands then, and wiped them on my clothes. I was upset."

Sam leaned forward. "Jeffrey, you did everything right. You were careful, and you called the authorities." He turned back to Meg and Seth. "Look, he's told you all he knows. He did not know this Novaro person, and he certainly didn't attack him. My son does not lie."

"We believe you, Sam," Seth said. "And we believe Jeffrey. We're just looking for another angle to follow. *Somebody* attacked Novaro, and at the moment we have no evidence pointing at anybody else."

Meg turned to Seth. "Did you hear anything new today?"

He didn't answer immediately, which led Meg to suspect he was trying to edit his reply. "I've lined up a couple more people to talk to," he said cautiously. Meg made a mental note to check with Seth about whether he had managed to set up a meeting with a teacher, or even the principal.

"Nothing new from the cops?" Sam demanded.

"Not that I'm aware of," Seth said. "What was it like at school today, Jeffrey?"

"Weird. Some people went out of their way to stay about six feet away from me in the halls. Other people who had never talked to me before were suddenly all over me, asking questions. A couple of guys tried to make fun of me—you know, calling me 'Killer Boy Scout.' Sounds like a bad movie, doesn't it?"

"Do you often have trouble like that at school?" Sam asked.

Jeffrey looked at his father. "You mean bullying? It happens, everywhere, I guess. I ignore it as much as I can. I'm lucky that I'm big enough to stand up to them. Some of the younger, smaller kids are easy targets."

Jeffrey didn't seem too disturbed about whatever bullying he had faced. Meg wondered how accurate his description was. While he wasn't a fighter, he was a six-footer, not some poor freshman still waiting for his growth spurt.

"How did you get involved in the Scouting thing?" Seth asked.

Jeffrey glanced at his dad again before answering. "Well, after Mom had trotted me through a lot of other activities, none of which stuck, I thought I'd try the Scouts, although I joined kind of late—a lot of the local kids started out together years ago in Cub Scouts, but at the Boy Scout level they combine kids from a couple of the local towns, so I wasn't the only newcomer. Of course, once I was in, Mom decided I should try to win some award for most merit

badges in a short time, or something stupid like that. But to
be honest, she wasn't so far off in this case. I like projects—
something interesting that I can finish. I like competing, and
trying to move up. And I learn a lot of stuff—like for this
history project. But nobody is pressuring me about it, and I
get to set my own goals, so that's good."

To Meg it looked like Jeffrey knew himself better than
his mother knew him. "Were you a Scout, Sam?" she asked.

"Yeah, years ago, but I never went as far as Jeffrey here.
He was telling me last night about that archaeology badge,
and how he noticed that skull during the excavation project.
If Jeffrey hadn't spotted them, that guy's bones might have
ended up in a landfill somewhere."

"Dad!" Jeffrey protested. "It wasn't that big a deal."

"You were paying attention, and that's important." Sam
turned to look at Meg and Seth. "Was there anything else
you wanted to talk about? Anything we're supposed to do?"

"Not unless the police have any more questions," Meg
said.

"Look, we're all tired, and Jeffrey probably has homework. We can regroup tomorrow," Sam said, and stood up.
"Thanks again for the hospitality. I hope we won't be in
your hair much longer. Jeffrey, you ready? You should call
your mother tonight, and we've still got to walk back."

"Yeah, let's go. Thank you, Meg, Seth."

Sam and Jeffrey went out the back door and into the
dark. When she had shut the door, Meg turned to Seth.
"What did you think?"

"I think Sam is a great guy, but he may be as blind to his
son's qualities as Karen is, although in a different way."

"Is that all?" Meg asked.

Seth cocked his head at her. "Why do you ask? Do you have a bee in your bonnet?"

"Nothing I can put my finger on," Meg said. "Oops, not a good metaphor, putting my finger on a bee. Or maybe it is, if by doing that I get stung."

Seth looked exasperated. "Meg, it's been a long day. What are you talking about?"

"There are things about this attack on Novaro that I don't understand," Meg said slowly. "Before you came home, Raynard brought Novaro's uncle Hector over so we could talk. Poor man—he only wanted to help his nephew. Anyway, Hector hinted that Novaro had had some troubles before he left Jamaica. I suppose the police will look into that, although Hector said he hadn't told the police everything, because he might have lied on Novaro's visa application and he was afraid he'd get in trouble. But the bottom line is, nobody has come up with a good reason why Novaro was at the feed store that night."

Seth nodded. "That's a good point. There's nothing there to interest a guy his age. It's out of sight, but it's on the main highway—so maybe he was meeting someone and didn't want to be observed?"

"Someone like who?" Meg shot back. "Someone he couldn't meet openly in public?"

"I wish I had any suggestions, but I don't," Seth said.

Meg switched topics. "Did you get in touch with anyone at the school?"

"Yes, we're going to meet with his history teacher, Mr. Dillenberger, at five tomorrow. Mr. Dillenberger was teaching there when I was in school, and he's a smart guy—and observant. We couldn't get away with much in his class.

That's why I wanted to see him, especially since we know Jeffrey's interested in history."

"Okay, sounds good. What about the Scoutmaster?"

"Jeez, woman, you don't ask for much," Seth teased. "He said he'd see us after a meeting tomorrow evening, at eight. If we can stay awake that long. Which means we should get some sleep now, though first I've got to take Max out."

"I'll go on up, then. Seth, I don't mean to be pushy, but I want to see this thing solved. Jeffrey's got enough problems in his life without dealing with an assault accusation hanging over his head, even if he's never charged."

"Meg, you can't fix everything."

20

Another beautiful September day, one of those clear, bright ones New England was famous for. Was it Wednesday? It was hard for Meg to keep track these days. The good news: the weather was cooperating with the harvest. The bad news: there were still an awful lot of apples to be picked.

Seth had left early. Bree hadn't been happy when Meg told her she needed to quit a little early to meet Seth at the high school at five.

"You're seriously telling me that the police haven't already talked to everybody in town by now?" Bree said, banging plates on the table. Lolly jumped down from her perch and fled to a quieter place.

"I'm sure they have," Meg said, "but they don't know the people involved. Seth does, at least in a different way."

"So send him alone. Why do you need to be there?"

"I want to hear what people say," Meg replied. "In case you've never noticed, women hear things differently, and ask different questions. I'm still trying to get a handle on Jeffrey's character and personality."

"Okay," Bree said cautiously. "So what makes you think that a high school teacher will be able to tell you if one kid out of a couple of hundred is hiding a violent streak?"

"Seth knows this teacher—he had him in high school—and he trusts his judgment. He'll have seen a lot of kids go by in his time, and he may have some useful insights. So, pretty please, may I have an hour or two off at the end of the day?"

"I guess." Bree sat down heavily and munched on some toast.

Between bites of her own toast, Meg said, "I just keep coming back to the same question: why would Novaro be where he was found when he had no reason to be there, as far as anyone knows?"

Bree stopped to look at her. "Meg, the way I see it, there are two choices here. One, some random stranger beat up and killed Novaro Miller, and happened to dump him behind the feed store because it was an isolated spot. Two: Mr. Perfect Boy Scout Jeffrey Green gets into it with Novaro, for reasons unknown, and goes berserk. Heck, maybe Jeffrey had a psychotic break and doesn't even remember doing it."

Meg sighed. "Neither one makes a lot of sense."

"No, they don't, and there's no evidence for either one," Bree retorted. "But, of course, now that you know Jeffrey, you want to fix his life for him. What's the happy ending going to be?"

Meg smiled ruefully. "Jeffrey rides off to an Ivy League college a long way from home. And Karen gets some therapy.

And Sam finds a nice woman who appreciates him. And Seth and I can find time to plan a wedding."

"Good luck with that!" Bree snorted, standing up from the table. "Anybody extra going to show up at the dinner table tonight?"

"I doubt it. Seth and I are going to meet with Jeffrey's Scoutmaster in the evening, so we'll probably pick up something on the way."

"Great. Maybe Michael and I can get together," Bree said as they headed out the door.

As she picked apples all morning, Meg mulled over why she and Seth hadn't gotten around to doing much wedding planning yet. In some ways they seemed like an old married couple already—she could almost forget that Seth owned another house no more than a mile away and had lived there for years before she moved in next door. So why were they having such trouble setting a date and making plans? Because they were both busy people, she kept telling herself. But a niggling little voice kept saying, *Even busy people get married.* Instead of renting a hall and planning a menu, she was trying to solve a murder and remodel a teenager's life. *Prioritize, Meg!*

She worked steadily all day, then washed up before heading out around four thirty. She and Seth had agreed to meet at the high school parking lot on the other side of town, in time for their five-o'clock meeting. She pulled in just as the last of the students were leaving, and parked next to Seth's van, where he was waiting.

"Right on time," he called out. "Wouldn't want to make the teacher wait, now, would we?"

"I wouldn't know," she replied. "I was never called to

the teacher's office after hours. Or the principal's office. What's the teacher's name, again?"

"Howard Dillenberger. He's got to be past sixty now—when I took his class he seemed ancient, which must have meant over forty. He didn't suffer fools gladly, and he always knew when you hadn't read the assignment and nailed you."

"Sounds like fun. And you still came out liking history?"

"I did. He made it much more real than any textbook I ever read. And, of course, we're living in the midst of a lot of it here in Granford. Wonder if he's heard about the body under the Historical Society."

As they were speaking, Seth had led Meg to the front door. The building was modern, and as a nod to security Seth had to push a buzzer and identify himself before anyone would let them in. Meg stifled a sigh: life had seemed so much more innocent when she was in high school. And yet, she reminded herself, they were here to investigate a crime where a student was a potential suspect in the fatal attack on another teenager. Maybe times had changed, or maybe she'd just been naïve when she was in high school.

Seth led Meg to the main office, where he chatted with the staff and introduced her around—and where they had to sign the visitors' book—then he confidently guided her through the maze of hallways to a classroom on the far side of the building. There, behind a standard desk, sat a man who reminded Meg of what she thought a modern-day Nero Wolfe would look like: he was large and rumpled, with scrambled hair and an anachronistic mustache. Also like Nero Wolfe, his eyes were sharp and intelligent. He stood up and smoothed down his tweed jacket.

"Seth Chapin. How long has it been?" He held out his hand to shake Seth's.

"I've missed a reunion or two. Must be ten years since I've seen you. This is my fiancée, Meg Corey."

"Nice to meet you, Mr. Dillenberger," Meg said. "I'm glad we could get together on such short notice."

"I'm glad you came to me. Sit, both of you—get one of those wooden chairs from around the edge of the room. I won't insist anyone over the age of eighteen sit in those molded monstrosities the school insists on using in classrooms."

Seth brought over two straight-backed wooden chairs and set them in front of the desk. They sat.

"I'm happy to help out Jeffrey, and it's a treat to meet the woman who appears to be keeping the Granford police busy," Mr. Dillenberger said.

"That wasn't my intent, really," Meg protested.

"Of course not, my dear. But you have gone out of your way to involve yourself with young Jeffrey, haven't you? You have no other connection to him?"

"No, we only met last week. I haven't lived long in Granford, so while my roots go way back, I still don't know most people in town. But his family has asked us for our help, and Jeffrey looked like he could use it."

"So, what do you want from me?" the teacher said.

"On the surface Jeffrey Green seems like a perfect kid," Seth began. "Smart, hardworking, nice to his mother, a Boy Scout, and so on. But he doesn't seem to have any friends. And now he's somehow become a suspect in a fatal attack on a stranger—a stranger to him and to Granford, I might add. How do we get from A to B? I thought, since you've spent some time with him, that you may have seen something under the surface that others missed."

Mr. Dillenberger sat back in his chair—which creaked—and folded his hands over his belly. "For the most part, I'd say what you see in Jeffrey is what you get. He always comes to class prepared. He understands the material and makes some interesting connections. He even reads outside the syllabus, and that's rare. I wish he'd laugh more, maybe make a joke now and then. But as his teacher I can't complain."

"He's an only child, and his parents are recently divorced—I gather it was hostile," Meg said. "Does that have something to do with it?"

"Maybe. Only children often are more comfortable with adults than with their peers. I'm not privy to his home situation, but I've met his mother on several occasions and found her . . . difficult. She's complained to the school administration more than once that we don't offer more AP classes. I could be charitable and say she wants only the best for her son, but she's pushing him as hard as possible toward a big-name college." He glanced quickly at the door to the corridor, but there were no people in the hall. "I sense she's more concerned with her boasting rights than with finding a good fit for Jeffrey."

"Has he told you what he wants to study?" Meg asked.

"Not in so many words. Were I to be asked for a letter of recommendation, and I probably will be at some point in the near future, I would say his interests lie in the humanities rather than the sciences. He has shown a real flair for history."

"Has he told you about the excavation on the green?" Meg asked.

"Not personally, but of course the rumors flew. It was a skull he found, wasn't it? Fascinating."

"It was, in pieces, and the rest of the body was recovered as well. Jeffrey volunteered to do some research to see if there was any way to identify the body. But that was before the . . . other situation."

"Is there anyone here that he's particularly close to?" Seth asked. "In class or out?"

"Among the boys in his class, I'd say there's a group of perhaps five or six who share similar interests and aptitudes, and I often see them together in the cafeteria or on their way home. But I see them as traveling in a pack, perhaps for protective reasons. There does not seem to be any one in particular whom I would say is an actual friend."

"Is there anyone who's shown antagonism toward Jeff?" Seth followed up.

"Ah, Seth, surely you know there are always those who try to knock the smarter boys off their pedestals." Mr. Dillenberger paused for a moment. "Before I say too much more, may I ask why you're so involved in this? After all, the state police are handling this investigation, are they not?"

"Yes, and I know they do a good job. But as Meg said, Jeffrey's family asked us to help, and sometimes someone who isn't connected to law enforcement can have better luck in simply talking with people. We're not doing anything that would compromise the investigation, if you're worried."

Mr. Dillenberger nodded. "Thank you, Seth. I do have to be careful. As I was going to say, the jocks aren't always kind to the nerds. I could give you the boys' names, if you like. We have our share of slackers, as we did in your day. *Plus ça change* and so on. But I can't think of any person or group that has singled Jeffrey out. He's a very self-possessed young man. If anyone has attempted to bully him, they've had little success."

"We've noticed," Seth said. "Anything else, Meg?"

"What about romantic relationships? Has he shown any romantic inclinations toward . . . anyone?" she asked. "Male or female?"

Mr. Dillenberger smiled. "Such a politically correct phraseology, Meg! We do have a cadre of gay and lesbian students—it's quite de rigueur these days. But I haven't seen young Jeffrey in their company. I'd venture to say he leans in the more traditional direction, albeit cautiously."

"Mr. Dillenberger, are you trying to say that you *have* noticed Jeffrey showing interest in a girl?" Meg said, surprised.

"That would be my educated guess, although I wouldn't go so far as to say they're dating, or whatever they call it these days," Mr. Dillenberger said, then added, "I must admit I despise the term 'hooking up'—it sounds so mechanical. I think in days past Jeffrey's current situation might have been characterized as an early stage of courtship, although I would venture to say that Jeffrey's aspirations are far higher than a brief fling."

"Does the girl in question appear to return his affections, or is he just worshipping from afar?" Seth asked.

"My, quite the turn of phrase, Seth. I'd say the former. She's a nice girl, kind of shy. She isn't in my class, but I've seen her regularly, and he often seems to be in her vicinity."

"Do you know her name?"

"Unfortunately, I don't. I believe she's a year or two younger. I'm sure I could find out, if you like."

"That might be helpful, as long as you don't rock the boat. If there is a girl he's interested in, I get the impression Jeffrey hasn't shared even a hint of that with either of his parents."

"Understandable," Mr. Dillenberger said. "I'm sure his

mother would declare the young woman unsuitable, sight unseen. In her eyes Jeffrey is destined for better things, and she wouldn't want him to be tied down to a hometown sweetheart. I don't believe I know Jeffrey's father."

"Sam Green," Seth said quickly. "He came back to town as soon as he heard about Jeffrey's problems—not from his ex-wife, I might add. He seems like a nice guy, which may explain why he and Karen aren't together any longer."

"Seth Chapin, I do believe you dislike Karen." Mr. Dillenberger said with mock horror.

"I'm afraid so. She's not helping Jeffrey at all."

"Which is why you and Meg have so kindly stepped in, I surmise. It's admirable of you, but I hope it doesn't complicate matters."

"What do you mean?" Meg asked.

"Jeffrey's loyalties may be somewhat conflicted at the moment, given his parents' situation, and he's facing all the hormonal torments of his age and gender. Add to that the stress of this being his senior year, and I would say he is in a rather vulnerable state. Perhaps it's a good thing that he has the two of you on his side—certainly he needs someone, and the fact that you are not related to him is a plus. All I'm saying is, tread carefully."

"That's what we're trying to do, Mr. Dillenberger," Meg said. "Can I ask you one more thing?" When the teacher nodded, she said, "I know the police verified Novaro Miller's identity, and we know that he was not a student here. But did you ever find kids of his age—eighteen—just hanging around the school? In the parking lot or whatever? Outsiders?"

"I can't say that I'm aware of anything like that, although perhaps I wouldn't be. However, my impression is that most students here try to get away from the school as quickly as possible—the parking lot usually empties out in under half an hour. In that case, any nonstudents would be rather obvious."

Seth stood up. "Thanks so much for speaking with us, Mr. Dillenberger, and so frankly. We won't share what you've told us, but I think it helps us to understand the kid a little better. If you can think of anyone else we should speak to, please let me know. And if you can identify that girl, it might help."

"I'll see what I can do. It has been a pleasure to see you again, Seth. You've turned out well, and of course I'll claim a share of the credit." Mr. Dillenberger grinned. "Meg, delightful to meet you."

They waited until they were back in the parking lot before speaking. "That was interesting," Meg said.

"Why do you say that?"

"Mostly the hint of a possible girl. If Jeffrey does have a girlfriend, he's been very secretive about it."

"Hey, that's what teenage guys do, keep secrets. At least the shy ones like Jeffrey. Believe me, I speak from experience."

"Aww, how sweet. Did you yearn after someone unattainable?"

"More than one. That's how we learn. But I didn't really connect with anyone until college. Besides, would *you* share anything sensitive with Karen?"

Meg shuddered at the thought. "No. Poor Jeffrey. He's having a hard time of things, isn't he?"

"For the moment. Let's hope we can fix at least one part of this before too long."

21

They picked up some sandwiches and drinks, and sat in the car to eat them, killing time until their eight-o'clock meeting with the Scoutmaster.

"What's his name, again?" Meg asked.

"Frank Baker. He's about my age, and I know him slightly from various town events. Married, a couple of kids, I think."

"If he's your age, is he old enough to have a son in Scouts?"

"Cub Scouts, maybe? If I recall, Frank was an Eagle Scout, and I think he wants to stay involved, but I'm not exactly plugged into that network."

Meg took a large bite and chewed, trying to picture Seth with a son in a Cub Scout uniform. Her son. Their son. Could she see herself in that picture? They'd agreed on the idea of having children sometime in the foreseeable future, but they hadn't gotten down to specifics, and Meg felt woefully out of touch with details like day care options, the quality of the local school systems, or setting up a college fund for little Ms. or Master Chapin. Corey-Chapin? Chapin-Corey?

"Meg, you're awfully quiet. Problem?"

"No, just thinking."

"Sorry I interrupted," Seth said, attacking his sandwich again.

"Don't be. Is your nephew Matthew a Cub Scout?"

"He is. It would be a different troop, of course, since they live in Amherst."

"Why do you say 'of course'? I have no idea how these things work."

"Well, you're going to be talking to someone who knows the answers shortly. Ask him."

"How is your sister Rachel, anyway? When's the baby due again?"

"I haven't seen her lately. She's due in, what, two months? Mom tells me she's pretty large already."

"I can imagine." Or maybe not—she'd been so career-driven, as had most of her female colleagues at the bank in Boston, that Meg had little direct knowledge of the stages of pregnancy. How ridiculous it seemed that she'd been so focused on her job that she'd failed to learn the basics of human childbearing! "We should get together with them soon—before the baby comes. Thanksgiving may be too late."

"We should. If we can find breathing room."

Meg bundled up her sandwich wrappings before turning to face him. "Seth, we're giving time to Jeffrey, who we barely know. Shouldn't we save some for family?"

Seth sat back in the seat and shut his eyes. "You're right. Sometimes I don't stop to think, and then things just happen, like this needy kid showing up."

Meg leaned against him. "It's the right thing to do. But let's not forget the family, okay?"

"Fair enough."

Frank Baker lived in a part of Granford that Meg was unfamiliar with, a pleasant, modern subdivision of mid-sized homes that looked comfortably lived in without being shabby. Frank was expecting them and answered their knock quickly.

"Hey, Seth. And this is Meg Corey? Good to meet you. I've heard a lot about you."

Meg laughed and shook his extended hand. "I won't ask for specifics."

"What can I do for you folks? Oh, come on in, don't mind the chaos. My wife took the kids to the mall to buy more school clothes—she'd be horrified to find out I let you in to see this." The living room was scattered with toys, both manual and electronic, and a few cast-off pieces of outerwear, but it looked normal enough to Meg.

"Don't apologize," she said. "I'm in the middle of the apple harvest, and I haven't seen some of my floors for weeks. Cleaning is on my calendar for December, I think."

"Well, see if you can find the furniture under this mess, and sit down," Frank said. He moved aside a sweatshirt and some kind of video game, and waited while Meg and Seth sat.

When they were all settled, Frank said, "You wanted to know something about Scouting, Seth? What's your interest? We can always use volunteer Scoutmasters."

"No, Frank, it's more specific than that, but I wanted to talk with you face-to-face. It's about Jeffrey Green."

"Ah, I see. What do you want to know? Or maybe I should ask first, why are you asking?"

"Have the police talked to you?" Seth asked.

"The police? Why would they talk to me?" Frank looked bewildered.

"Well, I guess we're doing what they're not—trying to get a handle on what kind of kid Jeffrey is."

"You mean, could he have hurt someone? Awful thing, that," Frank said. "I didn't know the victim—a seasonal worker, I heard?"

"Is it possible that Jeffrey could have known the kid who died?" Seth asked. "He swears he didn't."

"If he swears he didn't know the boy, then I'd believe him. Jeffrey has never lied in the time I've known him. So my opinion, for what it's worth, is that the other boy must've been a stranger to him. But you still haven't said why you're here."

"To put it simply, we're trying to find out what really happened, for Jeffrey's sake," Seth said. "We don't believe Jeffrey attacked the boy, but since we don't know him well, we've been talking to people who do, like one of his teachers. We've found his mother, uh, less than completely supportive, but his father's back in town and seems to be stepping up."

Frank smiled ruefully. "I've had my run-ins with his mom. She wants him to make Eagle Scout before he ages out. I tried to explain this wasn't a race or an achievement test, but I don't think she heard me. From what I've seen, Jeffrey's a good kid—conscientious, thorough, smart, hard-working. Everything we like to see in a Scout. I think he joined originally because he did like the idea of belonging to something. But lately I wondered if he's pushing so hard just to keep mom happy."

"I agree," Meg said, "although he did seem excited

about the history side of things. I don't think he's just going through the motions, or at least, not all the time."

"Good—we're on the same page. I didn't tell his mother, but the truth is, there's no way Jeffrey is going to make Eagle Scout. There are too many requirements he hasn't met, and he doesn't have time to complete them all. He knows that, although I don't know if he's told his mother. Not that I'm complaining. I mean, Jeffrey's a great Scout, but he's not a real group person, if you know what I mean."

"I think we do," Meg said. "He seems like kind of a loner. Does he have any particular friends in the troop?"

"Not really. Now and then he'll give one of the others a ride to a meeting or event, but it's not always the same one."

"Did you ever hear anything about a girlfriend?"

Frank shrugged. "It never came up. We don't talk about that kind of thing at our meetings, apart from trying to impart some basics—like 'no' means 'no.' But beyond what we've discussed at that level, I don't know what else I can tell you about Jeffrey. If he should need a character reference, I'll be happy to give him one."

Seth stood up, and Meg followed suit. "Thanks for your time, Frank. I appreciate your comments, and they pretty much match what we've heard from everyone else. That's what makes this whole thing so frustrating. There are no good suspects, and next to no evidence pointing at anyone. Look, if you think of anything else, or overhear anything from one of the other Scouts, can you let us know?"

"Sure will. And I admire you both for getting involved and trying to help—a lot of people wouldn't."

Meg glanced at Seth. "Maybe Seth is doing this just because he's a good person, but for me—well, I've been in

Jeffrey's position, kind of, so I know how it feels. So I'm paying it back with Jeffrey."

"Well, I can appreciate that. I'm glad to have met you, Meg, and it was nice seeing you again, Seth."

As they made their way back to their car and he started the engine, Seth said, "You know, this is almost like some bit of theater of the absurd. *Someone* killed Novaro—that's the one solid fact we've got. Nobody can believe Jeffrey would harm anyone, but it was Jeffrey who found the body. Unless Art has come up with something new, I think we're at a dead end here. We like Jeffrey, and we don't think he attacked anybody, but he's already got a crowd of character witnesses, so that's no help. You ready to go home?"

"I guess so." Meg couldn't think of anything else to do, or anyone else to talk to, and it was getting late.

"Bree home for dinner tonight?" Seth asked.

"Nope. Actually, she said she thought she might get together with Michael," Meg replied, adding, "They haven't seen much of each other lately."

Seth said, with a hint of dismay, "Please don't try to fix Bree and Michael."

"I wasn't planning to!" Meg protested. "I respect Bree, and she needs to make her own decisions. Sometimes I maybe even lean back too far because I'm afraid of ticking her off, and I need her. I ask her what to do next, she tells me, and I do it. With the crew, they know what to do, and she keeps an eye on them to be sure they do it, which they do. If I had to manage them, I'd be completely lost."

"I hope Bree stays around for a long time—you two make a good team. And you'll learn," Seth said. "You're a smart woman."

"I'm not so sure that's enough. Bree's got a lot of relevant education that I'll never have, plus I think that a lot of running an orchard comes down to experience and luck and maybe a touch of the mystical thrown in. I've been thinking about putting up a discreet shrine to Pomona somewhere on the property. I figure it can't hurt."

Seth pulled into their driveway a few minutes later, parked, then led the way inside and closed the door behind them. As Max loped up to greet them, Meg picked up a note Bree had left her on the kitchen table.

"I'll take Max out—he's been cooped up for a while," Seth said.

"Okay," Meg said absently, scanning the note. Bree informed her that there was a ninety-percent chance of precipitation the following day, so she thought they could take a break from picking. She'd already told Raynard, who would tell the others, and she was planning on staying at Michael's for the night. She'd also added that Seth's mother, Lydia, had called but hadn't left a message.

While Seth was out with Max, Meg called Lydia. "Hi, Lydia—were you looking for Seth or me?" Meg asked.

"You, actually. I'm planning to kidnap Rachel tomorrow and take her to lunch, and I wondered if you'd like to come along."

"Perfect timing! Bree informs me we aren't going to be picking tomorrow, so that works out just fine. When and where?"

"I'm going to pick up Rachel at her place, so want to ride over with me?"

"Great. How's she doing?"

"She keeps telling me she had forgotten all the details about being pregnant, and she feels big as a house. All perfectly normal. Should I pick you up at eleven?"

"It's a date. I'll be glad to see both of you."

Seth came back as she was hanging up. "Speak of the devil," Meg said. "Your mother just asked if I wanted to have lunch with her and Rachel tomorrow. Since Bree says she doesn't need me, I said yes. Don't feel left out—it's a ladies' lunch, and we're going to listen to Rachel complain about all her pregnancy symptoms. I don't think you'd enjoy it much."

"I agree. I've got plenty to keep me busy. Nothing from Sam or Jeff?"

"Nope. And Bree says she's staying at Michael's. The place is all ours."

22

After Seth headed out into the pouring rain on Thursday morning, Meg found herself at loose ends: she was so used to being busy, she didn't know what to do with spare time. She read the paper slowly, savoring a second cup of coffee while it was still hot. She cleaned up the kitchen, wiping down counters and cabinets whose greasy state was glaringly obvious by day. She ran a couple of loads of laundry, then showered and washed her hair. Which still left her time to kill before Lydia was due to pick her up.

Too little time to delve into her family history—every time Meg got started on that, she'd look up to find that several hours had passed. She was saving that for the long winter days when the harvest was over. Not enough time to shop for sorely needed food supplies—she'd do that after she returned from lunch. She could pull up her orchard spreadsheets and enter details of the most recent apples picked, but she wasn't sure she wanted to know the totals at the moment, especially since there was nothing she could do about it. The crop was what it was, and as long as the pickers handled the apples with their usual care, the fruit would all get harvested and then hauled off to the local markets she'd contracted with. In the end, Meg leafed through the magazines that had been accumulating for several weeks, finding little that held her interest, and then tossed them into the recycling bin.

She was ready and waiting when Lydia arrived at eleven. Meg liked Lydia, and was comfortable with the idea of her as a mother-in-law. Lydia had had her own problems with her marriage to Seth's father, about which both Lydia and Seth had shared a few details, but she wasn't offering Meg advice, thank goodness. Lydia and Seth got along well, as did she and Rachel—although, absurdly, Lydia saw more of her daughter Rachel, who lived twenty minutes away in Amherst, than she did of her son, who lived in eyeshot of her house.

Meg watched Lydia pull up close to the back door, her windshield wipers laboring. Meg patted Lolly, grabbed an umbrella, and dashed out to the car. Lydia opened the door for her just as she reached it.

"You're looking fit," Lydia commented, turning the car around and taking the road back toward town.

"That's because I get plenty of exercise. Lifting, reaching, and stretching."

"How's the crop?"

"About average, or so Bree tells me—down a bit from last year. Thanks for asking—I'm sure you're fascinated." Meg grinned, running her fingers through her hair to shake out the water droplets. "You know, I'd almost forgotten what rain looked like, but it's a great excuse to play hooky. I know that it's possible to pick in the rain, but I think everyone can use the break right now since there's no variety that absolutely has to be picked today."

"Well, whatever the reason, I'm glad you're free today. How's that son of mine doing?"

"Fine, busy. But it's good that he's got plenty of business, and we're both looking forward to when things will slow down in a couple of months." Meg sneaked a glance at Lydia. "It's all right, you can ask. I know you want to."

"Why, whatever do you mean?" Lydia said, but then couldn't contain a laugh. "No date yet?"

"Nope. For one thing, we haven't had time to think, much less sit down together and draw up detailed plans. For another, I've never been one of those women who goes all gaga over brides' magazines and agonizes over off-white versus ecru, or whether black is the new white."

"Do you know, I have never figured out what ecru is? Anyway, make up your own minds in your own time. I'll still be around—I hope."

They chatted happily about nothing important during the time it took to reach Rachel's bed and breakfast. She was waiting, seated in one of the ample wicker rockers on her Victorian front porch, and struggled out of it before they could help her.

"Don't worry," Rachel called out as Meg got out of the car, "I need the exercise. I feel like a whale."

Meg moved to the backseat so Rachel could sit in front. "Is that my cue to say you're glowing?"

"You mean I'm completely red in the face?" Rachel said as she sat down and struggled to wrap the seat belt around her middle. "You may now proceed, Mother dearest."

The drive to the restaurant took only a few minutes. Lydia dropped Rachel and Meg off in front, with Meg helping to haul Rachel out of the seat, then went to find parking.

"How's it going?" Meg asked, while they waited.

"I told Mom, there's a lot I had forgotten about the process. The brain is a wonderful thing—it erases a lot of the yucky stuff so that we can keep spawning new babies. You'll find out." Rachel glanced at her, a worried expression on her face. "Won't you?"

"Don't worry—you're not scaring me. Yes, probably, although the date for that is about as vague as the date for the wedding."

Lydia returned quickly, and she had had the foresight to reserve a deep, padded booth for them at the restaurant so that Rachel would be comfortable. Once they ordered, Rachel sat back and said, "Mom, I am tired of talking about my blood pressure and swollen ankles, so instead I figured we could talk about what happened in Granford instead. Some poor kid got his head bashed in?" Rachel turned to Meg.

Meg outlined what she knew, and reported how she and Seth had gotten themselves involved, though with little result so far. That carried them through soup and sandwiches.

"So, bottom line," Rachel said, "this young Jamaican guy is dead and the squeaky-clean Boy Scout is the only suspect, but there is zero proof that he had anything to do with it. And the police are officially stymied."

"That's it, in a nutshell."

Rachel grinned at her. "But you and Seth are on the job. Does that about cover it?"

"Sad to say, it does," Meg said. "And it's been nearly a week now and the trail is as cold as it gets. Nobody we've talked to believes that Jeffrey had anything to do with this.

If Jeffrey didn't do it, it has to be either random, which is an unsettling thought, or someone that Novaro met in the short time he was in the area. I guess there's a chance that a person or a gang came into town and did this, but there's no evidence of that, either."

"But of course the police are looking into that, right?" Rachel said.

"As far as we know—they haven't told us, no surprise. Nobody else seems to know who Novaro was hanging out with, after he quit his job. He just dropped off the radar, according to the other pickers, including his uncle."

"Well," Lydia said, "I admire you and Seth for trying to help."

"I'm glad you feel that way, Lydia. It helps. You two have fresh eyes or ears or whatever—anything we've missed?"

Their waitress had appeared and Rachel said quickly, "I want the cheesecake, please." The waitress took the rest of their orders and trotted back to the kitchen. "How about the theory of a damsel in distress?" Rachel said, once the waitress was gone.

"That's an interesting idea," Meg said. "As far as we know—and we've asked—Jeffrey isn't officially dating anyone, although there are some rumors that there's a girl in the picture. I gather his mother would pitch a fit if he got involved with a townie."

"*He*'s a townie, isn't he?" Rachel countered.

"Yes, but his mother has big plans for him and thinks that an 'inappropriate relationship'"—Meg made air quotes—"would interfere with those plans," she replied.

"His mother sounds like a real sweetheart. Have you asked Jeffrey?" Rachel said.

"No, not directly. Do you think he'd tell us?"

"Maybe, under the right conditions. Or you could simply observe his body language. If he turns bright red when you ask, that's a definite maybe. He might try to sneak around the answer, so you have to watch how you phrase your question."

"What do you mean?" Meg asked.

"You can't say, *Are you seeing anyone?* because that's too vague. If they've never actually gone on a date, he might try to get away with a no. So instead you say, *Is there any girl you're interested in taking out or have already taken out, with or without the knowledge of your harpy mother?*"

Lydia broke out laughing. "Rachel, listen to yourself. Have you been wallowing in old fiction?"

"Sure have. Mostly romance—my hormones have run amok. I keep plenty of books on hand for guests, and I've been refreshing my memory. Between that and watching reruns of *Law & Order* and stuff like that on television, there's not much else I can do at the moment."

Rachel thought for a moment, then said, "Seriously, the way you've described him, Jeffrey sounds like a sweet, innocent, shy boy—just the kind who is most likely to fantasize about saving the life or the honor or in some way coming to the rescue of the object of his affections, even if she doesn't know he's alive. God, I'm glad I'm not a teenager anymore," Rachel said. "Anyway, you should talk to Seth about it—he's a guy, right?"

"Uh, yeah?" Meg said. "And he did mention that he pined for one or two girls in his high school days without ever doing much about it."

"He was a late bloomer," Lydia said.

"He's a snail," Rachel countered. "I'm amazed he managed to ask Nancy to marry him. Oh, sorry, Meg—does it bother you if we talk about Nancy? You met her, right?"

"I did, and go right ahead. It's past history, right?"

"It is. Although, come to think of it, maybe Nancy proposed to Seth—she thought he was going to go on to bigger things. She wasn't planning on being a plumber's wife. Are you okay with that, Meg?"

"Hey, I'm a farmer, so who am I to throw stones? Seth loves what he's doing now—the whole restoration thing. He's really into the hands-on part, making things work or bringing them back to life. Sometimes I get jealous of the wood, the way he caresses it."

"Oooh," Rachel said, laughing. "Do tell. Actually, I think Noah feels the same way about the furniture he makes. But he comes home to me."

By the time they finished dessert, Rachel announced, "I'd better get back—the kids'll be back from school soon, and it's time for my nap."

"I'm glad we could do this, Rachel," Meg said. "Seth and I were just talking about how we need to spend more time with family. I mean, seeing you two should come before spending time checking up on a kid we barely know."

"We're not going anywhere, Meg," Lydia said quietly. "It sounds as though what you're trying to do for Jeffrey could make a real difference in his life."

Impulsively Meg reached out and laid her hand on Lydia's. "Thank you. And I hope that's true."

"Gang, can we get this show on the road?" Rachel asked. "Because I've really got to pee, and I don't fit into the stalls in ladies' rooms anymore."

"I'll go get the car," Lydia said.

By the time Meg had helped Rachel out of the booth and led her to the front, Lydia was waiting at the curb. They dropped Rachel off at her home, but before pulling away, Meg turned to Lydia. "Are you in a hurry to get home?"

"No, not really. Why?"

"I hadn't thought about it before, but now that I'm in Amherst, I could try to contact that archaeologist at the university and see if she has anything new for us. She could be busy, though—she's got classes to teach."

"Sounds intriguing. You have her number?"

"I think it's on my cell phone." On her phone Meg found the number she was looking for, then hit Connect. She was startled when Miranda answered quickly. "Hey, Miranda, this is Meg Corey, from Granford—Gail Selden introduced us?"

"Of course I remember you, Meg. What's up? Terrible what's going on there with that poor Jamaican boy."

"Yes, it is, and Jeffrey Green is still wrapped up in that whole mess. Anyway, I wondered if you'd learned anything more about the Granford skeleton."

"Nothing major—some interesting bits and pieces, though. Why do you ask?"

"I'm in Amherst at the moment, and if you had anything to add I could stop by."

"You want to visit the man?" Miranda asked gleefully.

"You mean the skeleton? I hadn't considered that. I suppose it would be interesting to see him reassembled, so to speak."

"I've got a lab at three where we'll be talking about him. Come on by. I'll tell you where to find me." Miranda gave detailed directions to the lab space, and Meg was glad she was already familiar with the layout of the campus, or she would have been completely baffled. When she hung up, Meg said to Lydia, "You up for meeting the skeleton?"

Lydia laughed. "Why not? Not exactly the way I planned to spend my day, but I'll admit I'm intrigued. Lead on!"

23

Miranda's directions, while convoluted, proved accurate, and Meg and Lydia arrived at the lab space just as the class of about a dozen students was gathering. The skeleton lay on a well-lit table in the center of the room, neatly arrayed. Miranda spotted them and held up one finger.

"Okay, kids, listen up. I know we've talked about this skeleton before, but for the moment pretend you don't know anything. I want you to take the next, say, fifteen minutes to write down everything you observe and what that tells you about the person. Then we'll compare notes. The clock starts . . . now!"

The students jostled around the skeleton while Miranda made her way over to where Meg and Lydia stood. "Hi, Meg—good to see you again. And this is?" She turned to Lydia.

"I'm Lydia Chapin—Seth's mother."

"Oh, right, Seth—I saw him at the Historical Society site, didn't I? And I keep hearing his name pop up—all good, I promise! Nice to meet you, Lydia. As you can see, our friend there cleaned up pretty good. Luckily the excavation stopped before much was damaged. How's Jeffrey doing?"

"As well as can be expected. He wasn't prepared for being part of a murder investigation, but then, whoever is?"

"I hear you. Hey, I've been held at gunpoint and accused of grave-robbing in my day, so I know something of what it feels like."

"Wow!" Meg said. "I'd love to hear about all that sometime. But for the moment, can you tell us anything more about our man than you could the last time we talked?"

"Like I said on the phone, only bits and pieces, but they're kind of interesting. I told you he was about sixty? I'm guessing he was in the ground awhile before the building went up over him, so that would put his birth date around 1700, maybe even before."

"That early?"

"Oh, sure. Bone and dental analyses show that he was born in Africa but spent most of his life in this country, probably right around here."

"You said he died of tuberculosis. Any other signs of disease or injury?"

"Nope. He was about as healthy as you could expect, for that time period. He was a physical laborer, based on the muscle attachment and bone wear, but he wasn't overworked or starved, if that's what you're asking."

"You can really tell a lot from a pile of bones, can't you?" Lydia commented.

"Absolutely, if you know what to look for. And modern technology makes it much easier. Look, I'm going to have to get back to my class and see what they've come up with. If you see Jeffrey, tell him I'd like to speak with him, would you? I think he'd be the best person to deal with the Granford history side—who the families were back then, what crops they raised, that kind of thing."

"Really? You've got a class full of kids here!" Meg said.

"Sure, but they all want to be CSIs, not historians. They're into the forensics, not the background."

"I'm sure Jeffrey would be happy to work with you," Meg said, then silently added, *once this other mess is cleared up.* "I'll tell him to give you a call."

"Thanks. Hey, you don't have to be scared of our pal there. You can get closer."

Meg looked at Lydia and they both grinned. "Shall we?" Meg asked.

"Oh, let's!" Lydia replied.

But when they approached, it seemed only right to Meg to maintain a respectful distance from the remains before them. This had once been a man who had lived where she lived now, who had seen the same views, plowed the same fields, maybe picked fruit from the same orchards. Would Jeffrey or anyone be able to find more about him? Had he had a family? Were there descendants? How had he come to be buried where he was found? Would they ever know? Meg looked up to see Lydia bearing a somber expression as well.

"We should go," Meg said quietly. She turned to wave at Miranda, and then she and Lydia left the room without speaking.

Outside the building, where the rain had slowed to a

drizzle, Lydia said, "Well, that was interesting. I wonder if we'll ever know who the man was."

"I was thinking the same thing myself. I'll speak to Jeffrey—maybe some historical research would be a good distraction for him. You ready to head home?"

"I am. Thanks for bringing me along, though." They reached Lydia's car and pointed themselves toward Granford. About halfway there, Lydia said, out of the blue, "Seth is happier than I've seen him in a long time. Part of it is his work, as you pointed out. But part of it is you."

Meg could feel herself blushing. "I'm glad to know that. I can't imagine my life without him now."

"And that's as it should be. I don't care when or even if you get married, but I think you two do belong together. And I'll stop with the mushy stuff now."

The rain had ended by the time Lydia dropped her off at her house, and Meg watched her leave with a smile. Seth emerged from his office at the end of the driveway, just as she was leaving. "Nice lunch?"

"Very nice. I like your family. Oh, and Rachel came up with a new theory: she thinks Jeffrey could be protecting a damsel in distress. Or at least he believes that he is."

"Could be, I guess. Although he hasn't mentioned anything like a damsel, nor has one come forward."

"Then he's doing a good job of protecting, isn't he?"

"Apparently so."

"And we stopped by to see Miranda on campus, and to say hello to our skeleton."

Seth laughed. "You took my mother to see a skeleton? You do have interesting ideas of entertainment. Anything new?"

"I'll tell you over dinner."

Inside they found Bree pottering around in the kitchen,

and joined her in putting dinner together. An hour or so later Seth's cell phone rang. He walked into the dining room to talk, but he was back quickly, with an odd expression on his face. "That was Howard Dillenberger, at the high school. He's put a name to the girl he'd seen with Jeffrey: Emma Stebbins."

It took a moment for the import of that to sink in for Meg. "You mean, as in Jake Stebbins?"

Seth nodded. "His sixteen-year-old daughter."

"And Novaro was found behind Jake Stebbins's feed shop. Tell me that's a coincidence."

"Unlikely."

They stared at each other. "Oh, wow," Meg said. "Rachel may have been right."

"It looks like it."

24

 "Okay, guys, back up," Bree broke in. "What's going on? Who's this Dillenberger guy?"

"Jeffrey's history teacher. We talked with him yesterday and asked if he'd seen Jeffrey with any girls."

"And what's this 'damsel in distress' stuff?"

"Rachel used the term today at lunch. She wondered if maybe Jeffrey was protecting someone, a girl, out of some sense of honor. Misguided or otherwise."

"Okay, but you two connected the dots from Novaro behind the feed store to the store owner's daughter and immediately stuck Jeffrey in the middle of it? Come on!"

"That's my first guess, and I may be way off base. Seth, what do we do now?" Meg asked.

"Let's not get ahead of ourselves," Seth said. "Mr. Dillenberger could be wrong. It could be a coincidence that they were seen together. It could be a coincidence that Emma happens to be Jake's daughter—I have no idea how many girls of the right age there are at the high school, or how many are Jeffrey's type."

"Yes, but . . ." Meg began, then stopped to think. "When we talked to Jake, he said his daughter works at the store, at least part-time, right? But Jake said his daughter was at home with him when he got the call about Novaro, didn't he?"

"Actually, I'm not sure," Seth admitted.

"Jeez, you guys," Bree broke in. "Why don't you just talk to Jeffrey?"

"Will he tell us the truth?" Meg said.

"About seeing Emma? Why not?" Seth replied.

"Because even if he was just yearning from afar, he might be embarrassed enough to lie about it—Rachel talked about that. And we still don't have any connection between Novaro and Emma. So what do we do, Seth?"

Seth thought for a moment before answering. "I see two choices: we talk to Jake, and Emma, or we talk to Jeffrey. Who is more likely to tell us the truth? Because it sounds to me like neither one has been completely honest. Or maybe Jake is clueless about his daughter."

"Or how about we talk to Art?" Meg asked.

"Why?" Seth said.

"Because we need to share what we know—or think we know—and I think we really need a law-enforcement perspective here. We need more information."

"I get your point. Want me to call him?"

"Please."

When he went into the next room to make the call, Meg turned to Bree. "You've been awfully quiet."

"What do you want me to say? You and Seth are playing detective so you can help your new buddy Jeffrey."

She's angry, Meg thought. "Bree, what's wrong?"

Bree took a deep breath. "I'm stuck in the middle again. I'm Jamaican, but I'm American. I work with the pickers, and they're great guys, but Novaro was a slacker. His own uncle didn't know what to do about him. What do you want me to say?"

Meg spread her hands helplessly. "Bree, I'm just trying to help Jeffrey, because I think he needs help. I don't have any other agenda. Like I said, if he's guilty, he'll pay for it."

Bree sighed. "Yeah, I know. I just wish somebody would figure this thing out so we can move on."

Seth returned. "Art said he could swing by later in the evening. So we should eat, right?"

"Yes, we should. Did you know that to become an Eagle Scout, boys are now required to earn a cooking merit badge?" Meg said sweetly.

"I'll take that as a hint," Seth said. "Let me take a look in the refrigerator."

Art rapped at the back door just as they were finishing up a dinner consisting largely of leftovers. "Am I interrupting?" he asked.

"Not at all," Meg said.

"I brought cookies," he added, holding up a white bag.

"Then we love you. Coffee?"

"Nah," Art said as he walked in. "It might keep me awake—that'd be a shame, right?"

"Hey, Art," Seth greeted him. "Thanks for coming. Sit down."

"Do you need me?" Bree asked.

"Yes, we do," Meg said quickly. "You can offer some insights that we might not have."

Art settled himself in a chair and snagged one of the cookies. "Okay, what do you want from me?"

"Art, we need to talk about what happened to Novaro Miller," Meg said simply.

"Yeah, that's what Seth said on the phone. Sainsbury put you up to this?"

"No. I met Jeffrey through the excavation of the Historical Society building. I didn't know who he was. Rick asked us to help before everything blew up. But you know all that, right?"

Seth spoke for the first time. "Art, we don't have an ax to grind. We like Jeffrey, but if he's involved in this, we aren't going to look the other way. And we aren't going to lie to Rick Sainsbury. I have to say, the more we learn, the more things don't add up. Look, why don't you tell us what you can about what you know?"

"You mean what crumbs Detective Marcus throws my way?" Art sighed, and took a moment to collect his thoughts. "Last Friday night, Jeffrey Green called 911 to report that he had found an unknown young man behind Stebbins's feed store, unconscious and bleeding from a head wound. Green requested an ambulance and administered basic first aid. The victim had no ID on him. He was taken to Holyoke Hospital, where he was declared dead.

"Meg here helped figure out who the victim was—one Novaro Miller, an eighteen-year-old Jamaican national who came over on an agricultural visa obtained for him by his uncle Hector Dixon, one of her former employees. Shortly after his arrival in the U.S., Miller blew off the job his uncle had gotten for him and his whereabouts were unknown until he was found at the feed store. Miller apparently drove himself to the store, in a car lacking in registration or valid license plates, which the police impounded. Inside the car, they found Miller's fingerprints and a number of empty beer cans. His uncle knew nothing about any car."

"Did the police talk to Jake Stebbins?" Seth asked.

Art swiveled toward Seth. "Of course they did. Jake's a good guy. Runs an honest business, knows most of his customers by name. His wife died of lung cancer a couple of years ago—really nice lady. One kid, a daughter named Emma, at the high school. The worst thing I can remember Jake ever doing is leaving his car parked on the street during a snow emergency. Do you really suspect him of having any part in this? Besides, he told me he closed up at the regular time, and he was at home with his daughter eating dinner when he got the call about the trouble at the store."

Meg and Seth exchanged a look, and then Meg said, "There has to be a reason why Novaro was found behind the feed store. Why there? Why behind it, out of sight from the road or anything else? You have any ideas about that?"

"Not a clue," Art replied. "As far as I can tell, nobody here in town knew him. He could have been involved in something illegal, but there's no evidence."

Meg said, suddenly, "You know, I've never seen a picture of Novaro. Do you have one, Art?"

"Right here in the file. I kinda figured you might want to know what's in it, even though I shouldn't be showing it to you. But it was taken when we found him, so it's not pretty."

"That's all right." Meg held out her hand and took the picture from Art, turning it around to look at the face. Then she looked harder: something was not right. "Art, are you sure this is the right photo? Novaro was Jamaican. This man is light-skinned."

Bree looked over Meg's shoulder and snorted involuntarily. Meg looked at her, and saw Bree's expression seesawing between amusement and frustration. "What?"

"You never heard about skin bleaching?" When Meg shook her head in bewilderment, Bree explained. "A lot of the poorer kids in Jamaica are into it. You know that old nonsense that light skin is better than dark skin? Bunch of idiots—it's not safe. Anyway, looks like that's what Novaro was into."

Meg thought again about that day a week earlier on the green. "Damn," she whispered to herself.

All eyes turned to her. "What?" Seth said.

"Art, I told you about how at the green, on Friday, I was there when Jeffrey drove up. And as soon as he stopped, another car pulled in behind him, and a guy his own age got out. They started arguing, and then there was a girl who got out of the second car and seemed to be trying to stop them. I couldn't hear anything, and I couldn't see them well from that distance. But the second guy had light skin. When you identified the kid at the feed store as black, I never put the two together. I only told you because I wanted you to know that Jeffrey apparently had issues with someone in town. When I asked him about it, he said some guy had been hassling the girl at school, but since they drove off together, I didn't think anything more about it."

"And now you're thinking that was Novaro Miller?" Art asked

"I'm saying it could have been."

"Let me get this straight," Art said, his tone sharper than before. "Last Friday you saw Jeffrey Green and another boy arguing on the green in town, and there was a girl in the mix. Novaro Miller was killed later that same day, and it was Jeffrey Green who found him."

Meg felt like a fool. "Yes. I'm sorry, Art. I did tell you about it on Monday."

Art sighed again. "You did. And I didn't see the connection either, and then I got distracted by another police call. You got any more bombshells for me?"

"I'm afraid so, Art," Seth said reluctantly. "We talked to one of Jeffrey's teachers at the high school, and he said he thinks Jeffrey was seeing Emma Stebbins."

Art stared at him. "Oh, crap. When did you hear this?"

"Just this afternoon. And, no, I don't know anything more, and we haven't asked Jeffrey about it."

"Where's Jeffrey now?"

"He and his father are staying at my place up the hill. Want me to call ahead?"

"No, I want to go over there and talk to them." Art morphed into his official role as police chief. "Will you all promise not to attempt to contact Jeffrey Green or his father before I get there and talk to them?"

"Of course, Art," Seth answered. "We know what's at stake. Do what you have to do."

"Thanks." Art left without any pleasantries.

"I'm sorry," Meg said, to no one in particular. What had Jeffrey really done?

They hadn't heard from Art by the time they went to bed.

25

"Today's Friday, you know," Seth said at breakfast the next morning.

"Why does this matter?" Meg asked, watching her toast so it wouldn't burn.

"The Harvest Festival is tomorrow."

"Oh, damn and blast. I signed up for a booth, didn't I? And I haven't done anything about it beyond asking Raynard to set aside some nice apples, but things have been so topsy-turvy that he may not have remembered. I should have some old baskets somewhere; I'll need to dig them out. Then I have to find booth decorations and bags and, oh yes, apples to fill them with. Shoot, I'll also need some small bills to make change, if I'm selling apples. And a scale would be nice—"

Seth interrupted her. "Take a breath, will you? I've got a vintage hanging scale you can borrow—it'll look good.

You'll have to be there at your booth from ten to three, so you'd better remind Bree. Either that or tell her to take a shift at the booth."

"Why are you so organized this early in the morning?" Meg asked him.

"It's in the genes, I think."

"Is Gail still planning a big display for the Historical Society?"

"Last I heard. It's not quite as dramatic as it was a few days ago, now that the building has been lowered onto the new foundation, but there are plenty of pictures documenting every step of it. I think she said something about a computer slideshow."

"I'm glad that project is working out," Meg said. She stood up. "I'd better get moving. I've got to go pick another million or so apples."

Meg was putting on her work sweatshirt when her phone rang. She cast a worried glance toward Seth. "It's never good news when the phone rings this early, is it?" she said anxiously.

"Want me to answer?" Seth asked.

"No, it's my phone." She took a deep breath and answered. "Hello?"

"Meg? It's Art. You and Seth had better get your butts to the police station—Jeffrey Green just walked in and confessed to killing Novaro Miller."

"What? No! Didn't you talk to him just last night?"

"I did. This morning he said he'd had all night to think about it and decided to come clean."

"Is Sam there?"

"Not yet. I called him, since Jeffrey kind of slipped out under his nose."

"Are you going to tell Marcus?"

"Not until I've heard what Jeffrey has to say. You coming?"

"We'll be there in ten." She hung up, then turned to face Seth. "Jeffrey just confessed to the killing, and he's with Art at the police station in town right now."

Seth stood up quickly. "Oh, crap. Why would he do that?"

"You mean you don't think he did it?"

"No, I don't. So why would he say he did?"

They stared at each other for a moment. "Because he's protecting someone else?" Meg said softly. "Like Emma Stebbins, maybe?"

Bree stood up quickly. "You don't need me for this, so I'm going up to the orchard. I won't mention anything to Raynard and the guys until you figure out what really happened." She grabbed a jacket and left. But no sooner had she opened the door than a truck rolled into Meg's driveway and Meg found herself staring at Jake Stebbins and a young girl who had to be his daughter, Emma. "Where the hell is Jeffrey Green?" Jake demanded. "He's not at home and he's not answering his cell. I gotta talk to him right now."

Seth came up beside Meg. "Jake, calm down. What do you want with him, in such a hurry? And why do you think he'd be here?"

"He told Emma he was staying at your house. And then he said that he was going to turn himself in for killing that kid at the feed store."

"I can't let him do that!" Emma wailed. "He didn't do it. I did!"

"Emma, don't say that!" Jake yelled.

She turned to her father. "Why not? It's the truth. Jeffrey was just trying to help me."

"Whoa, everybody," Seth said firmly. "First, Jeffrey and his father are at the police station in town—he just turned himself in. We all want to hear what really happened, but I think we should head over there and sort this out together. Jake, you take Emma with you. Meg and I will follow."

For a long moment it looked as though Jake would protest, but in the end he just nodded. "Come on, Emma, let's go."

Watching them leave, Meg said, "A damsel in distress indeed. Rachel was right. We'd better get over there before these kids dig themselves in any deeper."

"I'll drive," Seth said.

The ride to the police station took no more than ten minutes. "Do you have any idea what the legalities are here?" Meg asked Seth.

"Nope. I suppose we should turn the whole mess over to the state police and let them sort things out."

"You can't want to do that!" Meg protested.

"Not until I hear what they have to say. Not that I have any right to put off telling Marcus, but I have the feeling they'll be more willing to be open in a less scary setting, and our station is friendlier than the one in Northampton."

"Amen to that," Meg said.

When they walked into the police station, the receptionist smiled. "The party's in the conference room. Go on back." Meg and Seth knew the way. Inside the room, Art had taken the head of the table, with a view of the door. On one side stood Sam and Jeffrey; on the other, Jake and Emma. It seemed as though everyone was talking at once, although they hadn't reached the point of yelling—yet. Art smiled grimly at Meg and Seth.

"Everybody, just shut up, will you?" Art said loudly.

Surprisingly, everyone did. "Looks like we're all here—unless you want to call Karen, Sam?"

"No!" Jeffrey and Sam said in unison.

"All right, then. This is not a formal interrogation. You are not being recorded. I may get into hot water with the state police down the line for doing things this way, but it seems best for me to know what the story is before I hand anyone over to them. Or should I say, which the story is? Who wants to start?"

"Let me," Jeffrey said, his eyes on Art. When Sam reached out to lay a hand on his arm, he shook it off without looking at him. "Last Friday evening, I stopped by the feed store to pick up an order, like I said. This guy Novaro was there, and I thought he looked suspicious—I mean, he had no reason to be there—so I asked him what he was doing and he kind of came at me. We fought, he hit his head, and he went down. You know the rest of it."

"Jeffrey—" Emma protested. Art silenced her with a look.

"Why didn't you come forward with that story from the beginning, or tell someone at any time since?" Art asked, not unkindly.

"I got scared, I guess. I mean, at first I didn't know if he was dead or what. I never meant to hurt him, but he came at me first and I just defended myself. And after that it kept getting more and more complicated. I was wrong, sir—I should have spoken up at the start. But I'm here now."

"He's lying!" Emma burst out.

"Emma!" Jeffrey cautioned her.

Emma ignored him. "No, Jeffrey, I'm not going to let you do this. I know you're trying to help, but it's not right."

Meg looked at Emma's father, who appeared baffled by the whole thing. "Emma, maybe we should talk to a lawyer before you say anything," Jake said tentatively.

"No, Daddy. This has to be done now. I can't stand it anymore, and I won't let Jeffrey ruin his life over me."

"Okay, everybody, listen up," Art said. "Sit down. Anybody want coffee? Soft drinks? Because I think this is going to take a little time."

Meg was glad for the break, because the atmosphere in the room was intense. Sam and Jeffrey were engaged in a muttered argument in one corner, heads together, voices low. Emma remained seated at the table, her arms wrapped around her, while Jake looked helplessly on. Art stuck his head out and told someone to bring in coffee and sodas, and Meg seized the chance to talk to him.

"Did this all come out last night?" she said quietly.

"Nope, none of it. Jeffrey stuck to his first story. How'd those two"—Art nodded toward Emma and Jake—"end up here?"

"They came by my house looking for Jeffrey. I gather he got in touch with Emma after you talked to him. And I get the impression that *all* of this is news to Jake."

"Maybe," Art said noncommittally. "I want to hear the girl's story."

When they were all settled again, with drinks, and apparently calmer, Art said, "Emma, tell us what happened. Take your time."

Emma managed a small smile. "I guess I kind of have to go back to the beginning." She looked sternly at Jeffrey. "Please don't interrupt me—just let me tell this my way, all right? You, too, Daddy. Please?"

Jeffrey nodded reluctantly, and a moment later, so did Jake Stebbins.

Emma turned back to Art. "Jeffrey and I have been kind of seeing each other for a while now. I think Jeffrey's mom made it pretty clear that she doesn't want him getting serious with anybody around here, so we kept it quiet." She turned to her father. "Sorry, Daddy, but there didn't seem to be any way to tell you, either. I didn't know what you'd think, and I was afraid you'd go all protective on me, or tell me to stop. Not that there's been much to stop, really."

"Emma—" Jake started to protest, clearly distressed, but Emma held up one hand to silence him.

"You're a year behind Jeffrey at school?" Meg asked. "So you're a junior?"

Emma nodded. "We sort of got together over the summer. I mean, mostly we hung out, or went to Amherst or Northampton, once Jeffrey got his car. I don't have a lot of free time anyway, between school and helping my dad out at the store. I don't mind, really—I want to help, and I'm glad to do my part with the business."

"Emma, what's this got to do with what happened to Novaro Miller? Did you know him?" Art said gently.

"I'm getting to that, Mr. Preston." Emma picked up her story. "Novaro didn't go to the high school, I'm sure you know by now. But like I said, I work in Dad's store after school, and some weekends. One afternoon this guy came in, looking for Dad, wanting to know if we were hiring part-timers. I told him I didn't think so, since I *am* pretty much the part-time staff, except for a few other guys who work now and then. We kind of got to talking—you know, just killing time. The store wasn't busy. He told me his name was Novaro and that he was from Jamaica and had come over with the pickers, which I could totally tell from his accent. He said he'd come with his uncle, but all the guys his uncle knew were old and boring. He seemed nice, and kind of lonely—he didn't seem to know many people his own age around here. That was it. We just talked for a bit and then he left, and I didn't think anything about it after that."

Emma stopped to take a swallow of her drink. "Then he started dropping by the store when he knew I would be there. After a while I began to wonder if he was watching to make sure my dad wasn't around, like checking to see if Dad's car was parked there or not. It felt kind of creepy, but I didn't see what I could do."

"You could have told me," Jeffrey muttered, not looking at anyone.

"Did you tell your father?" Art asked.

"I didn't tell anyone because I didn't think it was that big a deal. But he kept coming by. I figured Novaro would get bored or find another girl to bug, and besides, by then I was back in school. Then I came out after school the first week and there he was, waiting for me in his crappy old car. I think he thought it was, like, romantic or something, but it just kind of creeped me out, even though he didn't try anything. He offered me a ride home or to the store or wherever I wanted to go. I said no, and he left. But then he was there the next day, and the day after. Finally I just said yes, and told him to drop me off at the store. Okay, maybe that was stupid, but all the other Jamaicans around here are really nice guys, so I wasn't worried. He dropped me off like I asked, then he left, so I thought things would be okay. But I didn't want it to be an everyday thing, because then he might get the idea that we were together. Which I didn't want. So a couple of times I asked Jeffrey to give me a ride instead. And Novaro probably saw us together."

"Like that day at the green?" Meg asked.

"You saw us?" Emma looked surprised.

"I recognized Jeffrey because I was expecting to see him," Meg said. "I didn't know you or Novaro, but it was pretty clear even from a distance that there was some sort of argument going on."

"Like Em said, I gave her a ride home or to work sometimes," Jeffrey spoke for the first time since Emma had begun talking. "On Friday Novaro was waiting at the school and he followed us. I pulled in by the green because I wanted to show Em what the dig looked like, but then Novaro pulled up and got in my face. I guess he figured he had some claim on Emma."

"And I didn't want it to be a big thing," Emma chimed in, "so I said I'd go with Novaro."

"Did he take you to the store that day?" Art asked.

"Yeah, he did, but then he left, or at least, I thought he did. Maybe he came back again—I was busy working."

"Your father didn't see who dropped you off?" Seth asked.

"No, he was in his office, not out front."

"I never noticed a damn thing," Jake burst out. "She said a friend dropped her off at work after school, and I didn't even pay attention."

"Jeffrey, you stayed at the dig site and worked with that archaeologist for the rest of the afternoon, right?" Art asked.

"Yeah. We didn't find anything as interesting as that skeleton, but Miranda showed us lots of good stuff about archaeological techniques. It was really cool."

"When did you leave?" Seth asked.

"About six, six thirty, maybe? It was beginning to get dark, so she sent us all home, but first I had to pick up that stuff at the feed store for my mother. So I drove over there and parked in the back, where Jake said the bags would be. And that's when I found Novaro. And Emma."

26

"Jeffrey, you have to let me tell the next part, okay?" Emma said in a low voice. Jeffrey wavered, then slumped in his chair. "It wasn't your fault," he mumbled to Emma.

"I know, Jeffrey, but it happened." Emma turned to the adults. "Look, here's the real story. Novaro dropped me off at the store, like I said. He left. I worked for a couple of hours, and then Dad said he was heading home and did I want him to fix dinner? Which for him usually means picking up a pizza. I said fine, because I needed to finish restocking some of the shelves. I said I'd let him know if I wanted him to pick me up, but when the weather's nice it's easy to walk home—it's not far, just over the hill. So then Dad left."

"And Novaro came back?" Art asked.

"Yeah, around six. He knew we were closed, but I guess

he knew I was still in there. He was pounding on the door, so I let him in."

"Why?"

"Honestly, I didn't think there'd be a problem. He'd been pretty easygoing up until then, at least until he got into it with Jeffrey earlier that afternoon. Maybe it was a dumb move, but anyway, I opened the door. All the lights were still on, and I had my cell, so I guess I wasn't worried. At least, not until he came in and I could tell he'd been drinking. I could smell it on him."

"Then what happened?"

"He seemed pissed off at me. I think he'd been stewing about my being with Jeffrey earlier. He started asking stuff like, wasn't he good enough for me? Was it because he was black? Or not American? I told him that didn't matter to me, but that I already had a boyfriend. Then he started making fun of Jeffrey—you know, wimpy white boy with a fancy car."

"And he got physical?" Meg asked.

"Yeah." Emma looked away; she had tears in her eyes. "I mean, I wasn't expecting it. He hadn't touched me before, but I think he really thought I owed him something. He didn't exactly stop to explain, you know—he just came at me and then he was all over me. I kept yelling at him to stop but he backed me up against some shelves, toward the back of the store, where we couldn't be seen from the street, and . . ." She paused and swallowed before going on, "He *wouldn't* stop, so I shoved him. He fell backward and hit his head hard on one of those heavy metal shelves, and then he just . . . lay there."

"Oh, baby, I'm so sorry," Jake said. He looked shell-shocked. "I should have been there. You should have told me."

Nobody spoke for a few moments. Then Jeffrey picked up the story. "It was right around then that I arrived. I was out back, getting ready to load the stuff into the trunk of my car, and I heard this scuffling inside the store. I knew nobody was supposed to be there and I thought it might be a robbery or something. I tried the door in the back and it opened, and that's when I saw Emma inside, and Novaro on the floor."

"Jeffrey just came in," Emma agreed, "and he looked at Novaro, and then he said something like, 'Did he hurt you?' and I shook my head no, and then we kind of stared at Novaro and didn't know what to do. I know, if I'd been thinking straight, we should have called the police right then, but . . ." Emma swallowed. "I mean, my clothes were kind of ripped, and I knew people at school had probably seen me with Novaro, and maybe they'd think I had let things go too far. This is a small town. People talk—even decent people. They're always going to wonder, did he really do that? Or, did I lead him on and then change my mind?"

Meg felt a stab of anger. It was hurtful to hear something like that coming from a teenager, that people would blame the woman, or girl in this case. That had been true when she was their age, and things hadn't really changed, not enough. Meg couldn't sit still for that. "Emma, I'm sure you didn't mean to kill Novaro. That was a terrible accident, but don't *ever* blame yourself for thinking you'd led him on. He would have raped you if you hadn't stopped him. And I can understand why you wouldn't want to try to explain that to your father and the police, and you don't even have a mother to turn to."

Emma looked at her, tears spilling down her face. "Thank you, Ms. Corey. I know that's what they teach us these days, but it's different when it happens to you, you know? And

Jeffrey was only trying to help me, honest. I'm sorry, Daddy, but she's right—how could I explain it to you? I know what Jeffrey and I did was wrong, but right then I couldn't see any other way."

"And then I told Emma to go home and try to act like nothing had happened," Jeffrey resumed, "and I checked to see if there was anything like evidence—you know, blood and stuff—inside the store, and then you know the rest of the story from there."

"So it was you who moved him outside? Why?" Art asked, keeping his tone neutral.

"I guess I figured if the body was found outside, the police might think there was somebody or something else involved. I didn't want anything to point to Emma or her dad."

"Kid, you are something else," Sam finally said in a voice that mingled awe and frustration. "You really thought you could cover this up? Make it go away?"

"Dad, I just wanted to protect Emma. That's all. I knew I hadn't killed Novaro, so I didn't see how they could pin it on me."

Meg sneaked a glance at Jeffrey's face, and her heart ached for him. Maybe he'd done something wrong by covering up what had really happened, but he was only trying to protect this sweet girl who he obviously cared for. But the trade-off for Emma's reputation remaining clean was that Jeffrey now had the shadow of an unexplained murder hanging over him.

Art looked down at the tabletop for a few moments before he spoke. "So let me see if I've got this right. Novaro Miller came back to the feed store once everyone except Emma was gone. There was evidence that he'd been drinking. And then he . . . attacked Emma. Emma fought him off, and he fell, hitting his head, and that blow was what ultimately killed him. Arguably, that was self-defense. Jeffrey then happened to show up at the same time, and helped Emma cover it up by moving the body. Have I got that right?" Art looked up at Jeffrey then.

Jeffrey and Emma returned his gaze. "Yes, sir," Jeffrey said.

"Tell me again why you didn't just tell the police what really happened," Art said.

"It was for Emma, sir. Okay, I know nothing happened— I mean, he didn't really do anything . . ."

"That's okay, Jeffrey," Meg interrupted. "We know what you mean. Go on."

"So I figured that I could just keep her out of it," Jeffrey continued. "I told her to go home and act like nothing had happened."

"I didn't want Jeffrey to do it," Emma said, still fighting tears, "but he convinced me it would be better all around. Maybe I was in shock, but I believed him."

"It's okay, Em," Jeffrey said softly to her. Then he faced Art again. "I told her I'd report finding the body, and there was no way anyone could prove I had anything to do with it, since it's not like I'd ever been seen with Novaro. Or, well—I guess I hadn't realized that Meg had seen the three of us together."

"Chief Preston," Emma interrupted, "I would have gone to the police, really. I mean, I know I didn't do anything wrong, and it was self-defense. But then I guess it all seemed unreal to me. I wasn't thinking straight. And I have come forward now. I'm not going to let Jeffrey get in any more trouble because of what I did."

Art turned to Jake. "Jake, you didn't notice anything odd

about your daughter's behavior when she got home that night?"

Jake shook his head. "God help me, I didn't. That makes me a lousy parent, doesn't it? Emma was home right around six, or close enough that I didn't notice. She didn't say much, and then I got the call from the police and had to run off to the feed store."

"When did you talk to Jeffrey again, Emma?" Art asked.

"I talked to her Saturday afternoon," Jeffrey volunteered. "I thought it was weird that nobody had identified the body yet."

"But you knew who it was," Seth said.

"Yeah, kind of. I mean, I only knew his first name because Emma told me, but I didn't know where he was working or where he was staying. I didn't tell the police, because I was afraid someone might put Novaro and Emma together. I mean, he'd been waiting for her right in front of the school, where everybody could see. Somebody must have noticed."

"Maybe we didn't ask the right questions, or the right people," Art said. "We checked whether he was a student, but I can't say if the state police showed his picture around the school."

"I assume the police also talked with you, Emma?" Seth asked.

She shook her head. "Just to my dad. The police called him right after seven, when they found the body. Dad asked me if I'd seen or heard anything before I left, and I said no. I lied to him, to his face, and he believed me." Emma's tears were back, and she brushed them away impatiently.

Another thick silence fell. The story hung together, sort of, Meg thought. Novaro had been bored and out of his element. He'd developed a one-sided interest in a girl who'd done nothing more than talk to him and be friendly. After a couple of weeks he'd gotten frustrated and tried to move too fast—and she'd fought him off, with tragic consequences.

So where did that leave them? Meg wondered. She wanted to believe Emma and Jeffrey, although it was possible that Jeffrey could have been the one who pushed Novaro, or worse, intentionally hit him with something. That would be up to the forensic people to decide. Could this go to trial? If so, who would a jury see on the stand? A couple of teenagers who tried to get away with a crime, or two nice young people in a bad situation? "Art, what happens now?"

"We talk to the state police," he said flatly. "Kids, you and your parents, you tell the detectives exactly what you've just told me. It's up to them whether or not they'll bring charges, and if so, which charges. You have to know you've both been guilty of obstruction of justice, at the very least. There is, however, at least one mitigating factor. It appears that Novaro Miller did have a police record back in Jamaica—information his uncle omitted from his visa application—and it involved an assault on a girl."

Meg felt a jolt of surprise: Hector had told her that Novaro had some sort of record back in Jamaica, but he hadn't said it involved a girl. Would that make a difference to Detective Marcus?

Jeffrey stood up. "Do we go to Northampton now, sir?"

"Might as well get it over with. Unless you kids want to lawyer up."

Jeffrey glanced at his father. "Can I think about that? And will you go with us, Chief? Maybe you can talk to the detective and see how things look from his angle."

Meg wondered what that angle would be. Young love wasn't likely to sway Detective Marcus's attitude—he wanted a simple answer. "I'll be there," Art said.

Then Jeffrey turned to Meg and Seth. "Thank you for what you've tried to do for me—for both of us. I'm sorry if I misled you, but I was thinking about Emma. But I won't hide anything anymore."

"Let's go, then," Art said. "Seth, I'll call you two later."

With that, everyone trooped out of the conference room and split up to go their separate ways.

It was lunchtime by the time Meg and Seth trudged into Meg's kitchen. Bree was at the table, finishing her own meal. "Where've you two been? Don't forget, you've got that thing tomorrow."

Shoot—Meg had managed to push the Harvest Festival out of her mind again. Was there a penalty for defaulting on a booth? Would she be long remembered as a no-show? Because at the rate things were going, there was no way she could prepare much of anything between now and morning.

"I did forget. And I am *so* not ready, but it can't be helped." Meg dropped into a chair. Her mouth twitched. "But for once I can honestly say that this is a matter of life and death. Unfortunately."

"What are you talking about?"

"We were at the police station. Jeffrey Green confessed to killing Novaro Miller. And then Emma Stebbins, who apparently Jeffrey's been seeing for a couple of months, confessed that *she* was the one who killed Novaro, although she didn't mean to. So we all adjourned to the police station to tell Art, and then Art and Jeffrey and Emma and Sam and Jake took off for Northampton to tell the state police. I don't envy Detective Marcus, trying to sort this out."

"They covered up a crime, didn't they?" Bree demanded.

"Yes, they did," Meg admitted, adding, "but they did finally come forward. I wish I knew what outcome I wanted here. Part of me wants to say that their main crime is being young and stupid, but there is still a dead boy to be considered."

"Exactly," said Bree. "You gonna tell Hector?"

Meg considered. "I should talk to Raynard, actually. I'm pretty sure the police will get in touch with Hector soon themselves. I don't know how he'll take the news, but at least we know what happened now."

"Well, good luck with that. I'm going back up the hill." Bree stood up and headed for the door. "Oh, and I won't be home tonight—Michael and I are getting together and I think we're going to a movie later. Don't wait up."

When she was gone, Meg looked at Seth. "You're quiet."

He rubbed his hands over his face. "I'm still trying to fit all the pieces together. Jeffrey and Emma start hanging out over the summer. Fine. They keep the relationship quiet, so his mother won't find out. Probably useless, but I can see why they tried. Emma smiles at this Jamaican kid who's at loose ends, and Novaro takes it the wrong way and tries to rape her. Emma fights back and accidentally kills him. Jeffrey rides in on a white horse and tries to protect Emma. And now these two nice kids are facing who knows how many criminal charges? It just doesn't seem right."

"Vastly oversimplified, but I agree with your outline. I feel terrible because I don't know whether to feel relieved that this is over or guilty because I didn't pass on what

Hector told me about Novaro's troubles in Jamaica or glad
that those same troubles back up Emma's story. How much
leeway do the state police have, do you think?"

"I'm not going to try to guess. I imagine Emma has a
case for self-defense, but they were both party to the
cover-up. We'll just have to wait and see."

After they'd eaten lunch, Meg made her way slowly up
the hill, seeking out the tall form of Raynard among the
trees. She spotted him at the end of one row and approached.
"Raynard, can I have a minute?"

"Of course," he said, as he climbed down the ladder. "Is
there a problem?"

"No, not exactly, but I have some news about Novaro's
death. The police will be speaking to Hector, I'm sure, but
I wanted to tell you that a teenage girl has come forward,
admitting that she was the one who killed Novaro. It was
an accident. She says that he was . . . aggressive with her,
and wouldn't take no for an answer, and that she just shoved
him away but he hit his head hard. And then Jeffrey arrived
on an errand and helped her to cover it up, to direct attention away from her, because he and the girl have been sort
of seeing each other. They're all over at the state police
station in Northampton right now. But I thought you should
know."

Raynard looked away from Meg. "Tell me, will charges
be brought against those young people?"

"I can't say. It's certainly possible. Why, do you have
something to add?"

Raynard spoke slowly. "I have told you, and I believe the
police already know, that Novaro was in some trouble
before he came here. It involved a young girl who was, shall
we say, less willing than Novaro. So I can believe this girl's

story. Hector's family tried so hard to help Novaro turn his life around, but he was not interested, I suppose. Thank you for telling me, Meg. At least you have given us an answer."

"I was trying to help, Raynard," Meg said. But, she wondered, as she donned her picking bag and set to work, why didn't she feel better about it?

27

Meg dragged herself back down the hill at the end of the day, feeling exhausted both physically and emotionally. It was funny how sometimes she welcomed picking because it left her mind free to roam; today she'd wanted nothing more than to not think at all, and the rhythmic repetition of picking had become soothing and mindless. Or it would have been, had she been able to tear her thoughts away from whatever was happening at the state police offices at Northampton.

Meg had always believed in following the rule of law, but since becoming involved in more than one crime after arriving in Granford, she was more aware of the gray areas these days. Not that it was ever right to take the law into your own hands. But was it always right to punish someone when a crime was committed—or overlooked—with only good intentions? Who could make those decisions? Still, the bottom line here and now was that both Emma and Jeffrey had committed crimes, even if they had not set out to do so, and there had to be consequences.

She was sitting in the kitchen with a glass of wine in her hand, staring at nothing, when her phone rang; the caller ID read Police Department. Art? She debated not answering, but that would be cowardly, and she'd rather know what he had to say. "Hello?"

"It's Art, Meg."

"I thought it might be. What happened?"

"I think the outcome was as good a one as we could have hoped for. Marcus says they're not going to charge Emma with murder, because she was acting in her own defense, and no one's going to look at her and think she used undue force. Jeffrey is most likely going to get slapped with a fine, and he'll get probation—with a misdemeanor on his record. But at least it's not a felony, and no jail time."

"Wow, that is lucky for them. How did Marcus react to all this?"

"Let us say that collegiality was maintained between our respective departments," Art said evenly. "Pass the news on to Seth, will you? I'll see you both at the Harvest Festival tomorrow."

"Will do, Art. Thanks for letting me know."

"Thank *you*, Meg. You made some pretty critical connections along the way."

All in a day's work, Meg thought, after they'd hung up. In reality, the cliché was true: she'd been helping neighbors, and as it happened the crime had splashed over into the Jamaican community, which was part of her work scene. Plenty of connections there.

Seth came in half an hour later, by which time Meg was

wrestling with dinner. Boil water: check. Open jar of . . .
something or other. Check. Boil spaghetti and drain. Add
B to A and call it dinner. "Any word from Art?" Seth asked,
as he helped himself to a beer.

"Yes, not long ago. I think the bottom line is that the
kids are getting off lightly—no trials, no jail time. Not scot-
free, but fair. I managed to talk to Raynard as he was leaving, and I asked him to spread the word among the pickers
that the police had settled things. How are you doing?"

"Tired. Sometimes wrangling construction projects is a
lot easier than dealing with human problems."

"I hear you."

"You ready for tomorrow?"

"I have no idea. At this point, what will be, will be."

A few minutes later, there was a knocking at the back
door. Again? Was there anything left to be solved? She
opened it to find Jeffrey Green and his father Sam.

"I'm sorry to barge in like this, but I thought we ought
to thank you for all your help," Sam said.

"You're welcome," Meg said. "Although it would have
been easier all around if your son here had just told the
truth from the beginning," she added, more tartly than
she'd anticipated.

"I know that, Meg, and I'm really sorry," Jeffrey said,
and he looked like he meant it. "But I'd only wanted to help
Emma, when she was so upset."

Meg raised a hand. "Don't worry, I understand. I think
I was young once, although it's getting harder and harder to
remember it. And I'm pretty sure teenagers don't think too
clearly. Hey, have you two eaten?"

"Not yet," Sam said quickly, "but we really aren't des-
perate enough to show up and beg for food again."

"Dinner tonight is about as simple as humanly possible, so it's no trouble. Did Emma and Jake go on home, or should we expect them to show up any minute, too?"

"Home. They have a lot of things to talk about." Sam and Jeffrey followed Meg inside, and greeted Seth. "Hey, Seth. We came by to thank the both of you," Sam said. "We should have brought gifts or something."

"Don't worry about it," Seth said. "I'm glad it worked out as well as it did. So, what now? Sam, are you going to stick around for a while?"

Meg handed a beer to Sam and a glass of cider to Jeffrey, eager to hear Sam's answer.

Sam smiled. "After seeing what kind of trouble this kid gets into when I'm gone, I think I'd better. Not that Karen and I are likely to get back together, and Jeffrey knows that, but I'll be around. I'll have to find a job, though."

Meg sneaked a glance at Jeffrey, who looked happy at the idea of having his father nearby. "Speaking of Karen, has anybody talked to her yet?"

"That is a pleasure I have still to look forward to— although I did leave a message on her voice mail. Kind of an odd message to leave, you know? *Our son was almost arrested but it's all right now*?"

Jeffrey snorted. "Dad, if it hadn't been for mom, Emma and I could have seen each other in public, like normal people. Instead we've been sneaking around and hiding. I should have been there to make sure that Novaro didn't let things get out of hand, but I knew Mom would make my life miserable if we went public. She probably would have called the health department and had Stebbins's store shut down for some made-up health code violation. For all I know, she would have declared Emma a witch and had her burned at the stake on the village green. All I ever wanted was to spend time with Emma."

Meg noted Sam clearly trying to suppress a smile at Jeffrey's vivid imagery, but he collected himself enough to put his foot down. "Jeffrey," Sam said firmly, "cool it a bit, okay? What happened was *not* your mother's fault. Your mother loves you as best she can. She wants you to be happy, really. Unfortunately, she can only understand happiness by her own terms, and her vision for you doesn't include someone like Emma." He sighed. "But I tell you what—if I have anything to say about it, you'll be able to see each other openly from now on. Emma seems like a pretty decent kid."

"She is, Dad. And it's not like we're going to get married or anything. I just like her."

Meg dumped a huge mass of pasta into an equally huge bowl, poured what seemed like a gallon of sauce over the top, and thunked it on the dining room table. "Here's dinner. Help yourselves."

They busied themselves with distributing food for a few minutes. After she'd inhaled half her serving, Meg said, "You know, Sam, you must feel very strange, with so many people in town tramping through the details of your personal life. I know—I've been there." She smiled briefly at Seth, who returned it. "Do you know, not even this guy here trusted me when I first arrived?"

"It's kind of nice to know that things—and people—can change. I mean, take the two of you now—you started out butting heads, and now you're getting married." Sam sighed. "Look, I'm not proud of how I've handled things. Karen and I went through a nasty split, and I took the easy route and cleared out—feeling guilty all the way. I knew in my gut that leaving Jeff with Karen was a bad idea, but I couldn't stick around, and I needed a job."

"Hey, Dad, I understood," Jeffrey protested. "And I was the one who wanted to stay here."

"Nobody's blaming you, Sam," Meg said.

Sam jumped up and started pacing around the kitchen. "*I'm* blaming me! Jeff, you're a good kid, and you try so hard, and you didn't deserve all this. This thing with Emma, it breaks my heart. You should be able to date any girl you want, without sneaking around. I wish I could fix what I've done."

"It's okay, Dad. Really. *We're* okay."

"God, I hope so, son."

With the resiliency of youth, Jeffrey perked up as he changed the subject. "Hey, I found out some really cool stuff about that body on the green."

Meg recoiled in mock horror. "When on earth did you find time to do anything like research, Jeffrey?"

"There's lots online. And I've been e-mailing Miranda Marvin—she's great. She told me what I should be looking for, which helped a lot. You want to hear?"

"Go right ahead," Seth said.

"Okay. So, the stuff we'd learned already—that the guy was African but lived here most of his life, died in his sixties, and was buried on land originally belonging to the Moodys who we know from the census still had slaves in the 1790s—all points to him having been a slave, right?"

"Slaves?" Sam said. "Here?"

"Yeah, Dad. I'll fill you in later. But the thing is, I don't think our guy *was* a slave. At least not at the time of his death."

"Why do you say that, Jeffrey?" Meg said, leaning forward on her elbows.

"Because I found one of the Moodys' wills, from around 1740, I think. It says that the deceased had a slave named Richard, but made provisions for this Richard in the will, including that Richard had to work for a term of two years for each of his two sons, and at the end of that time he would be granted his freedom."

"And was he? Can you tell from the records?"

"I think so. There weren't any federal censuses early enough, but there are town tax records and that kind of thing—Mrs. Selden showed me some of those. There are records of tax payments by one Richard Moody, after 1750. So I think this guy was a *freed* slave."

"Did Richard Moody own land?" Meg asked, intrigued.

"I don't know that yet—I'd have to get over to Northampton to check the indexes there, because the early stuff isn't online yet. But it's possible."

"I don't suppose you've looked to see if he married or had children?" Seth asked.

"Not yet, sir, but I've just gotten started. I've been, uh, kind of busy this week."

"What did Miranda say?" Meg asked.

Jeffrey flashed a bright smile. "She said she'd be happy to have me as an intern anytime. And that she was going to call our skeleton Richard from now on."

"That's wonderful!" Meg said. "And quite a compliment."

The happy mood was shattered by a knocking at the front door. *Who could it be now?* Meg appealed silently to the gods. "I'll get it," she said out loud, and trekked to the front door, which when opened revealed Karen Green, arms crossed, unsmiling.

"Where is my son?"

28

"He's here, and so is his father. Come on in." Meg stepped back to let Karen enter, then led her to the kitchen. Sam and Jeffrey stood up when they saw her, wearing matching expressions that were equal parts sheepish and belligerent.

"Coffee? Wine?" Meg said to their guest.

"This is not a social occasion!" Karen said in a shrill voice. "I want to know what the hell is going on! Since you're all here, maybe one of you will be kind enough to explain?"

Wine for me, Meg said to herself. She held up the chilled bottle she pulled from the fridge, and Seth nodded his agreement. "You sure you don't want any, Karen? You may need it. And sit down, will you?"

"Fine."

Meg drew three glasses from a cupboard and placed

them on the table, then filled each one halfway. Then she sat and stared at Karen until she sat on the edge of a chair, back stiff, twisting her fingers in her lap.

"Sam, you want to take this?" Meg said, after a healthy swallow of wine.

"I will. Karen, you've got to promise to keep your mouth shut until Jeffrey and I have explained. Can you do that?"

Karen stared at him for a moment, then her shoulders slumped. "All right. Tell me."

Sam proceeded to outline the events of the day, starting with Jeffrey's unexpected confession and Emma's appearance, and ending with the trip to Northampton to explain. "So, bottom line," Sam finally wrapped up, "the kids are in the clear, more or less. There's nothing more that we need to share, is there, Jeffrey?"

"No," Jeffrey answered emphatically. "But I'm going to keep seeing Emma, Mom."

Karen looked pale and drained. Meg almost felt sorry for her: it must be hard to see the life you've so carefully constructed crumble to pieces in front of your eyes, in the space of a few short hours.

Then Karen picked up her glass and drained it, holding it out for a refill. "I . . . don't know what to say. How could my son have gotten himself into this mess? I thought you were smarter than this, Jeffrey."

Seth stepped in before Jeffrey could speak. "Karen, your son is a fine boy and a credit to you and his father. He acted out of the best intentions, but he's still young, and he's definitely idealistic, and he made some bad decisions. But he has a mind of his own and, thank goodness, a heart."

"Karen," Meg added carefully, "I know we don't know each other well. From what I've been hearing, I can understand that you want the best for your son. What you aren't seeing is that he's got to figure out how to make his own way in the world. Maybe he made some bad choices in this case, but that's how we learn. And he's going to fall in love, whether you like it or not."

Karen looked at Meg, her expression bleak. "You're telling me how to run my life? And my son's? You don't even know me, and I don't know you."

Meg held her tongue. From what she'd seen of him, Sam seemed to be a really nice guy. Sure, he'd left Jeffrey behind to deal with his mother alone, but she could definitely understand why. She was glad that Jeffrey had found some little corner of his life that his mother couldn't trample over: Emma was both his haven and his rebellion. Even better, she was a good choice for him, current situation aside. When they were together it was clear that Emma cared for him, and he obviously cared for her. But could any of that get through to Karen? If Sam stayed around, would that help?

There were no guarantees in life, were there? Good parents turned out rotten kids; self-centered, foolish parents produced good kids like Jeffrey. And everyone else just muddled along. If—when—she and Seth had children, what kind of parents would they be? She'd seen Seth with children, and thought he was great, but Meg had always had reservations about her own maternal aptitude. Loving them was easy—even icy Karen must love her son, Meg assumed—but shaping them and giving them the skills to be good human beings was something else.

Meg drained her glass and stood up. "I'm sorry if you think I was unfair to you, Karen, but I hope that you can see that we care about Jeffrey and we want to help him if we can."

Karen gave her a bitter smile. "I know you think I'm doing a lousy job of being a mother to him. Sometimes I think he's older than I am. But he has so much potential, and I don't want him to let that go to waste . . ."

"If you don't give him room to grow, that potential will be lost," Seth said. "You've given him a solid base. Now let him find out what *he* wants for himself."

Meg stole a glance at Jeffrey, who was contemplating his hands under the table to avoid looking at anyone. This whole conversation must be hard for him to hear. Sam was watching his son, and he finally said, "Karen—they're right. We have to give Jeffrey some space."

"It's hard," Karen whispered. "He'll be gone in a year, and what will I have left? No husband, no job, no family. You don't have to say it—that's all my fault. I've driven my family away. But it's only because I want so much for them."

What Karen needed was something to occupy her mind and make use of whatever capabilities she had, Meg realized. "Karen, what do you like to do? I mean, *really* like? Take pleasure in?"

Karen turned to Meg, surprise clear on her face. "Why?"

"Because as you just said, you know Jeffrey will be moving on in a year, and you need something in your life that interests you. You're a smart, capable woman, and you're not using half your abilities. Do something! Find something that matters to you."

"Like what?" At least Karen now looked more curious than mad. Had no one ever talked to her like this?

"Anything. Take up weaving. Write a novel. Save starving children somewhere. What's important is that you stop stewing and go out there and *do* something."

"But . . . I don't . . ."

But Meg was on a roll now. "Why are you on the board of the Historical Society?"

"Because it's an important organization in Granford, and I was invited to join."

Probably because they thought you could write a nice check, Meg said to herself. "Do you like history?"

"Yes, I do. What does this have to do with anything?"

Meg noticed that Jeffrey had now looked up and was showing signs of interest. She went on, "Look, your board and Gail have done a great job planning the renovation of your building, and you're going to have so much more space now, so it will be possible to bring together all the collections that nobody's seen in years. You can help organize and catalog them. You know how to use a computer?"

"Of course I do, but I don't have anything like library training . . ."

"It doesn't matter. Gail can show you how it works, and there will be other people working on it, who can help you. It's something that needs doing, and you can learn a lot about the town you live in, and the families here, going back centuries."

Karen was beginning to look stunned. "Would she . . ."

"Yes," Meg plowed on, without giving Karen time to protest. "Just ask her. You'd be great at it."

"What about Jeffrey?"

"Jeffrey will be fine. And in case you haven't noticed, he really likes history, so that's something you two could share."

"Mom, I'd be happy to help you learn," Jeffrey said eagerly. "You wouldn't believe the cool stuff you can find out when you start looking."

"Oh." While Meg watched, Karen appeared to pull herself

together: she sat up straighter and smoothed her clothes. "You've given me a lot to think about. Uh, Jeffrey, will you be coming home with me, or staying with your father?"

When Jeffrey hesitated, Sam said, "Go with your mother—I think she needs you. We'll talk later."

"Thank you, Sam," Karen said quietly. Then she turned to Meg and Seth. "And thank you, both of you. I . . . I think I'd like to get to know you better, if that's possible."

"Of course," Meg said, hoping she wouldn't regret it later. "I can help you learn how to catalog, too—but not until the harvest season is over, please."

Meg watched as Karen made her way to the door, with Jeffrey following closely. When the door closed behind them, she turned back to Seth; he began to clap, slowly, then faster, and then Sam joined in.

"That was amazing," Sam said.

"What? What did I do?"

"You told Karen some hard truths, and she listened. That may be a first in her life. You were great."

"Thank you, I think."

"I should get out of your hair and let you folks get some rest. It is okay if I stay at your place just awhile longer, Seth?"

"Sure, no problem. Come to the Harvest Festival tomorrow and maybe we can find time to talk."

"I'll do that. See you there." Sam left by the back door, and they heard his car start up in the driveway.

Meg refilled her glass and Seth's with what was left of the wine. "Is today over yet? Because I'm exhausted."

"We can declare it over if you like. I've got to be up early myself."

Bree came in a few minutes later, then stopped, as if

startled to see Meg and Seth sitting together in near-silence in the kitchen. "Everything okay?"

"Just dandy," Meg said, feeling that second glass of wine. "We just solved all the problems in the town, and—"

Bree held up a hand. "I don't need details. You still going to the Festival tomorrow?"

"I guess. Seth, you ready to go up to bed?"

He stood, held out a hand, and hauled her out of her chair. "Let's go."

Bree snorted as she went up the stairs to her room.

29

Meg woke on Saturday as sun filtered through the window blinds. She checked her clock: past seven, later than she usually got up. But she felt no desire to move yet. Yesterday had been exhausting, emotionally if not physically, but at least they'd reached an ending that promised some happiness down the line somewhere. The police knew how Novaro Miller had died, even if it was a sad and messy affair, and no one would be charged with killing him.

Seth had left earlier, while Meg was sleeping, no doubt to oversee the setup for the festival. She found it endearing how involved he was with all the activities in the town, and he seemed to truly enjoy all of them. Poor Karen Green fell at the other end of the spectrum, with nothing to occupy her, no friends or spouse to turn to. As a result, she'd gnawed over every imagined slight, and pushed her son as hard as she could. Meg firmly believed that it was never healthy to put all one's eggs in one basket, as Karen had with Jeffrey. She herself had been an only child, but her parents had always had interests of their own, and looking back, she thought they'd done a good job of balancing parenting and maintaining their own lives. It was a wonder that Jeffrey was as stable as he appeared to be, although only time would tell. Whether Emma stayed in the picture was another issue, but that was for the two of them to work out—without Karen's interference.

Finally Meg hauled herself out of bed and showered, dressed, and went downstairs, where Bree was just finishing up her breakfast.

"Wondered when you'd show up. What time do you need to be at the Festival?"

"It starts at ten, and I should be there a bit before that to make sure everything is in place." Bree gave her an odd look, but Meg didn't have time to think about it because someone was rapping at the back door. She was surprised to see Raynard on the other side of the screen. She hurried to open it.

"Hey, Raynard. Is there a problem?"

"No, no problem, Meg. May I come in?"

"Of course." Meg stood aside to let him into the kitchen, where he and Bree made some wordless communication that Meg didn't understand. "Coffee?"

"Don't trouble yourself," Raynard said. "I came to tell you that the police in Northampton, they called Hector and told him that he could make arrangements to send Novaro home. But there was something else that you should know."

Meg hoped it wasn't bad news—it was too nice a day to deal with that. "What is it?"

"Hector knew that Novaro was trouble, but he hoped that work and responsibility would straighten him out. As you know, that did not happen. Novaro got himself mixed up with the wrong people here. But you tried to help, and Hector wishes to apologize if his nephew caused trouble to you, and in the town."

"Thank you, Raynard. I appreciate it. But Novaro was eighteen—old enough to manage his own life. Hector couldn't be responsible for him, and certainly can't be blamed."

"But he's still saddened by it."

"Of course—we all are."

"Indeed. Thank you again," Raynard said, but he made no move to leave.

"Was there something else you wanted?" Meg asked.

To her surprise, Raynard's face crinkled into a smile. So did Bree's.

"What?" Meg asked, confused.

"You've got to see," Bree said. "Outside."

Bewildered, Meg followed Bree and Raynard out to the driveway. There stood her farm pickup, clean and polished to a shine, with a new magnetic sign on the door that said *Warren's Grove Apples*. Bree shoved Meg closer, and she realized that the back of the pickup was filled with apple baskets, and the baskets were filled with different varieties of apples, which looked as though they had been individually hand polished.

"For the Festival," Bree explained. "There's some basic varieties, like the Cortlands, and a couple of heirlooms. I made signs for the different varieties. Oh, and you'll need these." She fished a bundle of something out of the truck, which turned out to be a stack of white paper bags with handles, each also imprinted with the *Warren's Grove* logo. "That old scale that Seth mentioned? That's in the back, too."

Meg battled a huge lump in her throat. "Thank you. This is wonderful! I didn't know what I was going to do today, but I didn't expect all this."

"Part of the job, ma'am," Raynard said, still smiling broadly. "You and the orchard do well, we all do well. And we owe you thanks."

"So you'd better get moving," Bree said, "because you have to set up your booth. And I almost forgot," she added, reaching into her pocket and pulling out an envelope. "This is fifty in singles—I figured you'd want to make change."

Meg had run out of words, so instead she impulsively grabbed Bree in a hug. Bree tolerated that for about two seconds, then backed up. "Hey, don't get mushy on me. You all set? Because Raynard and I have work to do."

"I am definitely all set. Go!" Meg watched them walk up the hill, her heart full.

She drove to town, careful not to jostle her baskets full of apples, and pulled into the lane that ran along the green, then climbed out of the pickup and scanned the canopies for her place. Gail came up beside her. "You're on this side, near the Historical Society booth. Need help unloading? Before you say no, I'm so wired that I need to burn off some energy, so you'd be doing me a favor."

Meg laughed. "I've got a bunch of baskets of apples, and I'd love some help. Isn't this the perfect day?" After a lousy year that had featured a blizzard and a drought, New England had decided to make up for it by throwing in a storybook September day—not too hot, cloudless blue sky, maple leaves just beginning to turn around the edges. The green was filled with people bustling around carrying bins and boxes, and everyone looked happy.

Meg and Gail made short work of shifting the apple

baskets, and Meg found a convenient place to hang the antique scale—Seth had provided a hook, of course. She stacked some of the bags on her table, clipped the labels on the apple baskets, and called herself ready. After moving her truck to a more distant location to allow parking for visitors, she decided to take a stroll around the green, to see who else was taking part in the Festival and what they had to offer.

She was not surprised to find a campaign booth for Rick Sainsbury, staffed with a gaggle of fresh-faced college students. She was more surprised to see the candidate himself in conversation with some of his staffers. When he saw her, he excused himself and came over to greet her. "Walk with me?"

"Sure. How's the campaign going?"

"I think it's going well, but I'm not taking anything for granted. Look, I want to thank you for what you did for Jeffrey. I don't know if he could have dug himself out without your help—yours and Seth's."

"We wanted to help him. We like him, and he deserves it."

"I'm glad he had you on his side. And I don't know what you said to Karen, but she seemed really unsettled by it— which I think is a good thing. She needed a swift kick where it would do the most good."

"Happy to be of service."

"Look, Meg, I owe you and Seth, and that's personal, not political. Whether or not I win this election, if there's ever anything I can do for you two, let me know."

"I'll keep that in mind, Rick. And good luck!"

"Thanks again, for everything." With that he took off across the green. Meg realized that she was beginning to like Rick, despite their rocky start—and she would definitely hold him to his promise, if he was ever in a position to offer the kind of help they might need.

At the opposite end of the green, Meg found Seth talking with Art, pointing at different corners. When she drew closer, she realized they were debating heatedly about traffic control.

"This kind of day, lots of people out, we have to juggle parking and leaf-peepers with keeping the road clear for others who are just passing through," Art explained.

Seth looked amused. "How many years have we been doing this? We have the same discussion every year. You've called in your off-duty officers?"

"Of course I have. And I've got sawhorses and traffic cones marking off the restricted area. Hi, Meg—hey, your booth looks great."

"You can thank Raynard and Bree for that. They surprised me this morning with the whole setup, including the apples. Did you know, Seth?"

"Nope, although Bree did remind me to hunt down that scale."

As Art scanned the green and the traffic flow, Meg leaned closer to Seth. "Since I missed you earlier—good morning," she said, and kissed him enthusiastically.

"And the same to you. You look happy."

"I am. Rick thanked us for helping Jeffrey. Have you talked to him?"

"Nope, not yet."

"You still on the fence about him, as a candidate?"

"Not as much as I was. He did make an effort to help his family, even when there were probably plenty of other demands for his time and attention. Of course, that could have been a political ploy."

"But no photo ops, no headlines. I'm going to choose to believe him. Oh, and if we ever need a favor—he volunteered." Meg turned to the police chief. "Art, I don't know all the details about what part you played, but thank you for facilitating whatever went on in Northampton."

"Aw, shucks, ma'am. Just doin' my job. You know, Marcus isn't a bad guy, once you get to know him. At least he's not PO'd that you stuck your nose in again." Art checked the scene again. "Whoops, I've got to go. Catch you later, Seth, Meg." Art hurried off across the green, where some overeager tourist was trying to shift the traffic cones and snag a prime parking spot.

"Look!" Meg pointed toward the Historical Society, where Jeffrey and Emma were walking together. Karen was standing by Gail near the young couple, looking pained—but at least she was there, and trying.

"By the way," Meg said, turning back to Seth, "what are you doing the first weekend in December?"

"I have no idea. Why?"

"My late grandmother's birthday is that weekend. I thought it might be a good day to get married. The harvest will be over, it's after Thanksgiving but not too close to Christmas, Rachel ought to have had her baby by then, and I really liked my grandmother. I think she'd be pleased that I chose that date, and Mom can't complain. We can hold the whole thing at Gran's and ask Christopher to officiate. How does that sound?"

"It sounds great." Seth grabbed her and gave her a kiss that weakened her knees, and Meg didn't care if the whole town of Granford was watching.

Recipes

Harvesting apples is hard work, but people still have to eat. What's more, Meg Corey thinks it's about time that she should share a meal with the pickers who work in the orchard and get to know them better. So she looks for quick, simple recipes that don't require a lot of preparation, and that also highlight the last crops of the season.

Grilled Chicken, Indian Style

This recipe makes enough for one whole chicken (you can cut it up yourself), or two pounds of parts if you purchase your chicken that way. Of course you can multiply the amounts to serve as many as you want.

½ cup unflavored Greek yoghurt
¼ cup lemon juice
1 tablespoon ground cumin
1 tablespoon ground coriander
Pinch cayenne
1 teaspoon coarse salt
2 tablespoons minced garlic
1 tablespoon minced ginger

Combine all the ingredients in a large bowl and mix. Add the chicken pieces and coat them with the marinade. Let the chicken sit in the marinade until you are ready to grill (if you're doing this well in advance, refrigerate the container, covered, until you're ready to cook the chicken).

Set up your grill (charcoal or gas) and place your chicken on the grate, skin side down. Turn once during cooking, and baste with any of the leftover marinade.

Note: If your grill permits, cover the chicken during the first half of the cooking, to ensure that the meat is cooked through. You can leave the cover open after you turn the pieces. If you don't have a covered grill, spread out your coals so that the heat is not too intense, so that the chicken cooks completely.

Baked Grated Beets

This is a recipe that's easy to make ahead, then pop into the oven about the same time you start your grill heating. There are many delightful kinds of beets available these days, particularly at local farmer's markets, so feel free to experiment. The golden ones give a lovely color to the dish. Again, you can multiply the ingredients to make more if you're feeding a crowd.

> 5 Little Golden Beets, peeled and shredded (a food
>   processor's shredding blade does this well)
> 1 small onion, finely chopped
> 1 potato, grated
> 2 tablespoons vegetable oil
> 2 tablespoons white vinegar
> 2 tablespoons brown sugar
> 1 tablespoon water
> Salt and pepper

Preheat the oven to 350 degrees.

Shred the beets and place them in a greased one-quart casserole. Add the onions and potato and mix.

In a small bowl, stir together oil, vinegar, sugar, water, salt and pepper.

Stir the liquid mixture into the vegetables. Cover tightly and bake in a 350-degree oven for 30 minutes, stirring once or twice during cooking.

Apple Cream Pie

Meg and Bree were too busy to think about making a dessert for their dinner with the pickers, but if you want a sweet ending to your meal, here's an easy pie that showcases the apples from the harvest.

9" unbaked pie shell, chilled (buy a frozen one if
    you're pressed for time, or use premade piecrust
    and fit it to your pie plate)
3–4 large cooking apples (whatever variety you have,
    or mix them up), peeled, cored, and cut into large
    chunks
¾ cup sugar
Pinch of salt
¼ cup flour
1 cup light cream
1 teaspoon vanilla extract
2 tablespoons butter
Ground cinnamon

Preheat the oven to 400 degrees.

Prepare your apples and pile them in the pie shell.

Whisk together the sugar, salt, and flour. Add the cream and vanilla and mix until smooth. Pour the mixture over the apples. Dot the top with butter and sprinkle lightly with cinnamon.

Bake on the lowest rack of the oven for 15 minutes.

Lower the oven temperature to 375 degrees and continue baking for 45 minutes or until the pie filling sets, and the apples are easy to pierce with a sharp knife.

Let cool before slicing.

FROM *NEW YORK TIMES* BESTSELLING AUTHOR
Sheila Connolly

RAZING THE DEAD
A Museum Mystery

Between her demanding position as president of the
Pennsylvania Antiquarian Society in Philadelphia and
her blossoming relationship with FBI agent James
Morrison, Nell Pratt has her hands full. But when she
discovers a dead body on a historic dairy farm that is
being threatened with demolition, Nell will have to dig
into the past to solve a murder in the present . . .

"A witty, engaging blend of history and mystery
with a smart sleuth who already
feels like a good friend."

—Julie Hyzy, *New York Times* bestselling author

sheilaconnolly.com
facebook.com/TheCrimeSceneBooks
penguin.com

M1501T0514

FROM *NEW YORK TIMES* BESTSELLING AUTHOR
SHEILA CONNOLLY

Scandal in Skibbereen
A County Cork Mystery

As the new owner of Sullivan's Pub in County Cork, Ireland, Maura Donovan gets an earful of all the village gossip. But uncovering the truth about some local rumors may close her down for good. . .

"An exceptional read! Sheila Connolly has done it again with this outstanding book . . . [A] must read for those who have ever wanted to visit Ireland."

—*Shelley's Book Case* on *Buried in a Bog*

sheilaconnolly.com
facebook.com/TheCrimeSceneBooks
penguin.com